# Directive Ninety-Nine

## Judith Rolfs

# Directive 99

# Dedication:

To the countless men and women ages seventy, eighty and ninety who continue to make major contributions in fields of art, science and human affairs. Bravo! Long may you live!

# Dear Reader:

I began writing Directive 99 over twenty years ago as a futuristic novel. However, I put it away thinking the story line too implausible. At one point I thought the manuscript had been lost.

Not long ago I came across the file and realized the plot had become frighteningly current. It appears that the fictional premise of Directive 99 could easily become a reality.

## Acknowledgments

The assistance of many people made this book possible.

I'm grateful first and foremost to my husband Wayne for his unflagging encouragement and excellent editing.

Collecting research background for settings in Directive 99 and absorbing local impressions happened over a period of years. My appreciation goes to St. John's County Chamber of Commerce, the St. Augustine Visitor Center and the residents of the Old City who often made me feel welcome. Several members of the staff at the United States Capitol in Washington D.C. were gracious and helpful.

Many thanks to Steven Ostrander, Sue Drefs, Linda Austin and Roger Jadown for their critique of initial drafts of Directive 99 and their enthusiastic endorsements. The editors of our local community newspapers graciously published my articles encouraging my journalistic input on controversial issues. Bloggers and newscasters from both political parties whet my appetite for deeper probing into policy decisions that affect us all.

Golden Years Retirement Center, one of many excellent private care centers in the nation, gave me an accurate concept of what a Fullness of Life Centre can be when operating at its best.

I'm motivated to write by the biblical words of Habakkuk 2:2 "Write the vision and make it plain that those who run may read it."

*Prologue*

Relton studied his computer screen and highlighted the name "John Levinson, journalist." He pressed delete, his favorite key. Delete meant dead. He eyed the next name on his list- Nicholas Trevor - and started an information search.

## Chapter One

At ten to eight Jennifer Trevor slid onto the burgundy chair behind her glass top desk at the Fullness of Life Centre for the Elderly. She hunted for the aspirin bottle in her left-hand drawer and shook out two to dull the aching in her temple.

Her double-breasted navy suit, deep as midnight without a trace of shimmer, contrasted with her white skin. No problem wearing a rumpled rayon blouse, wrinkles were the vogue in natural fibers, the haute couture of the twenty-first century. Staying current in fashion and lifestyle was vital for keeping her professional edge, although today she'd scarcely noticed what she'd grabbed from her closet.

"Ellen," Jennifer monotoned through the wireless intercom to her assistant, "get me the latest data on Directive 99."

She'd taken her job five years ago when the new status of Head Administrator was a coveted, low-stress position. Mostly, she simply maintained the status quo, which worked well for her ego, forever fragile from word swords thrust by parents who drank and argued too much. Jennifer hated conflict and her peaceful work environment was about to erupt in controversy. It couldn't be helped. *It is what it is.* She soothed herself with the familiar mental slogan.

Ultra-efficient Ellen entered noiselessly, placed a manila folder before Jennifer and slipped away. Economy of words was practiced at all government work sites.

Reviewing the new material Jennifer concluded this latest policy change would be controversial but workable. It had to be.

***

"Ms. Levinson. I regret to inform you your husband is dead. I'm so sorry to be the bearer of this news.

"No!"

"Is someone with you?"

Blankly she looked around her serene bedroom with its peach walls and lime floral bedspread. The voice tried to give more information, wanted to send an officer over.

"From all indications we must conclude Mr. Levinson took his own life."

"You're wrong." Sarah refused to believe. The phone slipped from her hand and the call ended. His tone was kind, she remembered later and sounded official, but this was a mistake. John was in Boston on assignment researching a feature article. Suicide was unthinkable. John loved her and their children and claimed he had the best job in the world as senior editor of *Newspersons*.

Weak-kneed she collapsed on the circular king-sized bed where she and John slept and made love. Tomorrow night he'd be blanketed under the mountain of down reading and waiting for her to emerge from the bathroom.

A distant part of her longed to cry, but tears wouldn't come. She shook her head. Of course, because his death couldn't be real. John traveled often and always returned to her. He'd never leave her by his choice. Their marriage had never been better.

He'd even begun working out regularly at her urging. Oh, he'd been disappointed their sixteen-year-old son had made bad choices about friends, and their married daughter was struggling financially, but they had confidence these problems would work themselves out.

True, John hadn't called at ten-thirty, as usual, but occasionally a meeting went late. She lifted her head and stared blankly at the wall. Of course, he had his gun with him. He always did since he began carrying five years ago. He'd never use it on himself. The idea was ridiculous.

2

Sarah heard a loud knocking and forced herself to rise and stagger to the front door.

She turned on the porch light, looked out, before opening to the policeman. How long had he been pounding? Suddenly, her tears broke like a summer storm.

***

Jennifer viewed the living areas for the elderly at the Fullness of Life Centre as she rode up and down in the glass-walled elevator making her rounds the first of two times for the day. One-way mirrors prevented residents from seeing her. Each had ten by ten feet cubicles, fancifully called rooms, with walls four-feet high creating an illusion of privacy. She sighed. *All is well; harmony prevails, at least for the moment.*

Returning to her mezzanine office perch on the third floor, she lit the six-inch spice candle on her desk. No matter how hard she tried to camouflage it, the smell of alcohol and pine cleaner permeated the walls and floor of the building. She'd grown to hate it.

Jennifer exhaled deeply before pulling out the new Directive 99 Manual, flipping through the pages. Of course, the change described in this material was being touted as an advance, one requiring tactful promotion. She could handle this.

Yesterday her boss reminded her she'd been selected for this key position because the unification planners preferred obedience to creative thought. Jennifer was above all a dependable organizational pup. She knew she excelled at management, not independent, thoughtful problem solving, having left her creative processes on the altar of graduate school. An independent thinker in private, at work her energy was poured into executing government directives. It was not her place to question, but in all honesty, this drastic new policy had shaken her.

She snapped the manual shut, squared her shoulders, and practiced the new Directive 99 jargon striving to reconcile her emotions.

Sarah dabbed at her swollen eyes.

All she'd ever wanted was to be a wife and a mother. She'd found her greatest contentment in anticipating the needs of her family and encouraging them in their activities.

Not that she didn't have her own interests. A Level Four tennis player, Sarah played weekly plus spent five hours a week at the indoor ice rink between her figure skating lesson and practice. Every Monday and Wednesday morning she volunteered at the food and clothing pantry attached to her church. But always her deepest joy came from being with her family.

Now a pain she could never have begun to imagine faced her. How do you tell your sixteen and eight-year-old sons their Dad's dead, he shot himself in the head because he wanted to die, which absolutely couldn't be true. At least her newly married daughter would have the comfort of her husband when she heard the news. *Your father didn't commit suicide*...this is what she'd tell her daughter and sons. She stiffened her shoulders and walked toward the boys' rooms to wake them.

What had the policeman said about getting her husband's computer and other personal things - downtown at the station, day after tomorrow, wasn't it?

John was a writer and Sarah desperately needed to see his laptop.

***

Broadleaf silk plants and cherry wood bookshelves holding ceramic and brass curios strategically arranged made the corridors seem homey at the Fullness of Life Centre. Americans had been thrilled when the federal government opened the first residential centre for the elderly. "A home away from home" is how it was promoted.

As one of the first administrators, Jennifer had helped hundreds of family members place their loved ones and she'd hired caring personnel to care for them. Her job description required her presence when a resident died to offer the condolences of the facility. If the death occurred outside her work hours she made contact by phone, which she preferred.

None of Jennifer's functions required deep, personal relationship building - the heart of the standard counseling process she'd been trained for. Jennifer rationalized she guarded her emotions by not getting too close to the residents so she'd have more emotional energy for her family. Today she wondered if her ability to feel anything at all had atrophied.

Her life between home and work was one big game of catch-up. Tomorrow will be better, Jennifer told herself, sighing. *I'm one of the new breed of women. Self-fulfillment above all else. I've seen my own godliness evolving.*

\*\*\*

Sitting in his comfortable recliner Pirelli reread the printout his boss Howard Relton had mailed him. The mob leader used the postal system because fax and e-mail left an electronic trail. He chuckled. No one would ever suspect important information would be sent the old-fashioned way.

And if you considered Nicholas Trevor's life of any value this mail was highly important. Pirelli would never ask Relton how Trevor became his mark. He preferred no unnecessary knowledge. He burned the paper and envelope as directed, and enjoyed watching the flames expire in his metal waste can.

Pirelli looked up the address of Nicholas Trevor's law office, researched further for his wife Jennifer Trevor, looked up her occupation and jotted down Fullness of Life Residential Centre and its address. His study of the local map pleased him, everything was close. He called Embassy Suites to arrange a two-week rental, which should give him plenty of time.

He could be there by late afternoon.

The cleanliness level at the Fullness of Life Residential Centre was superb. Jennifer demanded this for her residents because she wanted them comfortable.

She stared mindlessly at the familiar activity in the pictorial landscape-laden halls as she sipped her coffee. Attendants wheeled listless, chair-bound residents to the sunrooms at the ends of each quadrangle. The more active, energetic residents walked or wheeled themselves.

She tapped her fingers on the Directive 99 file on her desk. Ninety-nine went a step further than the government had ever ventured before. Pushing a stray hair back, Jennifer mused how her own idealism had originally pulled her toward this new twenty-first century government philosophy.

Human consciousness and goodness continuously evolving blended with her naive desire to perfect herself, the perfect career woman, wife and mother in this order. Not uncommon goals for an unaffirmed middle child from a dysfunctional family.

Her jaw tensed. How would her husband, Nick, react to the new plan on her desk? Would he disagree and call her unfeeling, maybe even unethical?

*So what? Utilizing the mind's fullest potential was key,* Jennifer glanced back at the bowed grey heads traversing the corridors beneath her on foot or by wheelchair. Despite the numerous morning activities available, there were always those residents content to do nothing, satisfied to simply sit in their rooms and "be."

Better Nick didn't know yet, Jennifer concluded. Her self-examination over, she drank deeply of her now cold coffee.

# Chapter Two

"Ellen, send in Miss Bolter."

Jennifer crossed the name off her appointment calendar, before focusing her attention on the twenty-seven-year old, non-descript woman, who nervously tiptoed in.

"Slightly overweight," Jennifer wrote on her private intake form, this assessment wouldn't go into the personnel file. Miss Bolter wore the muted pink uniform of an attendant-in-training.

Jennifer pointed to a chair, wasting no time on small talk.

"Miss Bolter, you've passed our initial screening. I need to know first of all, are you familiar with our residential care rationale?"

"Yes."

Jennifer barely waited for her answer. "At an institution of our size, it's important to be consistent in our philosophy with the residents. Is that clear?"

Miss Bolter fidgeted and pulled on her sleeves before she nodded.

"Your compassion for the elderly and sick, even those who die prematurely must be tempered with the realization these phases are simply stages of life on the way to perfection. Our goal is simple—to make our residents as comfortable as possible."

"Uh-huh, sure." The applicant nodded agreeably.

"Excessive sympathy is not appropriate, it only encourages self-pity. You're to be kind, but our residents are not to be pitied. They're fortunate to be here."

The young woman's eyebrows arched. She seemed about to say something, but bit her lip and stared at the wall behind Jennifer.

Jennifer ignored the body language, although she jotted a comment on her notepad. How might she handle indoctrination, that is, training, Jennifer corrected herself. Was Miss Bolter thinking, *what a bunch of gobbledly-gook?*

The sudden silence appeared to panic Miss Bolter.

Jennifer studied her more intently at length. Carlie Bolter gulped before saying, "Ms. Trevor, I hear you. I work and mind my own business. It gets me by just fine."

"I see."

Miss Bolter let out a sigh.

Jennifer hadn't slept well last night, and this routine interview bored her. She'd already examined Carlie's application and decided to hire her. Help was hard to find. She stifled a yawn and adjusted the clip on her thick, auburn hair pulled sleekly back. Jennifer gripped her pen tighter.

Perhaps encouraged by Jennifer's silence, Miss Bolter added, "I know these people are in the residential care center cause they're sick from their own unwise choices or because they're old and soon to die. I read those words in the manual," she said proudly, tugging on her sleeves again, her eyes not making direct contact with Jennifer.

"True," Jennifer said approvingly and scratched a notation on her pad. At least the girl made an effort to prepare herself.

"I can't help notice, Miss Bolter, you seem distracted?"

"Ms. Trevor, I need a job badly, that's all." Her tone changed to pleading. "I support my six-year-old daughter. There's just me and her, nobody else. My rent's due, and my daughter's private school tuition." She caught Jennifer's glance, and looked away again. "Err, what would be my responsibilities?"

Jennifer's face softened. "You're to be courteous, and thorough in executing procedures, but not overly friendly to the residents. It makes interactions much simpler, Miss Bolter. No need to ask questions about their earlier life. We don't want clients dwelling on their past. The good things of earlier years are lost to them as they age and remorse for the bad they may have done is unnecessary. The guilt concept for wrong-doing has long ago been eliminated."

Miss Bolter looked puzzled. "I never heard this, but it sounds good."

"Guilt is archaic. We all simply do the best we can. You can be assured" —Jennifer's jaw tightened— "in some loving fashion a sort of forgiveness will be meted out to all. Self-recrimination is a waste of energy."

"Yes, ma'am. Will I pass out medications, and that sort of stuff?"

Jennifer glanced up sharply and saw her pull at her sleeves again. A mental bell chimed. Another addict looking for an easy way to get drugs? Oh dear! One out of three job applicants was a druggie nowadays.

The supply of drugs in the "outside world" couldn't begin to meet the demand since legalization in 2012. Well, Miss Bolter would find out soon enough drug stealing wasn't easy here with the ironclad meds control system.

In the meantime, reliable workers were hard to come by and Jennifer was moved by the woman's desire to care for her child. Being in this positive environment could help Miss Bolter and the center might get good work out of her regardless of whether or not she reformed.

Jennifer wrote *APPROVED* on the outside of the file, gave Miss Bolter the good news, and stood up.

"My secretary will direct you to the practical phase of your training."

\*\*\*

In the next forty-eight hours, Sarah Levinson's neighbors brought dish after dish of pies, cookies and casseroles. She hated the pitying way they looked at her. No one believed her when she said John had met with foul play, not even her lawyer.

Despite Sarah's protests the police had assured her not finding a suicide note wasn't unusual. At the station when she'd collected John's things, she overheard one officer tell another, "It's natural for a spouse to be in denial for at first." She'd pretended not to hear as she'd hugged his computer to her chest.

Sarah desperately hoped for a clue on John's computer and planned to spend an entire day when the boys returned to school going through every file. Thank goodness she'd taken the computer classes provided by the library and achieved at least average skill.

No autopsy had been necessary. *Gunshot to the head leaves little doubt as to cause of death,* she thought grimly.

She chose to postpone a memorial service appreciating afresh she and John had left their Jewish faith three years ago to embrace Catholicism. Otherwise cremation wouldn't have been an option.

After her boys, Jacob and Eli, received the news Sarah observed they spent much of their time at home staying in their bedrooms or walking around the house in shock. For the first time in their young lives she had no words of comfort to give.

\*\*\*

Jennifer added ethnographic data to the report ordered by the health czar responsible for Directive 99.

Next Thursday, she'd appear before the Congressional committee in Washington for final approval, a mere routine because of the respect she held with her impeccable credentials in elderly care. With almost a thousand pages of medical terminology the pending bill was nearly impossible to decipher.

She thought back five years ago to when the government appointed a nursing home czar and he began a massive promotional campaign insisting federal centers could do the job cheaper and better than private. Citizens genuinely believed this. Many politicians saw it as an opportunity for a power grab. Private centers, unable to compete with the government's low costs, had to close their doors. Now corruption and poor control measures made costs zoom fourfold. In addition, no one had fully anticipated the impact of increased longevity.

Checking her spreadsheet Jennifer estimated how many rooms would be required for the increasing elderly population in the coming year. The task was easy, just time-consuming. Only so many beds and no one could be denied. Some residents would not live out the year. Never did it enter Jennifer's mind she would be doing a disservice by helping their death along.

Directive 99 set a cut-off time for this process of identifying perfection, the age when you'd become all you were meant to be. Life beyond this point might only result in unnecessary pain, suffering, and loss. Elderly-death advocates had a poetic phrase for the end, "If the seed does not die, further life is impossible." There comes a time when human fullness has been achieved and it's time to revert to the earth. Under these circumstances surely death could be facilitated. She knew the beautiful prose, but still winced when she thought of it.

***

Sarah hugged John's laptop before placing it carefully on her kitchen desk. Holding her breath, she opened it and pressed the power button.

She looked at the screen in horror, gasping as she pressed first one key, then another, and finally several at once. To her intense dismay it remained totally black. How could the hard drive on John's computer totally crash? Or, her stomach churned, had it been erased?

She rested her head on her arms and remained motionless as hot tears soaked her sleeves. After a time, she managed to rally herself and place another call to her lawyer. Surely, someone would believe her now.

"Sarah, I understand you're upset, but it's no use. I spoke to the police. They said the door to his room was locked on the inside with a dead bolt."

"There must have been some other entrance to his hotel room, a balcony?" Her voice was insistent.

"It was ground floor and the patio door also was locked from the inside. I know this is hard for you, Sarah."

"Will you ask the Boston police to check if the patio door could have somehow been locked after exiting, please?"

"Sure, if it will give you peace of mind, but Sarah, for the sake of your children, you need to accept what happened and move on."

"Never mind, I'll call myself." She slammed the receiver down, furious with him and the world.

***

At five the Centre's administrative staff offices closed. Jennifer usually stayed later, but tonight couldn't wait to go.

Outside, she shuddered despite the warm, but windy October air.

She drove home like an automaton becoming energized again only when she pulled into her three-car garage. The radio oozed out the words to "I'll love you forever," an international top ten song.

Jennifer stiffened her neck hurrying along the long walkway of crunching leaves between her garage and the impressive magenta entry of the main house. The air smelled of apples and wood. A comfortable serenity settled momentarily over her until she thought of her husband and groaned.

When she'd married Nick, he'd been her entire world. Their life had been nearly perfect until, her face twisted and she spoke into the silent air. "Nick staggered crazily into this mid-life morass!" What could it be if not some change-of-life kookiness? He'd become religious, of all things. How nonsensical and embarrassing. No amount of talking would change his mind. Once totally like-minded, now they argued about everything.

She fervently hoped Nick would adapt to the current culture. *We all must*, she thought. His idealism is passé.

Denying Nick's concept of a personal God was easy for Jennifer. She hadn't found the idea of God particularly helpful in her life thus far. Not that she'd ever seriously opened herself to Him. God was a global thought, too vague for her to grasp. He didn't fit with her straightforward "live for today" philosophy.

Life, death, everything blurred into an endless round of virtual unreality. Like a precision tightrope performer, Jennifer rejected any unbalancing thoughts.

12

When, as so often happened, "today" fell short of its desired euphoria, Jennifer consoled herself there's always tomorrow. They'd been perfectly happy before. No need to hide in this fairy-tale world of Nick's golden god. She remembered their recent argument when her lawyer husband insisted Christianity was based on facts and Christ brought him peace and a purpose for living he'd never known!

Jennifer complained his outdated beliefs were driving them apart.

Tossing her auburn hair, Jennifer looked up at the majestic twin turrets on her house piercing the sky like stately sentinels on alert. Her pace quickened as her stride became defiant. I work hard and deserve a lifestyle like this. Nick talks as if a divine being on a heavenly perch drops our financial benefits upon us. How insane.

Her harshness softened when she observed the turquoise and orange beauty of the setting sun. She rehearsed what she'd say after Nick got home. Picturing his naturally tan face with its handsome, broad jaw, she imagined it relaxing into a smile.

Oh God, if only it could be that easy! God? She vented with renewed anger. Directive 99 at the Fullness of Life Centre will be one more wedge between us!

Jennifer bit her lip. Her resolve not to mention this strengthened.

*** 

Pirelli ducked into a convenience store for the local paper and coffee.

Back in his car he scoured restaurant ads for later. He considered himself a connoisseur of food secretly idolizing two careers - food critic and gourmet chef. Pirelli didn't ask anyone for recommendations to avoid calling attention to himself, which was rather futile since he was six foot three and weighed almost 300 pounds.

On his way to Trevor's office, Pirelli stopped his Praxis electric car to let a grey-haired lady cross the street. "Courtesy only takes a moment," his favorite English teacher had often said. She'd insisted on thoroughness in evaluating literature which served him well every time he analyzed a new target's daily routine. At sixteen, Pirelli had abandoned school as too boring and confining for a brilliant mind like his.

Circling the block, he scoped the law offices and checked for Trevor's car, a BMW. He found three in the back lot and checked his printout for the license plate number, a necessary precaution. They were all shades of grey and silver. Don't these guys have any originality? Pirelli's Praxis rolled into a spot about ten spaces from Trevor's car.

He set his notebook on the seat beside him, opened his paper and waited.

*** 

Jennifer used her fingerprint to activate the keyless lock on her front door. Her heels clicked on the marble foyer floor, breaking the late afternoon silence.

She arranged her Kamali trench coat on a padded hanger in the foyer closet, and wandered into the living room. She dropped her slender body across one of two matching peach leather chairs.

Gazing out the sparkling twelve-foot window toward the stand of pine and oak woods gracing her backyard usually calmed her. Not today. The emotions she'd hidden through eight and a half hours of work broke through her fragile reservoir.

She despised having her feelings out of order - like clutter on her desk. Her fragile serenity was easily troubled. It was easy to pin down the primary cause - her fragmenting relationship with Nick, added to the new directive at work and three challenging children about to descend upon her sanctuary. She checked her watch. Nick should be home in an hour and a half, the kids in twenty minutes.

Jennifer shivered. Life hadn't always been this complicated.

Her eyes fell upon a pearlescent seashell lying inside the built-in, gloss-black bookshelves. A forgotten trophy from shelling with Nick ten years ago on Sanibel Island off the west coast of

Florida. She reached over to pick it up and ran her fingers slowly across its silky surface. Sunny, carefree mental pictures of beaches topped with surf-smoothed shells and grass-scented summers drifted together.

It seemed an eon ago she'd read Anne Morrow Lindbergh's *Gift From the Sea* about types of seashells representing different periods of a woman's life. Her life now, she concluded, was a half shell. Aloud she murmured, "Am I missing a part somewhere?"

How many years since she'd enjoyed unhurried leisure? Her days now were crammed like an over-filled toy box. Fun, lots of it, and challenges, but a few too many. Keeping the strands of family and profession untangled demanded enormous energy and an architect's knack for intricate planning. Jennifer reassured herself, *I'm doing fine, I manage well and the money I earn is marvelous.*

She tossed her head back with a defiant air, sat still and allowed herself a few moments to be completely honest. She feared she was missing something significant, intangible but real. Hating the thought, she immediately stuffed the unpleasant idea. After all, she was in the business of rechanneling ideas and feelings - wasn't this what counseling was all about?

She knew some, but not all, of the factors which had affected her. A crazy, dysfunctional childhood. Post-partum depression briefly after Jenna, their third child, was born.

Her parents' divorce after twenty-five years of marriage shortly after the birth of her change-of-life baby had scared Jennifer. She had trouble believing Nick could love her unconditionally forever. Someday would he see her with all her faults and inadequacies and want out of their relationship?

Although he continually assured her of his love, it was difficult to believe. Her love and respect for herself was based on performance and her appearance, why should his be any different? How silly she was, she told herself, to be overly focused on how much she accomplished and her looks.

Nick seemed to understand her insecurities, perhaps better than she did. He'd become her steel support emotionally. After Collin was in school, Jennifer had returned for a Doctorate in Psychology with his approval. In four years, she had a

15

dissertation attracting national attention in her field and highly marketable skills which earned her the position as Administrator of the Fullness of Life Centre.

All this gave her a sense of control over her future. Their combined salaries relieved her financial concerns. Not that she'd grown up in poverty. Still, she'd been warned as a child often to shut off the lights, take off her good clothes to keep them nice, since destitution might be only a day away to absorb some fears.

Jennifer had vowed when she married she'd never make Nick the center of her world. Now, since Nick had drawn closer to God he'd distanced himself from her or had she drawn away? Did it matter?

Her eyes began to blur and her head became heavy. She hadn't slept well. Last night she'd had her recurrent dream again of running into a blazing fire and being pierced by a dozen nails when she tried to escape through the door. If only she could recall more details, perhaps she could purge the dream rationally. Who or what was chasing her?

Momentarily hot all over despite the 70-degree-controlled climate she tilted her face toward the ceiling, painted soft blue to give the illusion of sky. Jennifer's gaze took in the peach-tinted walls surrounding her. Wind chimes tinkled on the deck and she inhaled the scent of roses. Her decorator had suggested piping the fragrance of flowers through the heating and cooling ducts. Jennifer congratulated herself on her wise choice of interior designers.

She relished these rare moments of aloneness, even as she eagerly anticipated the children's return home. She clicked her tongue on the roof of her mouth. Go figure. What a mystery she was, but wasn't every human being?

Jennifer sighed and turned on the TV for the day's news. Her eyes lingered on a story about the death of the editor of Newspersons newspaper. A suicide? She'd met John Levinson when he interviewed her for an article six weeks ago. He'd seemed professional and self-assured. CNA showed a picture of him, his wife, and two boys on a ski trip - you never know what's ahead, Jennifer reflected. How sad for the family. She flicked off the TV.

The front door thudded open and the sound of rushing feet filled the air. Time to enjoy her Mom role and try to forget her life had become terribly complicated.

*\*\**

After forcing down a few bites of scrambled eggs and toast for lunch, Sarah felt a little better. At least she could think again.

Her logic was simple. The hard drive on John's computer crashing at the time of her husband's supposed suicide seemed too coincidental. If someone wanted information erased from his computer, she wanted to know what.

There must be some way a technician could restore the data. Perhaps she'd find something to help her make sense of his death.

She carried her dishes to the sink and washed her hands before going to her computer desk. Clicking the screen on, she googled Data Recovery Software.

Minutes later, she discovered she could buy a recovery program, but how would she learn to use it? Further research turned up companies specializing in the process. Good, except none were local. Who might she call to help her? Her trust issue was huge. For a moment she wished her oldest son was less a jock and more a computer geek.

Sarah's face brightened. To the best of her recollection, John still used the same repair firm that had serviced his technology for years. If he'd trusted them, hopefully she could. Perhaps she'd find the number in John's old Rolodex he'd kept on his desk long after he got a Blackberry and iPhone. He wouldn't throw the Rolodex out, concerned about losing info on an old contact he'd need in the future.

She hunted through the closet in his study until she located the Rolodex in a storage box. Under C she found an entry for Computer repairs.

Sarah practiced speaking a few moments until she could explain her problem, while giving as little information as possible. It was 5:20 P. M. She prayed the shop would still be open.

## Chapter Three

Thirteen-year-old Tara charged in behind Collin letting the front door bang on her way to the family room tucked at the rear of the house. As Tara and seventeen-year-old Collin charged past Jennifer they tossed a careless "Hi, Mom" in her direction. Collin clicked his iPod on. Jennifer sometimes wondered if symbiotic electronics fused his body and brain.

Six-year-old Jenna, named after Jennifer, bounded in, ponytail in mid-air. The little leader, "Napoleona," her brother called her. "Mom, we're home!"

"Great, sweetie."

Jenna threw her arms around Jennifer's waist, and quickly wiggled away. Her sweet, warm hair, still shampoo-scented, filled the air.

"Kelly invited me roller blading Saturday. Can I go?"

"We'll see."

"What's for snacks?"

"Fruit and cookies on the kitchen table. I'll be right in."

"Not oatmeal raisin again!"

"Chocolate chip. Only eat two, we'll have dinner as soon as Dad gets home."

Jennifer liked having the children remain at the After School Center until she arrived home. The popular centers provided supervision services through the teen years for the working population. Like, most moms nowadays she didn't trust her kids home alone for long periods. Unfortunately, most kids vegged out on music and sitcoms rather than do schoolwork at the center.

Jennifer cornered Colin leaving the kitchen with handfuls of M & M's. "That's enough, young man."

"Okay, Mom." He ducked past.

"Wait a minute," Jennifer called after him, "Tell me about your day."

He glanced back at Jennifer lazily. "What about Tara? She's off doing what she wants and doesn't have to sit and talk," Collin complained.

He had his Dad's lankiness, thick, sun-streaked brownish-blonde hair, and grey eyes communicating a message of firmness in contrast to the flowing ease with which he moved his body. *On the outside Collin's all Nick,* but *it's my genes deep in there. He's independent and self-willed.* Jennifer recognized this, sometimes with joy – at the moment with regret.

"Tara, our budding socialite, is on the phone in the privacy of her room, she'll come talk later. She always does." Jennifer forgot for the moment it was inappropriate to make comparative statements about her children.

Collin spouted off two sentences about school before speeding out.

"Not so fast. Oh, never mind." She rose to change into her sweats. When she returned she inserted a Cindy Swanson low-impact aerobics DVD.

"1, 2, 3, 4, T-step, turn-step, over the top," her feet bounced up, over and down her step like a trained animal going through its master's drills, while her mind wandered to when her children were little.

Jennifer had filled their heads with literature and history, especially the Civil War and the World Wars. Tara loved words like Jennifer. Together they read all the classics Jennifer had missed as a child. She and the children read and studied together at the same table when she was home in the evening. Most of her doctoral classes had been at night.

Jennifer had been a good Mom, she told herself. She truly perceived mothering as an art. Learning how to motivate, excite, dispel fear while finding the keys of encouragement for each precious child had both consumed and satisfied her like nothing she'd done.

Now she couldn't spend her days in a huge, empty house waiting for them to bounce in and be gone again. And keeping the bills up required more and more money with the huge tax burdens on families.

Jenna, their surprise baby, born after Jennifer had started work, had developed into the family's social butterfly. She had an entire family to fuss over her and the knack for making every moment a celebration. Nick's vivacious, younger sister, whom Jennifer had never met, had died at age twelve. Perhaps Jenna carried her lively spirit, Jennifer often thought.

Thirty minutes later, sweat soaking her shirt, Jennifer dragged herself into the kitchen to wash her hands and assemble dinner.

The kitchen phone clanged for attention. Jennifer reached for it absentmindedly.

"Ms. Trevor, this is Dora."

"Yes?" Why was Nick's secretary calling?

"Mr. Trevor asked me to tell you he won't be home for dinner. He said something unexpected come up."

"Why didn't he contact me himself?"

"The battery went out on his phone."

*Or he didn't want me to question him.* "Did he give a time?"

"Sorry, he didn't."

"Thanks."

Jennifer rearranged canisters on the counter while considering Dora's message. *So, this is the game we're playing. Normally Nick would have called himself, but perhaps he didn't want to speak with me yet. It's not like him to hold a grudge. I guess I shouldn't be surprised he's not rushing home after last night! I was particularly cruel during our most recent argument. Lately arguing seems to be our normal activity.*

"Daddy's going to be late," Jennifer, announced through the intercom. "We'll eat without him. Tara, come set the table!" Jennifer yelled thirty decibels above her professional level.

"Do I have to?" came Tara's answer several minutes later.

21

"Watch out, Mom's hot, I can tell by her voice," she heard Collin warn Tara who was traipsing down the hall.

"I'm coming. Cool it, Mom."

"Tara, any verbal exchange between us becomes a conflict. Even a simple "Set the table" is taken by you as an intrusion into your private world. Stop it!"

"Mother! You're impossible!" Tara banged the cabinet door. She plopped plastic disposable dishes and silverware around before scurrying back to the family room.

Jennifer followed her into the beige and brown jungle-wallpapered room. She couldn't remember when she and Tara last had a civil conversation.

"Mom, I'm busy. Can we talk later?" Tara's cell phone buzzed and she flitted out without waiting for Jennifer's answer or noticing her mother's silent fuming.

Jennifer decided a major scene wasn't worth depleting her energy. She'd need it for her confrontation with Nick later, which she dreaded.

Jenna sensed her displeasure and danced by. "What's eating you Mom?"

"Nothing, Sweetheart." She sighed, glad Nick wasn't here to witness her interaction with their children. She often let them do as they pleased. Correcting them, was contrary to the new nurturing adolescent psychology book she'd just read.

Besides with her time with them so limited why deal with the added guilt of making it unpleasant even for a moment? Taking her irritation out on the children now wasn't right either, Jennifer realized, but at the moment wasn't ready to stop.

Later, after dinner and the children's homework and bedtime ritual, Jennifer slipped into the Jacuzzi. For some reason the ominous words of her college sociology teacher, Ms. Harder, came to mind. "Love for a man could destroy your potential fulfillment as a woman. Be careful, Jennifer, you have much to offer our world."

"Our world." The words had sounded weird, even then. Unmarried Ms. Harder existed in a world of female against male, and thirsted for female dominance.

22

Never having felt subjugated in the first place, Jennifer didn't understand Ms. Harder's obsession for liberation. *Is the feeling I'm experiencing now what she meant? If my standards and values are different from Nick's, what does it matter? Does Nick expect me to buy into a belief system enslaving my own mind to appease him?*

At eleven Nick still wasn't home. Jennifer punched the pillows in their king-size bed and drew them close to her body. Not even the vibrating waters of the whirlpool had relaxed her tonight. She didn't like admitting how important Nick was to her happiness.

Staring out the window at the peaked roof slicing the background sky, she finally drifted into a fitful sleep.

A quarter past midnight Jennifer half-awoke feeling Nick's warm skin press against her body. She emitted a low moan, and turned on her side to slip into the curve of Nick's arms and was sound asleep again instantly.

Nick was relieved his wife was asleep. He didn't want to tell her about the man who had followed him from his meeting or what the meeting had been about. It had taken almost an hour to lose the car. He'd gotten the license number and tried to trace it from his office, to no avail.

Why alarm Jennifer when he didn't even know what was going on? He held his wife close and wordlessly stroked her hair.

Tomorrow he'd investigate further.

## Chapter Four

At six the next morning, fresh from sleep and au naturelle, Jennifer's beauty was marred only by tiny tension lines around her eyes. A peach velour robe wrapped her body like a queen's cape, its texture matching the softness of her skin.

She finished her first cup of coffee while poring through the local paper. She needed to keep current on any happenings possibly impacting public relations for the Fullness of Life Centre she administrated.

Collin and Tara, rushing as usual, stampeded through the kitchen grabbing breakfast granola bars enroute to the front door, shouting "Byes" into the air. Jennifer turned her attention to prodding six-year-old Jenna.

"Almost ready, darling?"

"After I say goodbye to Daddy."

"He's still asleep."

But Jenna had already darted up to the master bedroom. She dove onto her Dad, gifting him with a Cheerios-fragrant kiss.

Nick groaned, "Who's waking the giant?"

"Me," Jenna squealed delightedly.

"Now I've got you." Stretching his arms he caught Jenna in a quick bear hug. "Daddy loves you, princess. Remember that always." Jennifer watched from the door.

Nick adored his children, and connected with them better than Jennifer lately.

"I know you do! Bye, Daddy! Will you be home tonight?"

Jenna ran down the stairs leaving a trail of words. She seldom waited for her questions to be answered.

"Hurry, Jenna," Jennifer scolded.

At the front door, Jennifer inhaled the morning air with its surprising fragrance of mint and waved goodbye to Jenna. She stood smiling, watching Jenna wave backward as she zipped out for the bus.

Jennifer prided herself on knowing the meaning of her little girl's every expression, change of posture, tone, although lately distance had been creeping into her parenting. It was hard to stay close to the kids during the school year. Friends and sports strip away empty evenings to sit and talk. She brushed away a niggling thought - maybe some of her own extra activities should go.

Jennifer glanced at her watch and hurried back to the master bedroom suite. She'd showered, but it would take twenty minutes to dress and put on her face. She untied her robe and absentmindedly pulled a suit from her closet as Nick strolled out of the bathroom. He dug both arms under the soft velour of her robe until his hands rested on her bare waist.

"Morning, my love." His face nestled against her shoulder as he began to kiss the nape of her neck.

"Nick," Jennifer murmured a soft protest, before relaxing in his arms for a moment. She pulled back to gaze at him, her expression puzzled.

"When you didn't get home until late last night I worried. Where were you?" She screwed her face into a pout. "Am I being punished for our recent disagreement?"

She looked coyly into his bright eyes under blonde, bushy eyebrows. Of German descent, Nick's controlled features had an annoying stubbornness to go with them. She teased people looked twice to make sure he wasn't a mannequin. When he walked his shoulders angled from years of working at a desk made him look older than his age forty-seven. She liked his slim physique maintained by good genes coupled with personal effort.

He answered in his reassuring tone. "I admit I hated quarreling over my pro bono work, but darling, you know I don't play silly, get-even games. I was detained, that's all."

Nick didn't like secrets, but why stress his wife, he reasoned. She'd be upset unnecessarily if he told her where he was and what happened afterwards.

Nick breathed in her sweetness while nibbling on her ear. "I still don't know why you dislike my helping Christian organizations defend their rights."

"One huge reason, your conservative connections could put me in a bad light at work! You know how important image is there. Before I took the position at the Fullness of Life Centre, you weren't involved in any controversial issues or I'd never have gotten the job. I don't want it threatened now. Clear enough?"

"No! You know I think for myself and choose my own activities."

"Maybe this is about something else. With the approach of middle age, are you reverting to the fantasies of your childhood! Isn't it a Robin Hood syndrome to be a rebel?"

"Churches are being shut down on trumped up charges. Many lose tax-exempt status for ridiculous reasons; without this status they can't afford to operate. I intend to help them appeal. Whether you believe it or not, churches and faith-based organizations are still important to society."

"Why must it be you who intervenes?"

"Why not? I've told you I've rediscovered traditional belief, Jennifer - not a philosophy but a relationship with a living God. I intend to be of service to Him and His people."

Nick's patient, even reply made her face redden. "A relationship with an invisible God who exists in your imagination. I'm uncomfortable with old-fashioned thinking."

Nick's warm grey eyes searched her face. "Jennifer," he began, "you're intrigued with the concept of human beings having enormous untapped potential. Me, too, but God's far superior to our resources. Since you're in this so-called process of advancement, you've become passive in your professional role. The existence of a personal, creative God is logical if you study the evidence. In fact, I've been meaning to tell you it would be wonderful if you would re-introduce church services for your residents again."

"I can't in a federal institution - not now." The cord at the base of her skull tightened. "Besides my residents don't need God, nor do you or I. With education and counseling, people can discover coping mechanisms for all their problems. The world within self is sufficient for happiness."

"Yeah, sure."

"Even if I wanted to believe what you're saying, I can't deviate from the national consensus and put my job in jeopardy. Why keep pestering me with these outmoded ideas? This is the twenty-first century! Get real Nick! Every professional person is responsible for advancing society. As a partner in the Jessell and Davidson's progressive law firm, you know that."

This wasn't going the way Jennifer had intended. She resented Nick's ideology intruding on her neat little package of human completeness. The issue ripped at the core of her personhood and separated her from him leaving a pain she'd never known before. How could Nick believe in a personal God? She'd tried giving him time, thinking his enchantment would wear off. She crossed her arms as anger darted between them.

"Enough!" Nick opted for peace. "Let's not argue, precious, for now let's agree to disagree and talk it through another time. How about a kiss and...?"

Jennifer pushed his shoulders back. "Sorry, I have to get to work." She went into the bathroom to fix her hair. Clearly, he must never hear about Directive 99.

"Anything on for tonight?" Nick followed her in and started to shave at one of the side-by-side marble sinks.

"Nothing special." Jennifer answered absently, as she framed the top of her head in purple instant rollers.

"Good. Let's go to the special school board hearing."

"I'm going to take a pass." Jennifer spread thick alabaster foundation over her face and powdered it without adding blush. She applied heavy blue-black eye makeup to create a stylish, if startling colorless mask. When stark white complexions first appeared on models in Avant Magazine a year ago, they became the rage immediately. She'd hated the look at first, but within three months had grown accustomed to lifeless faces, as one would adjust to faces without noses if they were commonplace.

"I think we should go. Anne Stasen is on the docket."

Jennifer lowered her eyes to hide the thud of her heart. "I know. I read about it in CNA."

"The Controlled News Association rag," Nick mocked, "I'm surprised they bothered to cover the story."

Jennifer ignored his comment. "You know what fanatics Anne and Michael have become." She refrained from adding, just like you.

"Darling!" Nick sounded personally wounded. "This is Anne we're talking about, your best friend in college and you know Michael and I are close. The least we can do is support them by going."

Jennifer spoke louder than necessary. "You know I don't want to get involved. It's a volatile situation, why even ask me! "

Nick slapped his metal razor against the side of the sink brusquely. A faraway look shaded his eyes briefly. He dried his hands and turned to Jennifer. There it was again, the separation invading their lives.

He reached out and cradled Jennifer's chin tenderly in his large palms. "Sweetheart, please."

The pain of all their recent arguments flashed over her nerves. She freed herself and stomped past him. "I suppose I could go for an hour or so, that's all. I've got paperwork to catch up."

"A deal."

Her back turned, she groaned. "I can't believe I said yes. Now I'm out of here. I can't be late for work."

"One for the road." Nick grabbed her and planted hungering lips gently on hers.

She shut the front door, along with her emotions, and headed for her car.

\*\*\*

Sarah hadn't been surprised K & M's work day ended at five, only disappointed. The previous night was forgotten now as she placed her 9 a.m. call, when she returned from morning Mass.

A man with a deep, kindly voice answered on the third ring. "K & M Technology, Tony here."

"Hi Tony. My hard drive crashed and I desperately need to recover some important data. Can you help me?" when she described John's laptop as "hers' she grimaced. Of course it was now.

"It depends how 'lost' it is, M'am. We have recovery software we can run in our shop. However, if the hard drive is badly damaged we'll need to send it to our specialist in Chicago."

"What do they do you can't?"

"Lots. Put it in what we call a clean room and take the hard drive apart. It's a delicate, time-consuming process and isn't cheap. We're talking anywhere from $1000 to $3000, possibly more. You'd have to need your data pretty bad."

She restrained herself from saying that money means nothing to me. My husband's life, his reputation, the legacy our children will carry with them forever are worth any price. Instead she asked, "Where are you located?"

Sarah jotted down the address and was about to hang up, when something else popped into her mind. "I'd like to stay while you work on it."

"It could take a while."

"No problem. I'll bring a book."

She didn't see him shrug his shoulders in a "whatever" gesture. He was used to the people's possessiveness over their hardware.

"Hopefully, I can get to it about eleven tomorrow."

"Is that the soonest?"

"I'm afraid so."

"Give me a break, mam, People often wait a week to get their stuff in."

"I'll be there."

Only, Sarah prayed, let there be information helping me make sense of John's murder. She refused to believe his death was anything else.

## Chapter Five

Pirelli had never been in Relton's office before. The modern black leather furniture edged with stainless steel looked impressive. If the large orange and yellow abstract painting, the only wall hanging, was supposed to portray something, he couldn't figure out what. On a pedestal to the right of the huge desk was a black statue about three feet high of a man bent over with his chin in his hand. A small, engraved sign under it, read The Thinker or The Killer, he guessed but couldn't be sure.

From Relton's circular desk he could swivel to any one of the six computers around his semi-circle.

He turned to face Pirelli now. "I don't want our current target to look like a suicide. Levinson's is enough for now. There must be no sign of a crime involving Trevor. A clean disappearance, that's all, and nobody turning up ever. Work with Shak and Bruter to set it up."

"What's the time frame?"

"Tomorrow."

Pirelli winced.

The laser printer next to Relton's right arm spit out a page with contact information for his accomplices. The words became a death warrant in Pirelli's grasp.

\*\*\*

Jack Danzing waited for Jennifer in her office. She'd personally selected all the staff at the Fullness of Life Centre except Jack, her chief assistant, a federal appointee, as she was.

Technically Jack was under her control but only to a point. She critiqued his performance, but her evaluation was a formality. Jack sent his own reports on her to his command chain at national headquarters. Jennifer didn't like the process, but endured it as one of many unpleasantries she'd learned to tolerate.

She knew because she was top of her class and had been made national liaison for all the nursing homes' Congressional affairs, responsible only to the managing federal health czar. All major decisions at individual locations were made by this czar and his staff in DC. Jennifer, like all heads, controlled implementation and crucial on-site details of operation.

Charming and nice-looking, Jack was loved by the residents. Jennifer might have appreciated him more if she didn't know he wanted her job. He now assisted even more with daily operations so she could focus on writing the procedural changes coming with the new directive.

The original job bulletin describing Jack's position said, "Assignment five years in duration, supervision of staff and standard protocol." Proper administrative training supposedly took that long, but if Jennifer messed up, she'd already trained her replacement.

Those five years were nearly up. The question was where would he go? Unless an administrator died they rarely were replaced. She could be stuck with Jack ad infinitum.

After the ritual of morning greetings, Jack inquired, "Did you read about John Levinson?"

"I saw the news on TV. How tragic for his family." It was easy for Jennifer to feel sympathy for any woman who lost the man she loved.

"The name didn't register immediately. Then I remembered I met Levinson when he did an article awhile back on the federal elderly care centers." Jack's eyebrows shot up. "Rumor was he'd been working on a book. Did you know?"

"No." Was he pumping her? "All I know is he was a vocal opponent of federal government involvement in elderly care. Haven't heard much from him in the news lately; supposedly his paper kept sending him around the country on assignments."

"Listen to this," Jack's eyes were still glued to the paper. "His wife is asking anyone who had contact with her husband during his last trip to Boston or information regarding his death to get in touch with her. She doesn't believe the police report he committed suicide."

"I'm surprised she found someone at the paper willing to humor her."

*** 

Sarah Levinson drove directly to the computer shop after dropping the children off at school. For now she needed the security of driving them each day and picking them up herself. They'd both complained, but she was adamant. Knowing how great her grief was, her oldest son persuaded his younger brother not to continue making a fuss.

Maybe if she arrived at the shop early, a cancellation would open a time slot sooner. She brought a new book on the Civil War along, *No Peace for the Wicked*, if only she could focus enough to read it.

Sarah waited, not patiently, but with determination and persistence allowing her to be nowhere else.

Tony finally started work on John's computer at 10:45. She forced herself not to keep asking how it was coming and did they find anything yet.

The book stayed in her bag. Leafing through magazines filled the time and made her look absorbed in something else at least.

*** 

Nick spent two hours toward the end of his workday with representatives from the Coalition of Charities, which faced shutdown if the proposed tax law eliminating non-profit's tax-free status went into effect. Most simply couldn't afford the additional expense of a property tax. He was a half hour late getting home.

Jennifer heard the front door slam. "Ready for the board meeting? I'll eat later. Let's go, sweetie."

Nick stuck his head in the refrigerator and pulled out a couple slices of cheese. He grabbed a package of Triscuits in the pantry and ripped open the inner bag.

Jennifer sauntered into the kitchen from the bedroom. "Hi, Love."

She folded her arms sweetly around his neck, kissed his lips, and nuzzled her head against his neck. She brushed her lips over his right ear. Maybe she could charm him into staying home tonight by a trip to the bedroom.

"Where are the kids?" Nick asked, surprised they hadn't come running to greet him.

"At my Mother's. Darling, how about staying home instead?" Subtlety was never Jennifer's strong suit. "I'll make you a nice dinner. We won't have to rush out."

Maybe if she'd skipped the words and relied on body language she'd have won, but her voice made Nick's body freeze. "You said you'd go."

Jennifer frowned. He'd used his strong, lawyerly tone.

"Why the switch?" he added a touch more sensitively.

"I'd rather keep my distance from Anne. You know I care about her, but I like to protect myself from her antiquated thinking. Also, she expresses her feelings so passionately. I hate excessive emotion. It's so...so sloppy."

She viewed any close liaison with Anne like associating with an emotionally disturbed person, so far had their beliefs changed. Yet Jennifer still valued her friendship, more than she'd admit.

Not being able to completely cut those ties disturbed Jennifer. Usually she could make her mind respond like an obedience-trained shepherd. A smidgen of guilt intruded, but why? Anne changed, she didn't!

Nick responded sarcastically, "That's right, emotion is outdated, isn't it, in your popular world-view of non-involvement?"

"Nick!"

He shook his head. He wasn't letting her off this easy. "Motion denied, you promised. Anne thinks of you as a friend," he reminded his wife.

"So?"

"What about all the things Anne has done for us? Remember how she came to help when you had the emergency C-section at Tara's birth? For a week she watched Collin, did our laundry, and cooked double meals until you got back on your feet. She's always been there when we needed her. Tonight could be tough on her. I understand she's got plenty of vocal opposition." Nick finished his cracker and cheese micro-meal and washed his throat with ginger ale.

"Alright, I'll go, quit the guilt trip." Jennifer sighed. Honorable, as vaguely as Jennifer now conceived honor, she remained a woman of her word, and Nick was holding her to it.

She pulled her coat on and followed him to the car.

A handful of protesters marched outside the municipal building carrying homosexual banners. Feminist groupies shouted random obscenities as Jennifer and Nick entered.

They followed the arrows pointing to the room for the special meeting of the board.

Jennifer wished even more fervently she'd followed her first instinct and refused to come. She'd become less sensitive toward people who, in her estimation, caused their own problems, shutting one door after another in their lives.

Nick guided Jennifer toward some open chairs in the fourth row from the front, smiling at people he knew as they passed by.

Jennifer nudged him with a sharp elbow. "I'd have preferred a seat near the back."

Nick squeezed her hand as he answered her objection. "We want Mike and Anne to know we're here supporting them."

She responded with a dirty look. "Whatever controversial event is happening, Nick Trevor, you need to be in the thick of it." Jennifer looked around, sat down gingerly and pulled a magazine from her shoulder bag. She nonchalantly flipped the pages of Avant for Women while waiting for the proceedings to begin. The diversion didn't work. Her mind kept returning to the scene. Minutes later she twisted in her seat as Anne and Michael came through the door.

Anne's husband's hair was peppered with grey at his temples making him seem older than his forty-five years. His deep blue eyes held a serious look, energized by a magnetizing smile.

Jennifer noted Anne's heather blue skirt and matching silk blouse. Even without make-up she looked stunning.

Jennifer's face softened. "Anne's pretty enough to be a Clairol model."

Anne was deep in conversation with a woman walking at her side.

"Mike says her high school students adore her," Nick said.

"Of course, they would, she's wonderful!" Suddenly Jennifer was ashamed of her reluctance to come. Fearing Anne might really suffer from trying to better their community made Jennifer ashamed. She murmured, "Anne seems so composed. You'd think she'd be threatened by all this hoopla. How strange." Jennifer spoke to herself, more than Nick.

"You're right. I spoke with her yesterday. She said she's trusting God, no matter what. I'm praying whatever happens will somehow turn out for the students' good. I know Anne and Michael are doing the same."

Ella, Anne and Jennifer's mutual friend, walked in behind Anne and Michael. Ella caught Jennifer's eye, and sent a tiny wave in her direction.

Ella looked years older since Jennifer had last seen her six months ago. Was she ill? Ella Farwell often attended their mutual friend, Becky's, social gatherings.

Ella leaned heavily on her second husband Larry, a kindly man is his early 50's. Her first husband, a history professor from a local college, had died of a heart attack. She appeared noticeably shaky. Rumor was Ella had "a drinking problem," genteel terminology for full-blown alcoholism.

Ella and Larry dropped onto two chairs several rows over. Jennifer was glad they weren't sitting too close. She wasn't surprised Ella had come. She kept abreast of any social gossip.

Jennifer caught herself. Perhaps her assessment of Ella was unfair. Maybe it was important for Ella to come for Anne.

Jennifer, Ella and Anne had been college buddies. Their friendship motto was, "All for three and three for one." How times change, Jennifer mused.

People continued to stream in chattering noisily.

"Michael and Anne are in the midst of proceedings to adopt a five-year- old girl from Chile," Nick whispered.

"Oh." Jennifer knew Anne was unable to have children, but hadn't known about the adoption. It must have come up suddenly, as often happens. She knew Carolyn, Mike's seventeen-year old niece, lived with them following the death of her parents in an auto accident several years earlier. Suddenly, Jennifer felt guilty she hadn't returned Anne's calls lately.

"Nick, maybe it's better for Anne not to be working now with the adoption coming up. Does she work because they need the extra income?"

"No. When Mike gave up his position as a marketing executive with Crandall Chemical to become a pastor, his salary dropped, but they manage fine."

"On donations? What kind of financial security is that?"

"You'd be surprised. Genuine Christians believe generous giving is a privilege. They pay their ministers respectably."

Nick leafed through the Daily News while waiting. His eye caught the subtitle of the column on the upper right page, "John Levinson's Suicide Upheld." Beneath he read "despite stricken wife's protests." The article disturbed him more than he would admit. Nick tore out the article, pulled out his Daytimer, and slipped the tiny paper inside.

He half heard Jennifer saying, "I can't imagine wanting to throw ten per cent of my money away."

Nick let his arm drop from the back of her metal chair onto her shoulder and said tenderly, "No, not you, Sweetie." He didn't bother to add he tithed that much and more for both of them. Jennifer never paid the household bills and had no idea. Nick would have told her if she'd asked but it never occurred to her.

As long as Jennifer had enough money in her personal account, she was satisfied, thinking the rest of their income after bills went into savings and investments. *Which was true,* Nick thought. *What better investment than God's work?*

Jennifer shifted position to look around the room. Her chair scraped across the tile floor. Over a hundred people had already filed down the aisle.

She scanned the faces around her. Certainly, Anne's position didn't warrant this much attention?

"Nick," Jennifer whispered in his ear, "Look at the trouble the Stasen's weird lifestyle has caused them. These people don't want her teaching their children because she's such an extremist."

Nick squeezed her hand. "Anne and Pastor Michael certainly are fascinating, you must admit."

"Not to me!" Jennifer shot back.

One protester dressed in a linty black gabardine overcoat ran up to Anne and spit contemptuously at her before anyone could grab him. He missed her face and hit her sleeve leaving a dark, wet spot on Anne's blue silk blouse.

Instantly two men appeared, members of Michael's church, whom Nick recognized. They pulled the shoddily dressed, unshaven man back and out the door. Anne looked down quietly at the spot before gazing compassionately toward the person being pulled away. Michael took her arm and escorted her to the washroom.

Michael's associate pastor walked across the room to greet Nick and Jennifer. After introductions, Jennifer asked, "Why is Anne willing to give up teaching?"

The pastor was only too willing to discuss the intricacies of Anne's position. "The schools were lost in regard to sound moral values a generation ago but she stayed as long as she could to help."

"How did she manage to hang on so long?" Nick interjected.

"That's the question." Pastor Dan smiled. "Anne was secure as a tenured teacher. She'd won several Outstanding Teacher Awards years back and was well liked. The board couldn't simply dismiss her. They'd hoped to avoid going through this huge process and risking a counter suit." The pastor shrugged. "Perhaps now she can do more good on the outside."

"It's sad only a small number of Christian families remain in public education across the country. The majority long since abandoned the public system in favor of private schools and home schooling."

"Right," the pastor agreed. "The DEC organization did a lot to put fear into people who kept their kids in Christian schools."

"What's DEC?" Jennifer asked.

The pastor hurried to explain. "Supposedly, it stands for Decisive Education for the Community. Really it should stand for Discredit Every Christian. The government wants more control over children, among other items on its agenda. The Christian Underground opposes its programs, but must be cautious."

Nick leaned forward out of Jennifer's peripheral vision and subtly shook his head at the assistant pastor.

Jennifer ended the discussion for him. "Spare me the details. Politics doesn't interest me."

Michael's assistant pastor got the message. "Nice to meet you, Ms. Trevor."

Jennifer sat back and pondered her friendship with Anne and Ella.

Their lives intertwined more than she liked to admit. They'd met long before husbands entered their worlds. The three had shared a suite at Esther Waters Dormitory, the bastion of serious female students at the University of WI Madison.

They cavorted as a group with a mysterious synergistic energy none possessed separately. Friends complained they whipped around like three tennis balls on one court, plenty of action but no depth, unless you got one of them alone.

Anne and Jennifer developed into strong individuals in their own right. Ella remained dependent, clutching possessions and people for security.

In college each had the same quick pat answer for the "What are you going to do with your life?" query. They'd chant, "We're going to make an impact!" On what or who was never clearly established. The threesome had vowed to put off marriage until they'd made their mark, whatever that was.

But life, in all its enticing reality, deluged their goals with greater force than the flood of Noah.

Jennifer gazed at Anne's dainty figure framed in nearly perfect posture, and thought, *we've all changed a lot, Annie, not on the outside, but inside where others can't see.*

When their princes rode up one by one, they journeyed into private fairylands. Only the storylines were different.

During her senior year, Anne had joined Campus Crusade for Christ and her spiritual education began. The mystery and wonder of a relationship with a living Jesus fascinated her. She'd told Jennifer, Ella and anyone who would listen she'd experienced the triune Godhead, come to understand the Holy Spirit and found what she'd yearned for all her life.

The college luster had ended for Ella and Anne by senior year. They clutched their diplomas and took off but Jennifer changed her triad room for a single efficiency and plodded on to graduate school finishing summa cum laude with a Master's in psychology. She'd found a stability and inner strength to complete her education that surprised her.

Jennifer's reverie was interrupted by the sound of men putting up another row of chairs across the front of the room for the burgeoning crowd. As her glance wandered over the crowd, she wished this meeting would get underway and be done. The need to continually produce additional seating, seemed to be delaying its opening.

She resumed her memory trip. How coincidental in the years following graduation all three former roommates moved to within five miles of one another near Milwaukee, Wisconsin, as if an invisible bond held them together. Although the three weren't emotionally close any more.

Jennifer waxed poetic and grimaced, "friendship the flower lost," wasn't this line in an old poem? Oh, the three had an excuse – time, too busy. But the real reason, by age forty-five they'd spread poles apart in the values motivating their lives.

Anne and Michael approached the empty chairs at the conference table opposite seven board members and Superintendent Oleston. The five men and two women sat in a grey and navy blur of suits shuffling papers and looking as distant as a block of Antarctic ice. A recording secretary manned the chair on the end. An unsmiling female newswoman with the warmth and posture of a wooden ruler flanked their right.

A gavel pounded. Conversations hushed. Nick shifted in his seat beside Jennifer.

Jennifer looked at Anne with pity, thinking *you were the smart one, how could you fall for the fanaticism that got you here?*

*** 

Sarah relived her conversation at the computer shop for the tenth time as she stood in her kitchen making her sons' school lunches for the next day.

"Sorry, Mrs. Levinson, we did our best, but can't retrieve anything from your husband's computer. If you'd like we can send it on to a specialist we use. Unfortunately, I can't give you a precise cost estimate, but as I said, it will be pricey."

She'd hesitated. "May I drive it there to assure its safety?"

"They don't have an office accessible to the public. We ship UPS so it will be insured. No need to worry. They use shipping boxes with at least a 200lb burst strength. We've never had a problem."

She'd slumped down on the chair in the waiting room. "Let me think a moment."

John's laptop seemed like an extension of him. He'd brought it everywhere, even when they vacationed. She hated letting it out of her possession even temporarily.

"You have a choice to have it returned here or sent directly to your home. I'll be in back. Ring the bell on the counter when you decide."

"Wait!" She'd stood. "Send it." Sarah knew she had to try. Hopefully, she'd salvage a piece of his life if this could be restored. "Please mark it urgent."

He looked at her with raised eyebrows. "A rush job will cost more."

"No problem." She pulled out her credit card with shaking fingers. "Let's begin the process."

Tony had looked at her with sympathy. She realized she must appear weary to him, grey circles under her eyes and drooping posture. Perhaps he thought she was a poor wife trying to find out if her husband had been unfaithful to her. She didn't care what his conclusions were.

"This hard drive data must be extremely important to you?"

"You can't imagine."

*I hope I did the right thing,* Sarah mused as her knife sliced peanut butter and jelly sandwiches. Money will be tight without John's income. She shook her head. *Of course, I did.*

## Chapter Six

A sudden brightening of the lights drew the noisy crowd to attention.

Those still standing slid to the closest unoccupied chair as the meeting was formally called to order.

In the back of the room a large man wearing a vertical striped sport shirt designed to minimize his tremendous girth slipped his six- foot frame into a seat. If anyone asked why he was there, he'd have been hard pressed to come up with an answer - not being a local citizen or a member of the protest groups.

By coming late, he'd avoided chattering with anyone. He despised small talk. Aloofness was an asset in his business, although that wasn't the real reason he preferred it.

Pirelli pulled a snapshot from his inside coat pocket, and started looking for the man in the picture.

In the harsh glare, Anne blinked rapidly, but not fast enough to keep rhythm with her quickened heartbeat. *Jesus, help me settle down*, she prayed silently.

After brief introductory comments, Superintendent Olston addressed Anne. "Ms. Stasen, I'll get right to the point..."

"Thank you," she replied immediately. He raised his eyebrows searching for sarcasm in her simple phrase, but moved on.

"It has come to our attention you opposed the approved social studies curriculum which you were required to teach. Is this correct?"

"Yes." Anne lifted her head.

Jennifer watched Anne's demeanor of quiet composure and boldness with amazement. She appeared undaunted by this confrontation.

A vocal majority of the crowd jeered in unison until the chairman rapped his gavel.

"Unless the onlookers are respectfully quiet, I'll request the security guards clear the room." The superintendent's angry, schoolmasterly voice conveyed his edge of authority.

Jennifer glanced at Nick. "Anne reminds me of someone, who?"

His face, with its Indian tan complexion, radiated approval as he studied Anne. "I know." Nick whispered in Jennifer's ear, "A five-foot-three Joan of Arc."

Jennifer frowned experiencing a shiver of jealousy as the crowd stilled. "She's a fighter. I'll give her that."

"Subsequently, you were fired. However, the fact of being a tenured teacher has created a complication. The purpose of this hearing is to remove your tenure Ms. Stasen. Please tell the board what objection you had to the curriculum goals approved by this school board?"

"Superintendent Olston and Board Members, the school curriculum assumes all students are already sexually active. Students are to take health-oriented safeguards, specifically the use of condoms, which are known to be only partially effective. Past research results on similar curriculums demonstrate promiscuity, venereal disease and unwed pregnancies increase when this material is taught."

Anne directed her reply to the questioner before turning to visually sweep the audience. She spoke with authority as though lecturing one large class.

"Furthermore, young people are encouraged to explore fully every alternative method of sex to discover their preference, including homosexuality and bestiality."

"Bestiality, Miss Stasen?" The chairman interrupted. "First of all, we cannot determine what is offensive to the morality of our community. For some that may include sex with animals. However, I'm not sure that's currently taught in our program."

Anne sweetly corrected him. "My name is Mrs. Stasen. If you'll examine the teacher's manual and student material for the curriculum under discussion you'll observe it differs from the misleading introductory data reviewed by the school board earlier and sent to the parents for approval."

His face reddened.

"She better watch herself," Jennifer whispered.

But Anne was on a roll. "We need a curriculum stressing commitment in marriage and the dangers of physical union before the emotional intimacy of a relationship," she paused for breath, then continued, "with warnings of the consequences of illicit sex, particularly for girls. I don't just mean pregnancy. An STD, sexually transmitted disease, for a man is often a minor irritation, but a woman risks painful uterine infection and permanent infertility. This afflicts one of every three girls with STD's. Way back in the 90's there were 30,000 new cases of STD's per day. No one even is even willing to state in print the increase in those statistics now."

Anne turned to the group holding feminist placards like, "Equal Sex!" "Women Deserve to Have Fun Too!" She asked rhetorically, "Is ignorance and misinformation what you want for women?"

"Mrs. Stasen, let's hurry this along. There are other items on our agenda. Will you bring your remarks to closure?"

Anne was not deterred. "I was told I'd have adequate time to present my position."

The chairman glanced at the city attorney in the front row. He shook his head in the affirmative.

Not wanting legal repercussions, the chairman said, "Go on."

"Thank you. I object to the phrase on p. 10 of the Teacher's Manual. I quote, 'If students have any reticence discussing sexual alternatives, they're to be referred for long-term counseling to undo the 'psychological barriers created in their psyche by the outmoded concepts of sin and prudish morality which prevent them from achieving full personhood.' Sin will always be a relevant concept."

A husky voice from the crowd yelled, "You're a prude. That's your problem lady!"

Several "Yeahs!" followed.

Anne circled the room with her voice, "Childhood inhibitions are healthy protective defenses. It's not our job as educators to tear them down and leave students vulnerable to valueless choices."

A protester yelled from the side of the room, "How students behave sexually is their choice, Stasen. If they get pregnant, abortion is the law of the land!"

Anne appeared not to notice the hostility around her. She smiled calmly and went on. "After conception occurs the best choices become adoption or parenting. Students need to know the joys and challenges of teen parenting and the wisdom yet difficulty of adoption options."

A woman school board member in a grey suit stood up, her face flushed with anger. "Who are you to criticize our program! This curriculum has the backing of the National Learning Association."

Another female from the audience chimed in, "Of course it's good! The NLA has the best interests of the students in mind, don't they?"

"Perhaps the NLA did initially, but no longer. It's a political arm of government with an agenda for manipulating the minds of our children."

Anne's point was disregarded.

Nick raised his hand to speak. To Jennifer's relief, he was ignored.

"You may cancel my tenure if you wish, but I won't alter my stand." Anne's voice assumed additional strength with every word. She sat down quietly.

Michael immediately put his arm around her. "Super job, honey," he said loudly.

"Mrs. Stasen, you have made your position perfectly clear." The Chairman sighed. "I regret you have been so thoroughly misguided." He called for the vote against her continued employment.

The decision for Anne's dismissal was unanimous.

The President of the Board stood. "Your well-known and succinctly expressed commitment to an intolerant and long-discredited world view damages your credentials. You leave us no choice but to terminate you, effective immediately."

Most of the audience cheered.

Jennifer glanced at Anne. Was that a tear trickling down her face as a photographer rushed over for a quick shot?

Nick disliked the picture was taken during what would be seen as a show of weakness, rather than during her powerful presentation of ideas. He muttered, "This ignorant board's perception of success is a farce. The parents don't understand losing Anne is their children's loss. They're too propagandized to know truth."

A few students from Anne's classes ran up and huddled around her. Soon she was smiling, not crying.

"You would think she won rather than lost the decision," Jennifer whispered with surprise as she and Nick approached Anne.

"I'm sorry, Anne," Jennifer ventured, "at least it's over." These were the only words of comfort Jennifer could think to offer.

Anne hugged her spontaneously.

Jennifer hoped no one was watching.

Anne looked toward Nick. "We lost."

"Anne, you didn't lose, they did." Nick glanced at the retreating parents. "They think they're buying their children's lives with the false protection of condoms and unnatural sex, but in reality, they're losing their kid's souls, maybe their lives as well."

Jennifer squirmed. No way she was getting into any soul and damnation talk.

Anne ventured, "I'm willing to accept the ostracism, I just pray some good will come of this."

"You've expressed thoughts that haven't been heard for a long time here," Nick responded. "What's next for you?"

"I have an opportunity to teach as a substitute in the local Christian school for now. Our daughter's adoption will be finalized soon. I'll take time off to be with her. My days in public education are over."

"We'll appeal the board's decision anyway as we discussed, Nick," Mike said, moving closer. Nick wasn't eager for Jennifer to know he'd been giving Mike and Anne professional consultation.

"Can we buy you coffee?" Nick asked.

Jennifer groaned inwardly. Being seen in public with the Stasens right now was the last thing she desired.

Anne shook her head.

"Thanks, but we're beat," Michael answered, walking Anne down the aisle.

"Me, too," Jennifer added quickly and started edging toward the door. Feeling a tinge of guilt she called over her shoulder, "I'll contact you for lunch soon, Anne."

"See you Monday, Michael."

Nick guided Jennifer through the crisp night air to their car.

"Nick, what's on Monday? You're not still meeting with Michael for his men's breakfast Bible study group? You know I dislike your participation in activities like that in public."

"Yes, I know." He swiftly changed the subject. "C'mon let's get home."

Entering the highway, Nick looked cautiously into the rear-view mirror to see if any auto pulled out after theirs. He was still leery about his experience the night before with the blue sedan.

*I wish I could have seen a face,* he thought.

Nick missed the car at the school parking lot intersection sitting a long time to make a turn. When Nick turned, it moved out slowly. The large man who had tailed Nick the previous night sat behind the wheel.

Later in bed, before he fell asleep, Nick prayed, "Lord, whatever is going on, please protect Jennifer and the kids."

## Chapter Seven

Saturday afternoon Nick and Jennifer hiked among the massive oak and catalpa woods behind their five-acre estate. The rhythmic sway of the branches provided a soothing backdrop for Nick's thoughts.

Jennifer wore faded jeans and tennies, the casual attire transcending every social class and decade. Nick's green and tan flannel shirt and denim jeans provided natural camouflage gear as they hiked along the tree-studded ravine. When they stopped to rest, Nick wrapped his arms around his wife.

"Sweetie, we've got an indestructible cord of love around us. Through all these years it's held strong."

He looked at her with deep tenderness. Jennifer turned away self-consciously.

"Let me guess who's speaking, is it Robert Frost or Longfellow? I say Longfellow."

Nick hesitated, apparently choosing his next words with particular care. "Jennifer, you are infinitely precious to me."

"Nope, I was wrong, it must be Shakespeare."

"Hon, will you hear me out?"

She nodded, but a tingle of fear swept down her spine. Something inside her sensed she didn't want to have this conversation.

He went on. "During the first several years of our marriage we both went to church occasionally... a meaningless routine that turned me off. You wanted to go for social reasons and 'family image stuff.' Now when going to church and worshipping God means something to me, you want no part of it." Nick reached for her hand, but she withdrew it instantly.

She began walking again and he followed.

Jennifer didn't try to hide the frustration in her voice. "I'm still trying to figure out what happened to you. "

"I've told you. I discovered Jesus is for real."

She shook her head. "I'm not there, Sweetheart. We both went searching for spiritual meaning. I used my brain and found the new universal philosophy with its acceptance of many gods. That's reality, dearest. One God, no other, is pie-in-the-sky unreal and it's..." She searched for the word and finally came up with "...discrimination!"

"But there is only one genuine God of power and love." The path narrowed. Nick moved aside to let her go first.

"Illusion." She sighed, lifting her face to the streaks of sunlight pouring through the huge oaks. "You're deceived. You've mixed up dreams and goals crazily. We're eons apart!"

"I hope not. The Lord created us to be one."

Jennifer sensed a mournful, hushed darkness descend over her heart. "Face it, Nick. Since you became a Christian we're not just spiritually isolated, but emotionally, too. Our relationship has become a battleground."

"Someday I pray you'll understand," he murmured.

"Don't count on it." Jennifer thrust the last words over her shoulder and lowered her head to hide a shimmering film of tears.

"How can you be angry because I have intimacy with God?"

"What I dislike is our emotional separation." Jennifer couldn't hold back her tears now. "We had a closeness that was more than sexual. It was like being one, totally known and understood by each other."

The woods absorbed the sound of their voices and made each speak more freely than they ever had before.

"I sense the distance, too. I feel like I lost you. You're my best buddy, Jennifer. Let's not let this happen."

"I didn't. Your God did."

They stopped briefly. Nick kicked away a six-inch wide limb that had fallen along the path. At first, he didn't answer. He prayed silently, *Dear God! Is this the sacrifice you're asking? Where is it written I must give up unity with my wife? You revealed Yourself to me, show yourself to Jennifer, too.*

Stillness surrounded them. Nick dropped down on a tree trunk, looking sadder than she'd ever seen him.

"I've searched for a resolution to these differences between us Nick. There isn't any! I hate living with this tension."

"Me, too."

She gave him a frightened look. "What are you going to do?" She'd always been insecure about trusting in unconditional love. Was he implying he'd leave her over this?

Instantly sorry, Nick said, "Don't worry, we'll work this out somehow."

Decayed leaves and twigs pulverized beneath Nick's feet as he ground his boots in the dry earth and forced a laugh. "I won't let our marriage end over my relationship with God!"

They trudged back in silence.

After dinner, Nick went for a short hike alone. When he returned he knew he mustn't wait any longer to tell Jennifer his secret. He pondered how he should phrase it. He found her sitting in front of the fireplace reading a professional journal, La Psycholique, the latest international publication for psychologists.

Her trim body showcased her mauve sweat suit, enticing him to take her to bed, rather than confront what smoldered around them. But Jennifer had to be warned. Besides, it might help bind them together.

Jennifer patted the sofa cushion next to her.

Nick plopped down and encircled her with a squeeze. He hoped to re-establish a light-hearted mood. As he bent to kiss her, he felt the coldness of her lips. This wasn't going to be easy. He could depend on her to act civil at least. "I need to tell you something."

Jennifer raised her eyebrows.

"It's about Thursday night when I was late."

She put down her magazine to give him her full attention.

Nick studied his hands as if they'd give him the right words. "I believe I was being followed."

"Whatever for?" Her face expressed amazement.

"I'm not sure. Yesterday I received this letter." Nick withdrew a folded paper from his pocket. "I've received crank letters before, as you know, but this one I don't think is from a crackpot."

"Why not?"

He opened it slowly. "See for yourself." He handed the letter to Jennifer. "Notice the fine grade bond paper and perfect English grammar."

Jennifer read aloud. "Unless you immediately desist in your radical representation of unpopular causes, severe measures of reprisal will be instituted against you and your family. This is the only communication you will receive. Heed it."

Her hand was shaking by the time she finished. The letter, unsigned, had been specifically addressed in the heading to Nicholas Trevor, in care of his law office.

"I knew it would come to this! You're getting into big trouble. Who could have sent it?"

He shrugged. "Perhaps one of my twenty plus colleagues or a client who disapproves of what I do."

"For Christian organizations!" She added as though they were despicable entities. "You'd promised to be discreet."

"I am. It's true some of my associates oppose my beliefs, but I doubt they'd use this form of censure. Besides, my work thus far has been as a consultant. The American Center for Law and Justice handles actual casework."

Jennifer's flaming eyes were glued to Nick's face. Her look switched to tenderness. He basked in her love and concern like a parched flower receiving water.

Jennifer rested her hand on his wrist. "Darling, you're in danger! You must stop whatever you're involved in causing this."

Nick soaked up her sweetness. "Combined with my uninvited tail the other night, I'll admit I'm a bit worried. But I've racked my brain and can't think of anything I'm involved in now or upcoming issue warranting this kind of threat."

"Could it be Anne's school board appeal?"

"No, she's sure to lose, no matter what I recommend."

"There must be something!"

"Not that I can think of. Hopefully, it's nothing, but it won't hurt to use caution." Nick slipped the letter back into his pocket, wanting to downplay the severity of the situation. Still he wanted Jennifer informed and vigilant just in case.

"Right," she said, not convinced one bit.

"Our firm's private investigator will check it out. If any connection turns up endangering you, I'll hire bodyguards to protect you and the children."

"Bodyguards?" Jennifer's left eye twitched involuntarily, an annoying holdover from her stress-laden childhood. Instead of producing a feeling of security, news of a personal bodyguard distressed her more.

"What about you?"

"I'll be fine." Nick's tone was more confident than his queasy stomach. "Remember I gave the guy the slip. He hesitated, before adding under his breath, "it took me awhile though."

Jennifer's face was white. "I'm scared. Tell me you'll give up any dangerous activities."

"Let's forget about it now." He squeezed her shoulders.

Her skin prickled at his touch and her eyeballs became globes.

"What is it?"

"Maybe the threat you received is because of something I'm involved in."

"You? Darling, I hardly think so." He took her hand. She let it rest in his.

"I haven't told you because it's highly confidential. And," her jaw stiffened, "I don't want you to interfere."

Nick sat up straighter. "What is it?"

"I have a new directive at work to be phased in gradually over the next six months. Its full name is Future Enhancement Directive 99. Ours will be the first facility to implement it, an honor, probably because of the recognition I received for my PhD thesis on quality of life issues." A thrill of pride raced through her. "This is the purpose of my upcoming Washington trip. I've been asked to present the program in closed committee to Senators who are major decision-makers on the issue."

Nick let go of her hand. "Tell me more about it."

Jennifer hesitated only briefly. "The lives of residents over 85 are to be terminated by their own choice with medical assistance provided by our staff."

Nick drew back in shock. "Terminated!" Have you gone mad that you say this so calmly? Medical assistance!" He rolled the words off his tongue with disgust. "This is a desecration of what medicine is all about!"

She ignored him, caught up in her explanation. "That's Phase One. In the advanced phase anyone over 85 wouldn't have a choice. The age gets gradually lower..." Jennifer paused, seeing Nick's ugly facial distortion. He looked as if he'd been given poison he couldn't spit out.

"Dear God! You can't possibly consider being a part of this. You have to oppose it."

"Me? I have nothing to do with the decision. If I leave, someone else will implement it. I could lose my job if I don't proceed."

Nick's tone softened. "Jennifer, I thought you went to graduate school to help people, not destroy them!"

"Why is death so bad? We're all going to die someday and move into another state of being. Why should old people live meaningless lives?"

"We're back to the issue of values, are we? Why isn't life itself important to you? You're worried about me. Is my life more valuable than anyone else's?" He slapped his hand on the coffee table in front of them. "You better do some serious thinking. I won't stand by and let this happen."

"Great!" she said sarcastically. "Don't threaten me."

"How can you be so callous? You weren't like this before."

Her voice was almost a shriek now. "Perhaps I wasn't, but I am now."

Nick stood and began pacing and yelling at the same time. "So, I may be in jeopardy because I'm a threat to your 'work! I'll be number one guinea pig in Directive 99."

"Don't say such a thing. You're being unreasonable and hateful. This is my job."

She stalked out slamming the door behind her, glad Tara wasn't around to view her performance. Tears of frustration, mingled with sadness, spilled out of her eyes. She'd sensed the disgust in Nick's voice.

He didn't bother to follow her. As much as he loved her, he didn't want to see her now, let alone talk to her.

Nick settled himself on the sofa to think what to do. He clicked on the TV remote for a familiar sound in his world that had gone crazy. He sat for what seemed an hour, maybe two, mulling over every possibility of this horror. Eventually he fell asleep to numb himself to reality with a golf match playing in the background.

When Nick awoke it was early evening and the room was shadowed in semi-darkness.

"I knew TV was good for something," he muttered, turning on the immense brass lamps at either end of the sofa.

"I thought I heard you." Jennifer entered the room dressed in a bright pink and olive-green flowered Norma Kamali dress, one of Nick's favorites. Since florals weren't currently fashionable, she seldom wore it. "Becky's party starts at 8," she announced keeping her voice emotion-free. "It's okay if we don't arrive until closer to nine."

"I forgot all about it! Can we skip it?"

"It's the surprise farewell party for the Newtons. Ella will be there. Maybe Anne and Michael. I'm sure they were invited. Becky will be terribly put out if we don't show."

"Does it matter to you?"

Nick knew Becky and Jennifer weren't close friends. Becky liked to be the center of attention and made a career of throwing parties to guarantee herself an audience.

"Yes, it does. I could use a party tonight." Her eyes blazed.

Nick sized up the situation aloud. "It's the 'Let's pretend' game. Shove the pain deep into the well, and pull out innocuous small talk. Okay, I'll play, but remember the ultimatum I gave you earlier, my love. Give me twenty minutes to shower and dress."

"Skip the threats and hurry, " she replied coldly.

There would be a truce tonight at least.

## Chapter Eight

The ornate carved sign placed at the driveway's edge like a pompous sentinel announced Becky and Jed's property, Kirkland. The house, an immense two-story, castle-sized home, sat on a ten-acre lot. Jennifer counted four separate wings each built around a central garden courtyard.

"Jed's done well," Nick's words knifed the iciness between them. Even the efficient BMW heater hadn't removed the chill in the car.

Eager to make small talk to heal their rift, Jennifer jumped in. "Becky's wild about her new home, but Jed has to travel so much to maintain their lifestyle she says their relationship is hanging by a fiber."

Nick responded sarcastically, "As long as he provides expensive clothes and this gorgeous roof overhead, she puts up with his absence."

Jennifer rambled on, warming with the chatter. "They're both pretty independent, maybe they prefer this lifestyle. I, for, one am uncomfortable with the tension I feel around them. It spills out into angry outbursts at the slightest provocation."

"Too bad. They're both nice people." Nick reflected aloud. He eyed her sideways.

Did his look say, we are too, aren't we? Jennifer pretended not to notice and began to relax. Finally, a neutral subject, someone else's dysfunction, to deaden the fiery coals of their own emotional separation. "Becky and Jed's daughter, Lisa, functions as their unifying element."

"That must put a lot of pressure on her."

"She's a sixteen-year-old sweetie..." Jennifer stopped speaking as the car reached the end of the drive.

A doorman, hired for the occasion, welcomed Jennifer and Nick with a flourishing sweep of the front door, and scooped their coats away from them obsequiously. Nick handed over his car keys and watched him direct an attendant to park his BMW.

Jennifer inhaled at the site of the lovely decor. Kirkland had been custom-designed for entertaining, beginning with the spacious foyer, which opened onto a 24 by 40-foot living room. Multiple shades of gray with buttercup yellow accents in pillows and floral pieces provided a neutral backdrop for the multi-colored gowns the ladies wore.

Festivities were well under way from the sound of music and tinkling glasses emanating from the sunken bar.

Becky must have been keeping one eye on the door for late arrivals because she'd hurried over to greet them in a loose, flowing, purple caftan swishing over her silver metallic pants every time she moved. Her matching diamond studded earrings and necklace sparkled lavishly.

She grabbed both of Jennifer's hands, leaned across her and kissed Nick on the cheek. "Two of my favorite people! Nick and Jennifer! Come with me," Becky gushed, "I want you to meet some new friends." Another late-coming couple arrived and Becky turned away to include them.

"Don't bother about us Becky, dear," Jennifer insisted. "We'll introduce ourselves around. See to your other guests."

Becky smiled and was off.

"Peace," Jennifer said to Nick resting her hand lightly on his arm as a covert signal for a unity she hoped he wouldn't resist in public.

He smiled ruefully. "I'm not going to be a phony and pretend everything's hunky-dory."

Becky and Jed's older daughter, Lisa, approached them. Lisa had baby-sat Jenna as a toddler and Jennifer still kept up on her doings. Lisa led Jennifer to the den to meet her boyfriend, Ken, watching TV.

While Jennifer was occupied, Nick wandered to the buffet table where he found Becky's husband, Jed. "Are Michael and Anne here?"

Jed shook his head. "A meeting about their upcoming adoption, can't blame them for giving it preference," he said, wiping shrimp dip from the corner of his mouth. "At last I can talk football, buddy, where have you been?" For a few minutes they exchanged opinions on the local team and the new coach.

In his scrutinizing lawyerly fashion, Nick assessed the room. Men in tailored suits and women in shimmering dresses clustered in tight knots of three to five people. The fragrance of exotic perfumes, and expensive shaving lotions blended with wine and scented candles to produce a heady, sensuous scent.

Maybe it was his mood, but it seemed as if all those around him tonight wore cemented smiles and used artificial laughter. Nick decided the group would have made a great TV beer commercial, "Are we having fun yet?"

He found it surprising among the upper middle class house parties were in vogue again. He wondered if it was for the community experience because aloneness and technological connection wasn't all it was touted to be.

After a few hours of chit chat guests played games like Buzz Word and Now What or gathered around a fireplace to sing Irish ballads. Tonight he'd prefer singing to the games. If a party only lasted a couple hours it could be fun. After that the drinking often got out of control and revelers could end up losing their manners and embarrassing themselves. Nick wanted no part of this setting now, although he'd once been at its center.

He wandered into the living room and entered an inviting group with two of his former golf partners.

"No thanks," Nick said when a serving girl approached with a tray of champagne.

Nick had no intention of repeating his previous history of overdoing alcohol. He'd quit drinking altogether to avoid his previous excess, but friends rarely remembered or took him seriously.

Jed sauntered over with two mixed drinks. "Here you go, partner."

Nick said, "I've refused several drinks already, remember I'm a Pepsi guy, buddy."

"Sorry, forgot again." He didn't look sorry.

"Darling, can't you at least hold a glass for show?" Jennifer asked, slipping up behind him. "It's not like you're an alcoholic on the wagon."

Jennifer reached for a glass of Chablis.

Nick glared at her. He wanted to be patient and loving, but darn it, she was such a cultural puppet. Strong in ways where she should have allowed herself to be vulnerable, and stupid and complying when she should have been unyielding.

After about an hour and a half of mingling with the guests Nick cornered Jennifer privately. "Ready to duck out? Pretending lightness is stressful, when we have an engine of discord steaming between us."

She turned away and he observed her beginning to make her goodbyes. He did the same, but before they could reach the entrance, Ella grabbed their arms. "Wait, Nick and Jen. You can't leave till we each tell our favorite story about our dear friends, the guests of honor, the Newtons. They're leaving us the end of the month."

Jennifer mumbled, "We can only stay a little longer." She barely knew the Newtons.

Nick stationed himself near the door as the group assembled.

After a couple golf stories and reminiscences about Gloria Newton's excellent cooking, Ella Farwell, staggered to her feet.

Nick remembered Ella's condition at the school board meeting. Her husband, Larry, doted on her, and had expressed concern about her bouts of depression. He'd told Nick more than once, "I give her everything she wants. What else does she need? I don't get it."

Nick understood using vodka to fill the emptiness emerging as soon as one awoke in the morning. Today it would appear she'd exceeded even her growing capacity.

Slurring grandly, Ella said, "I'm going to tell you all a story." She tottered ever so slightly in her periwinkle pumps dyed to match her dress and waved her cocktail glass like a badge.

All eyes riveted on her, with apprehension rather than anticipation.

"My story's about a town called Self Central, like our town, only the name's different." A sickening sweet smile formed on her lips. "Two friends live there. Their names are Mefirst and Youlast and they work in the local business called World Good."

Ella pulled her words out slowly, stopping occasionally for a sip of her drink. "Together they've been to the seminar called 'Say the Right Thing' and they even took courses, 'Do Unto Others Before They Do Unto You.'"

Ella's husband, Larry, tugged on her sleeve, but she ignored him. Her eyes fastened on the more ruthless businessmen among them, "Can you hear me okay? Mefirst and Youlast are socially conscious. This makes them valuable employers and employees." She continued in a mocking tone slurring "s's" dramatically. Her voice was the only sound in the room.

"Are you wondering what that means? I'll tell you. They're altruistically dedicated to helping the Faraway Disadvantaged," she paused for effect, "because the nearby ones are too disgusting." Ella stopped to giggle in a sickly tone.

One woman uttered a quiet gasp. Ella's husband said, "C'mon, sweetie, you're done now."

Ella threw him an ice-like stare, and went on. "Mefirst and Youlast are fond of platitudes. One of their favorites is 'The green buck stops here.' Ella was warmed up now. Holding her glass unsteadily, she determined to finish. She tossed in the last line in her singsong voice, 'This means get whatever you can from whomever, however.' She stifled a burp and sat down.

Ella's really hurting, Nick noted. He prayed silently for her and resolved to tell the fellows in his Bible study group confidentially to pray. Maybe one of their wives could reach out to her.

Stillness, deep and intensely uncomfortable, followed Ella's little speech, like someone had opened the door to an ugly scene and no one knew how to respond. After seconds seeming like minutes, one man began to chuckle. A quiet murmur became a nervous trickle of laughter.

The tension broke when Jed jumped up and said, "I saw a bumper sticker that read 'Life isn't a dress rehearsal, it's the real thing.' Remember this, Newtons, when you move!" As if on cue the guests began heading for the door.

Jennifer and Nick slipped out wordlessly after he'd tried to find Ella to say goodbye. She was nowhere to be seen.

***

The day after the party, Sunday, Jennifer met Nick at the door when he and the children returned from church.

One look at her drawn face and he knew immediately something was wrong.

She drew him aside into their bedroom and said with a quaking voice. "Anne just called. Ella's dead. She OD'ed on sleeping pills last night. Her husband claims she accidentally took too many, and they reacted with her alcohol blood level."

Shaking, Jennifer fell against Nick. His long arms encircled her.

"God have mercy on Ella's soul," Nick said softly. He knew he and Jennifer were miles apart in their thoughts, despite their physical closeness. Yet she clutched him desperately for comfort.

Trembling, Jennifer forced herself to speak, rather than feel. "Of course, we must shield the children from this horror. We won't discuss it with them."

Later, at dinner, Tara began to chatter non-stop. "I saw this great brown knit, Mom. I need another casual school outfit," she insisted.

"Tara, you can be adorable when you want your way."

Nick and Collin discussed basketball. The children helped clear the table. Jenna's friend's Dad drove the two girls to a roller-skating party, and Collin disappeared in his room.

Nick offered to take Tara to her friend's to work on a homework project. It all seemed so normal, yet unreal.

On the way home Nick called Michael to commiserate over Ella's death. He told him about the new directive at the Fullness of Life Centre. "Keep this under wraps for now. I'm trying to figure out how to fight the proposal, if it passes."

"Does Jennifer have enough power to oppose it?"

"I'm not sure. The big question is, will she? I doubt it."

"Nick, you're one of my best friends. What hits you, hits me. On top of that, my eighty-five-year old Aunt Kathryn is a resident there. Count me in on working with you to stop this."

"I'm not sure how to go about it without alarming Jennifer."

"Why not visit my aunt with me?"

"Let's plan on Wednesday. I'll call tomorrow to arrange the time."

***

Jennifer sat alone at the kitchen table. An inexplicable sadness had settled over her following Ella's death. This was life in sedated suburbia, the life she wanted and loved, right? For once none of her usual leisure activities hiking, reading, aerobics, interested her.

Why so down, she asked herself? Why was the death of Ella like a personal loss? She barely knew Ella any more, despite their history as college friends. Yet Jennifer kept returning to the mysterious question eating at her. What was Ella's problem? Why was she so depressed?

She wondered, most of all, could this ever happen to her?

Of course not, she thought. Ella kept her world too small, her activities too narrow. Jennifer didn't have to worry suicide would tempt her. She had a creative, professional outlet for her energy, didn't she?

She shrugged. The things Ella said disturbed her more than she liked to admit. She wanted to forget this ever happened. Aloud she said, "I don't want to think any more about this now, maybe never."

A strong, unpleasant thought ripped through her. "Despite my free spirit," Jennifer spoke aloud, "maybe I'm not as inwardly confident as I think."

Later the same evening, under the protection of darkness, Nick spoke aloud to Jennifer as soon as they got into bed. Perhaps the words could more easily be heard than if said in daylight. "Jennifer, love, it's like we're on a teeter-totter pulling at each other from opposite ends."

"I know. I'm trying to find a balance without one of us falling off, like Ella."

"This distance isn't the way I want it."

She lay on her back wide-awake beside him. "Nor I, but I can't change," Jennifer stated sadly.

"Can't or won't?"

"Whatever, end of conversation." Her body tightened beside him.

Words had become treacherous weapons, best left in their private arsenals.

She dreaded their upcoming trip to St. Augustine to celebrate her birthday. The federal government gave everyone his or her birthday off and she'd added another personal day to extend the excursion. Going during the week made it easier to make arrangements to be away since the kids were in school and could stay with their friends. Jack, of course, would be delighted to be left in charge for two full days.

# Chapter Nine

Coffee cups rattled noisily in Goldie's Restaurant Monday morning as the men's meeting ended.

Nick checked his watch. "Pastor Mike, can I drop you at your church office?"

"Great, save me the walk."

"I'm parked around back," Nick grabbed his raincoat off the coat rack at the entrance.

They exited into crisp fall air filled with a whisper of winter.

Nick deactivated the security system of his BMW using his fingerprint code and Michael settled himself in the passenger seat.

Once they were on the road, Michael asked, "How's it going with Jennifer?"

Nick grimaced, "Same old spiritual struggles. Please keep praying God becomes as important to her as He is to me. Our talks seem to drive her farther away than ever."

Michael shook his head sympathetically.

"My wild liberal is so saturated in secular worldview propaganda at work, she believes she doesn't need a Savior. She's mixed Eastern religion with the New Age philosophy of the last century and who knows what else? She even believes she's a god! I give her good stuff to read but she won't touch it."

Nick gripped the steering wheel although he was in automatic cruise on a feeder lane requiring little steering.

"Jennifer and I made plans months ago to have a two-day get-away in St. Augustine, Florida for her birthday. She's home packing now. We leave this afternoon. It's obvious she's lost her enthusiasm for the trip, but doesn't want to be the one to call it off. And I won't either."

Nick turned off auto-drive and wove his car in and out of the morning rush hour traffic. He watched the road abstractly, focusing on the conversation.

"I can't blame Jennifer. I never seem to have the right words to get through to her. Lately, we constantly upset one another."

"Time away may help," Michael said sensitively.

Nick's sigh came from deep inside. "I hope so. When we talk about anything of substance like politics or religion, I can't give her the responses she's looking for, which makes her furious."

Despite the warmth inside the car, Nick pulled his coat collar up around his neck. The frosty image of his wife chilled him. "If I made Jennifer choose between her work and me, I'm not sure where I'd end up."

He focused glumly on the windshield.

Michael said, "I can imagine how tough this must be. Give her time. More importantly, give the Holy Spirit time."

They'd reached Michael's church, a tall brick building with a single bell tower emanating from the center topped by a modest cross.

"Got a few more minutes? Another issue is pressing at the moment, I'd like to discuss it privately."

"Sure."

Nick briefed Michael on being followed and the note he'd received.

"Any idea who would see you as a dangerous threat?"

"Hard to say. I could be viewed as a liability because of Jennifer's directive at work or my previous links with Christian organizations. I participated in a couple pro-Christian suits involving the ACLU and a few pro-bono, anti-porn cases. My name's out there. Even if I have tried to keep a low profile for Jennifer's sake. We're checking into this further when I return."

"Let me know how I can help other than praying."

On the drive home Nick used the time to pray, *Lord, let Jennifer become yours, not for me, for her and for You. As the trees sway and bow before you majestically, as your sun is brighter and warmer than any man-made source of energy, let Jennifer know the beauty and power of your love. Lord. With you nothing is impossible. May you be glorified in her, in me and in our family forever and ever.*

# Chapter Ten

Around two p.m. Monday Nick and Jennifer's direct flight taxied onto the landing strip at the Daytona Beach Airport.

Jennifer strolled off the plane leisurely, not at all sure she wanted to be here with Nick. A sense of melancholy had slid over her mind. She tried to push it away, but couldn't.

Nick addressed the clerk at the Avis counter. "You have a Lincoln town car reserved for me." He hunted through his wallet for the reservation number.

"Yes, Mr. Trevor."

Nick jerked his head up, suddenly suspicious. Had he been followed here? He looked around. "How do you know my name?"

"Sir, only one reserved town car hasn't been picked up. I guessed you were Mr. Trevor," the Avis representative replied innocently.

"Great. I'm not used to such personal service." He knew he was edgy.

"Avis tries harder, sir."

Nick laughed. "Right, I forgot."

"Just enjoy it, darling." Jennifer smiled sweetly, picking up the keys to their Town car.

Once outside, with a whiff of the breeze off the ocean and the prevalent smell of azaleas, Jennifer was hooked on enjoying her two days on Florida's east coast. She hugged Nick spontaneously.

"I'm glad we came. Let's pretend it's our honeymoon again, and forget everything else."

Nick pressed his cheek against hers momentarily and whispered, "You are so precious."

Following the directions offered by the Avis agent, they drove on A1A along the ocean to Palm Coast and on to St. Augustine Beach in light traffic. Jennifer pressed open the sunroof to catch the sound of waves. Inhaling deeply, she released her tension. "We're hearing resounding surf in 85-degree air. I love it!"

Jennifer read aloud from a brochure she'd picked up at the airport. "St. Augustine is the New England of the South, and a favorite getaway spot for Floridians. Ocean waters are guaranteed to work their magic as you watch our magnificent sunsets!'"

Nick grinned, "This is the oldest city on the North American continent, picturesque St. Augustine, where Ponce de Leon sought the Fountain of Youth in the sixteenth century."

"Hey we're seeking the Fountain of Happiness," Jennifer interrupted.

"In this distant place in time and space we're going to shake the dust off our love, and make it new again."

Jennifer laughed. "Oui, monsieur poet again." She leaned back and admired Nick's profile. "I must admit you're still the most handsome man I've ever met."

"Let's keep it that way. By the way, flattery will get you anywhere, lady."

Around six after stopping for a grouper sandwich at an oceanside open-air restaurant, Nick parked in front of the Casa de Plaz Bed & Breakfast across from Matanzas Bay. The architecture strongly indicated the Spanish influence during settlement. Their B & B consisted of two rectangles washed in pink with a black roof connected by a courtyard. A gracious shaded verandah intimately lit with antique oil lamps, beckoned guests with a gorgeous hand-painted, wooden Welcome sign.

Nick and Jennifer passed through French doors into a large parlor with a stone fireplace.

"Welcome to the Casa de Plaz, a site of heaven on earth." The dark-skinned Hispanic man behind the front desk flashed a congenial smile.

"Thank you." Jennifer smiled warmly.

His friendly handshake accompanied the words, which sounded sincere, not trite. "I'm Señor David, your Innkeeper."

Nick introduced himself and Jennifer, as he filled out the check-in forms.

Señor David extracted two antique reproduction keys from a locked drawer. "Now I will show you to your suite. On the way may I give you a tour of the Casa?"

Jennifer smiled. "Of course."

Señor David guided them past sitting rooms and alcoves to the dining room with its massive Spanish oak table already set for sixteen. "You may join us in here for breakfast or have it brought to your private courtyard outside each room at nine."

Nick raised his eyebrows in Jennifer's direction to ask her preference.

"We'll do the courtyard," she announced.

They walked down a corridor adjoining the second building, and entered a separate wing. "This," Señor David said with a flourish flinging open the door, "is the honeymoon suite, which you chose, Mr. Trevor."

Jennifer's eyes widened. Breathtaking views of the bay from three walls of glass stretched in front of her. The first room they entered, the sitting room, featured an oriental carpet over gleaming maple wood floors and a cozy sofa in front of a real wood-burning fireplace. Original brass lighting fixtures cast a soft glow.

In the next room of the private suite, also facing the bay, a four-poster cherry bed with a white lace canopy sat three feet above the floor on a raised platform. Like the windows, the bed had been draped in rose chintz and white eyelet.

A picture window on the opposite wall framed their view of the private courtyard, a walled in garden of wildflowers with a white iron table and two wicker rockers. Inside, an ivory marble Jacuzzi dominated the private bathroom enclosed with white painted wainscoting.

Jennifer gasped, "This is perfect."

Señor David said, "If you need assistance, either my wife or I will be at the welcome desk." He disappeared closing the door behind him.

Jennifer wandered once around the rooms before climbing onto the bed and flopping down on her back. Rising and reaching for Nick's hand she pulled him atop her. She pressed her lips to his, then pushed him back gently and scrambled up. "This is a promise of what you'll get later. We'd better get to a restaurant before they all close for the night."

"No problem! You'd be scrumptious enough!"

While the innkeeper gave Nick dinner recommendations at the front desk, Jennifer glanced through menus from the places he suggested and made a selection, Joie de Vivre, within walking distance.

The building stood out a block away in bright white stucco with a red awning imprinted with the name in gold. *This reeks of class,* thought Jennifer with pleasure as they were seated.

They ordered chateaubriand for two with an appetizer of Brie puff pastry in maple and brandy sauce. The chef added black linguini vegetable stir-fry as the evening's side dish, a house specialty the waiter said they must try.

"Real gourmet cooking, darling, just like at home," Nick teased. It was rare they had anything other than the latest, completely prepared micro-meals.

When the appetizer arrived, Nick bowed his head briefly to thank God for providing this special celebration and asked God's blessing on their getaway and the food.

Jennifer looked away, determined not to let anything annoy her.

During dinner they spoke only of pleasant, past stages of their lives. Nick covered Jennifer's hand with his own on the tabletop, recalling aloud the stirring of his first feelings for her and how they had deepened over the years.

She looked down for a brief moment with a mixture of shyness and sadness. Did she deserve to be loved so completely?

They lingered over coffee with pleasant small talk, a precious rarity in their busy lives. For a few hours, nothing else existed. Love became their world.

Over banana cream torte they planned their one full day in this marvelous old city with the waiter's help. He insisted, "The Lightner museum is a must, followed by a horse-drawn carriage ride through town."

As they stood to leave, Jennifer noticed an elderly couple in the corner and a cloud descended over her. She knew Nick would have been upset to read her real thoughts. Would they make it to 40, 50 years of marriage? These were nice moments, even romantic, but could her love for Nick remain strong, if he continued to disappoint her and she him?

She could justify her frequent, angry responses toward Nick, yet truly regretted causing him grief. Worst of all, she deeply feared losing his love.

Later in their suite, satiated in the afterglow of their physical union, Nick said aloud, "It must have been like this the first night in the Garden of Eden." Jennifer was already asleep in his arms.

*\*\**

Pirelli visited Nick's office on Monday according to the schedule Relton had set for him but was put out to learn Nick was out of town until Wednesday.

He immediately contacted his boss.

"The trip must have come up suddenly," Relton said. "It changes nothing except to create a two-day delay. I'll pass the word on - Wednesday." He clicked off without a goodbye.

*So much for manners,* Pirelli thought.

*\*\**

Jennifer was curled in a modified fetal position with one leg tucked up, the other stretched out straight, her head bent down. Nick's body encircled her side completely.

He'd awakened for prayer at five, and an hour later crawled back into bed against his sleeping wife. The smooth cotton lavender-scented sheets lulled him swiftly back to sleep. They slept till eight and made love passionately again, as if both sensed the preciousness of the relationship between them that could be lost.

After a scrumptious breakfast of French toast filled with cream cheese and strawberries, bacon, juice, and coffee, they toured the Lightner museum, marveling at the gorgeous paintings and ceramics. They explored the magnificent architecture of Flagler College as they strolled about town.

Back at the B & B sitting in the garden on wrought iron chairs, they ate sandwiches they'd picked up at a nearby deli.

Nick stretched his arms overhead and stood up. "Okay, love, it's time to hit the beaches to walk off this food."

"I just need a minute." Jennifer slipped into her one-piece melon-colored suit and loaded a beach bag and two huge towels the B & B provided.

Twenty minutes later, Nick turned the rented Lincoln onto the strip of oceanfront allowing vehicles. He found a place to park twenty feet from the roar of the rushing surf. Jennifer jumped out and ran barefoot along the white sand beach, half dancing, half running in and out of the waves.

The sight of his wife and the azure blue ocean with its surprisingly warm waters magnetized Nick. If anything on earth possessed the imprint of the awesomeness of God, it surely had to be the ocean.

Nick sauntered along behind her, renewing his spirit as he sidestepped the waves neatly without soaking his rolled-up sweats.

After they reached the public fishing pier, they circled back. Jennifer plopped down on the big yellow beach towel she'd brought.

Nick pulled off his outer pants, and whipped them down on the beach towel. Running to the water he yelled, "Cowabunga," before plunging into a four-foot wall of salt water. A primal sense of security rebirthed in the surging, relentless waves seemed to signify more powerfully than words the presence of His Creator in his world. Nick absorbed the presence of God without and within. Quite simply God permeated him. How could he ever describe this to Jennifer?

Jennifer saw it on his face when he returned. It was the distance she always sensed when he'd been in prayer.

Before heading back to downtown, they meandered out on the fishing pier extending what seemed a mile into the water.

Nick knew it would soon be time. He decided they had to talk again tonight. His thoughts wandered in rhythm with his steps while he chose words for later. He knew his tongue would feel like a bar of steel and he so hated to break the mood of their closeness. One of his favorite quotations as a high school student, was 'Veni, vidi, vici, I came, I saw, I conquered. He'd grabbed this as a kid venturing to make his mark'. That's what they'd say of me, Nick Trevor, he came, saw and conquered - work, women, he'd have it all!" Until he realized how empty it all was.

Now, he thought pensively, my motto is, "Jesus came, I'm His, and He's the conqueror."

He believed he'd given up too easily in the past when he tried to talk about spiritual issues with Jennifer. She always changed the subject or left the room. This evening he wanted to speak his heart completely one last time. He'd know he had done all he could and leave the results to God.

On the way back to their car, Jennifer shoved her rolled up towel at Nick and ran wordlessly off to the splurging, extravagant surf for one last dip.

She'll say my words are crazy and tuck them far away in her brain. But I have to try.

He watched her swim as if for her life. Looking refreshed, she jogged back to their car where Nick waited.

"What's next?"

"Is this a marathon, lady? Besides, I got you here. You're in charge of our itinerary."

"How about biking! I saw bikes behind the Casa de Plaz."

Forty-five minutes later they were exploring the ancient brick streets around the Oldest House Museum and the Oldest Store.

Jennifer called to Nick riding ahead, "I'm falling in love with this historic, little town."

"Me, too!" he shot back.

The quaint architecture of the buildings separated by only a few feet on each side, with walled gardens in front and back, enchanted her.

They pedaled toward St. George Street, a quaint main street blocked off to vehicular traffic with tiny branches jammed with stores shooting off each side.

"The guide book says St. George Street is a shopper's paradise," Jennifer called out. "Let's park and lock our bikes and get souvenirs for the kids." Nick took Jennifer into a boutique and watched her try on outfits. She decided on a coral, two-piece summer suit. "My favorite color. This will be perfect."

Nick handed the purchase to the young clerk and pulled out his plastic. "For my bride." Nick joked kissing Jennifer's cheek lightly.

"Bride!" Jennifer exclaimed.

"Well, we're staying in the bridal suite!"

Jennifer blushed, always a little uncomfortable with Nick's public affection, yet basking in it all the same.

After picking out colorful T-shirts and souvenirs for the children at another shop, they put their purchases in Nick's backpack and biked back to their B & B.

After showering together, they tenderly made love again.

At dusk they wandered over to a quaint Parisian restaurant on King St. for drinks. With them they devoured the best spinach quiche appetizer in the world, as the sign on the door proclaimed. Outside the hum of sightseeing trolleys circling the square and added to the festive aura of activity.

After dinner, Nick leaned back in his chair and surveyed Jennifer. She wore a powder blue, black, and white knit cotton sweater with white pants, tight at the ankles. No one would guess she had kids in high school, unless they got close enough to see the tiny wrinkle lines forming around her eyes.

Nick focused now on those bright, brown eyes.

"Nick, you make me nervous when you stare." Jennifer squirmed like a schoolgirl. It was as if she had a persistent, deep-seated anxiety maybe she wouldn't measure up if examined too carefully.

"You know you've hardly aged!"

"Keep it coming," she quipped.

"Must be because I treat you so well." Nick shot back.

"It's true you have spoiled me, but I'll let you in on a secret." Nick leaned forward.

"Though I sometimes object, I like knowing I'm under your blanket of caring."

Jennifer grew quiet, thinking about her past. "Before I met you, I never knew the feeling of being loved for myself. Anytime I messed up, my father would say, 'That's it, we're through,' and threaten to put me in an orphanage. I believed him!"

Nick knew Jennifer's father had fled from his failed business into alcohol. Jennifer had no escape until she was old enough to leave home. "Once you left, you never looked back, did you?"

Jennifer sighed. "Your love came as a surprise. Sometimes, I still don't quite believe it."

"You can." Nick reached across the table and placed his hand tenderly over hers. He stiffened his chin and added, "Wait till you experience the unconditional love of Jesus."

"Nick, you've accepted me totally until now. That's what scares me. You're trying to change me with this religious rigmarole, like I'm not good enough anymore."

Before Nick could answer, the clomping of huge workhorses' hooves interrupted their conversation. Jennifer parted the Battenberg lace curtains at the window adjacent to the table. She gazed on a horse-drawn carriage with driver mounted on the high front seat of the surrey with a blue fringe top.

"Nick, what fun! Let's finish talking on our carriage ride. I haven't been in one for years."

"Your every wish is my heart's desire," Nick said with exaggerated gallantry.

He nodded to the waiter to bring the bill and asked directions to the carriage stand.

"Two blocks to the street beside the St. John's River where they line up waiting for riders. Just south of the fort."

***

Outside evening shadows quickly descended like a grand finale curtain drop on the day's performance. The lights of the city popped on giving the streets and walkways an amber glow.

At the carriage stand no less than ten buggies were lined up, each uniquely arrayed in resplendent colors, some had silk flowers attached to the side poles of their rigs. The drivers were costumed as dramatically as the horses and carriages. The earthy smell of horses pleased rather than repelled Jennifer's citified nose.

Nick propelled her toward an off-white horse and buggy resembling Prince Charming's carriage. A woman driver in a long dress and bonnet bowed, "Carriage ride for milady, sir?"

"Perhaps."

Jennifer pressed Nick's arm. "I want to walk past them all, and pick my favorite."

He delighted in obliging her with little gestures giving her joy. That's why it hurt so much to initiate pain. Their changing values were creating a new reaction neither knew how to neutralize.

Jennifer selected the brown velvet surrey. The driver sported a slightly worn tux and top hat, but his bow tie was impeccable. When he opened his mouth, he sounded all cowboy.

"Howdy, mam, my name is Henry, this here horse is Buck. You'll want to wrap the blanket around your legs to keep warm. It's uncommonly cold tonight," he said kindly.

Smushed comfortably together like stuffed animals, Jennifer breathed deeply.

"I'm never going to forget St. Augustine," she nuzzled Nick.

He brushed his mouth across her lips tenderly and squeezed her tightly. "A perfect place is anywhere with you. Wait till we get to the last act," he intimated in his sexiest voice.

Henry was talking. "Excuse me folks. Would you like me to identify points of interest along the way or would you rather I remain silent so you can visit with each other?"

"Let's have your tour, by all means," Jennifer said eagerly.

"Great. Castillo de San Marcos is on your right, oldest fort on North America. Construction began in 1672. The walls are made of coquina stone quarried from nearby St. Anastasia Island. We're proud it's the only fort never taken." Henry droned on like a radio. "Every time General Oglethorpe's troops fired, the cannon balls bounced off or stuck in the walls. Finally, he gave up and withdrew." *God, sometimes that's what I'd like to do*, thought Nick. *Give me courage.*

Jennifer leaned against the once plush, padded carriage seat. "How perfect. The driver is agreeable and the horse is obedient. Darling, if only our children were as docile and easily guided as this horse."

"I don't think we'd want that."

"Try me! No, I suppose you're right," she wrinkled her face resignedly. "It is exciting to see their unique spirits developing. Even if it does add stress and uncertainty to life."

"We piled on plenty of stress ourselves." Nick had wanted to find a tie-in back to their earlier conversation. Was this his chance? He dreaded sledge hammering the mood.

*God, please keep Jennifer from over-reacting*, he prayed.

He'd be forthright, he knew no other way. "Speaking of the dynamics at home, I sure sense an electrical jolt when I want to talk about what Christ means to me. And I'm concerned maybe I've given you the wrong impression..."

Perhaps if he just talked about himself, and kept the focus off her, he could make her understand.

"Nick, I don't care if you feel a social need to attend a church. I don't have the same compulsion, although I'll go occasionally." Jennifer's body tensed beside him. "Let's leave it at this."

"What I don't think you understand is I attend church, not because it's the thing to do, the external façade of a good Dad, honorable citizen sort of thing." Nick mistook her silence for an invitation to continue. "I actually enjoy being there. Michael makes God's Word relevant through personal applications. I'm excited about applying God's principles to my life."

Jennifer's face twisted in distaste. "I understand Michael's your close friend and you want to support his work and charitable projects. But please don't try to talk me into a relational experience with this far-off God of yours. Nothing could convince me one-man's death two thousand years ago could affect my decisions today. That's not only ridiculous, it's bizarre!"

"Sweetheart, you're right, a relationship with our living God isn't something you can be talked into. As Paul said in 1Corinthians 2:4 'And my speech and my preaching were not with persuasive words of human wisdom, but in demonstration of the spirit and of power...' It's not like being a Christian is an altruistic, social or merely intellectual experience." He was becoming more animated now. "I get personal happiness from loving God nothing else can touch! And a concern for others, too."

"Nick, if God is real, He can prove Himself to me, without my inventing Him. He's got his work cut out because I'm not the naive person I was before new worldview enlightenment. I truly believe we can control life and death for the world good."

Nick shuddered involuntarily. "Jennifer, you use the new worldview terminology beautifully, but it's ugly, false doctrine that can destroy us all."

Jennifer threw her head back, stiffening, "I preferred to avoid this discussion, but you've apparently been gearing for it all during our trip. You mentioned happiness. Are you saying I'm no longer the most important person to your happiness?"

"Darling, it's not that at all. You're more important than ever."

Jennifer pushed Nick's arm off her shoulder and sat up straighter as the horse pranced down the narrow street. Henry's speech rambled on, but he'd long been forgotten.

She turned up her nose with exasperation. "I simply don't comprehend you!"

"Strange because I understand things I've never been able to figure out before. I see there's a right order to this crazy world, and a purposeful way to live bringing deep meaning to life."

"Like I don't live with purpose?" Jennifer threw off the blanket and slunk closer to her side of the carriage.

Henry's sightseeing monologue continued: "On your left is the church Henry Flagler, the great oil tycoon, once a partner with Rockefeller, built in honor of his daughter who died during childbirth..." In the distance two granite lions stood guard over the bridge spanning the St. John's River and led toward the ocean where restless waters rippled in the background. The wind had changed.

Nick breathed a deep sigh. "Jennifer, it's true, I'd like you to know God like I do for your sake. I can't make it happen. You've got to want and seek Him for yourself, but also I'm concerned about your changing values at work."

Nick reached for her hand, but she pulled away. Jennifer's voice faltered as she held back tears. "The bottom line here is, what if I won't change?"

Nick spoke firmly, "I have a real problem with this Directive 99. It interferes with God's plan for the lives of the people in your care. I can't accept this."

Jennifer's eyes caught fire. "Conditional love again! Just like my Dad! Is this your ultimatum? Are you saying squelch it or we're through?"

"I'm not using threats. You're my wife, Jennifer. I don't believe in divorce."

"Until now," she said painfully.

"All I ask is, will you at least consider what I've said and go over the directive with me?"

"We're in the process of an impact study. I need to wait for its completion." Her eyes were like black flames. "The Directive is based on what's best for the center. Nick, you know how hard I worked to achieve this position and how important it is to me." Jennifer used a calm, professional tone. She'd make no commitment based on his old-fashioned values.

He sighed. "Okay, I did my best."

"To ruin our trip, thanks, great getaway!"

Jennifer's words stabbed him with their bitterness. The anniversary weekend was over, even though they were still in St. Augustine.

Nearing the carriage stand, Henry guided Buck to the rear of the line of waiting carriages and said a prayer for his riders.

***

Later that night, under soft cotton sheets hemmed in yards of ivory lace, Jennifer and Nick's bodies avoided one another wordlessly. Jennifer sensed Nick's intense desire, longing to draw not just her body, but her mind, too, into unity with his. She'd resist with all her being.

## Chapter Eleven

On Wednesday, the day after Nick and Jennifer returned, he strode through the entrance of the Fullness of Life Centre. He'd dropped by a dozen times before, but today he studied the place as if for the first time.

He intended to find out more about Directive 99 and how close they were to implementing it. Jennifer had been too vague to pin down. Usually Nick hustled directly to Jennifer's office to see her, but today she was at a conference, which suited him fine.

The lobby resembled a mid-grade hotel furnished with light oak tables with barrel-back, rose tweed chairs set on tan tightly woven carpet exuding the smell of chemically produced fibers.

An arts and craft mini-show was in progress. Nick guessed Fullness of Life Centres were probably a good venue for them. The elderly knew the value of handmade articles and could contribute their own.

Nurses' heads turned as Nick passed looking handsome in his dark grey double-breasted silk suit, a style in and out several times over past decades, but currently in. His starched shirt looked like it had been donned five minutes ago, not at seven a.m. It wasn't often the residents saw a man dressed in anything other than pajamas or a jogging suit, except for Jack in khakis and doctors in white coats.

If Nick noticed the attention, he gave no indication. He avoided conversation by moving brusquely toward the elevator. When the doors opened on the third floor, a slight odor of bodily waste assailed his nostrils despite attempted cloaking with pine antiseptic.

A two by three-foot bulletin board dominated his view when he strode out on the fourth floor. The lengthy schedule printed in large type covered three-quarters of the board listing daily activities for residents from moderate exercise to basket making to spiritual enrichment, whatever that was.

Today's highlighted activity was a movie in the Gathering Room to his right. Nick peeked in and saw a large screen TV with VCR/DVD equipment. In a corner of the room an old-fashioned, red-capped, popcorn machine was already snorting kernels for residents with sturdy teeth.

*How comforting for family members to see the vast selection of time fillers,* he thought. Any lingering sadness at having placed their loved ones, or worse yet, guilt for wanting to be rid of them, could be doused by all the potential for activity.

Nick checked himself. That was unkind. Surely many people chose to live at the center because they truly liked the social aspect of being around staff and other residents during the day. Better than an empty household with working family members. At least at home they were safe from dangers like Directive 99.

Nick intended to find grounds for either stopping the Directive or shutting this place down before the assisted deaths began. Jennifer would lose her job and hate him for it, but he had no choice. He needed substantial evidence to challenge this new policy, enough to cause a public outcry. The government would never voluntarily shut down one of its income sources.

He continued his visual survey. Much as he'd like, he couldn't fault the appearance of this Fullness of Life Centre. The corridors were at least two wheel chairs wide, which gave a spacious feeling in contrast to the tiny rooms. The dominant decorating shades were blue and beige. Jennifer had told him research suggested these colors produced restfulness in patient psyches. An unending stream of soft music piped through the halls.

Nick had pre-arranged to meet Michael on the wing of the live-in, one-room apartment section for the more able residents. He paused at the door to Room 414.

Michael's aunt, who looked sixty-five rather than eighty-five, sat in a maple captain's chair, a picture of genteel maturity. Her soft gray curls circled a patrician face with skin like pink suede. She wore a classic outfit of long sleeve, embroidered white blouse and a pleated navy skirt, accented with a gold cameo medallion and matching earrings.

*An extremely attractive, matronly lady.* Nick assessed her as he entered.

"Welcome!" Michael rose and shook Nick's hand warmly. "Aunt Kathryn, meet my friend, Nick and Nick I'd like you to meet Kathryn Dobbs."

Because her face was bent over a large hardcover book, Nick thought Kathryn was dozing but she glanced up immediately and straightened into an alert posture.

"Nice to meet you, Kathryn." Nick extended his hand graciously. "You're looking lovely today. Michael has told me what a talented woman you are."

Kathryn looked at her nephew fondly. "He exaggerates, but it's his only fault. Otherwise he's perfect," she said in a thick, charming Scottish brogue.

Michael added, "My aunt's in excellent health. She came to live here temporarily to be with my uncle who's in the twenty-four hour care unit. She spends most of her daytime hours with him, but I coaxed her back to her room for a quick visit with us."

"What are you reading?" Nick asked settling into a chair across from her.

"I'm researching birthstones in my gem catalogs. Michael wants to order a keepsake ring for his adopted daughter."

"Aunt Kathryn, Nick has a couple questions he'd like to ask you."

"I hope I know the answers."

"Do you enjoy living here?" Nick's question was so unexpected Kathryn's eyes widened. He rephrased it. "I mean, my wife is the administrator, and I always wondered what it's like," he stammered, "from the viewpoint of a resident."

She thought for a moment. "Well, it's sort of like being in a protective bubble. Everything is taken care of, which can be quite pleasant or troubling depending on your perspective. Frankly, I look forward to returning to my home, which the church is watching over for me, and taking charge of my own life again. However, I made a commitment to Joseph not to leave him until he's with the Lord, which we expect will be soon."

"Kathryn, do you feel safe here?" Nick immediately wished he hadn't been so blunt.

She looked at him strangely before responding. "I'm never afraid anywhere. Fear wastes energy, besides it's a sin. I had one experience with fear, and that was enough. After I retired the first time, and settled into our house in Arizona I started feeling anxious. I didn't know why."

"Major change of lifestyle?" Nick guessed.

"Yes. I realized it was because I couldn't stand to be alone all day and do nothing. I like being an active member of society. Joseph and I opened up another antique shop and did well until he became ill. I closed the shop shortly afterwards to care for him and I only do appraisal work now. Much jewelry is synthetic now, often quite good, so only an expert can tell the difference."

Nick followed her eyes to the neat stack of correspondence and catalogs on her little desk. Eighty-five years old, still using her skills and earning income! He marveled. "I have a fondness for antique furniture and jewelry, but my wife likes the current decorating trend which is rather stark and simplistic."

"Too bad. If you like antiques, you like history. I've certainly seen a lot made in my lifetime."

"I bet!" Nick whistled. "What changes stand out in your mind?"

"Technology of course, which has its merit. I think one of the most detrimental is probably the change in the way we deliver education. Children used to learn while listening to stories and wisdom of their elders. Today their most significant learning comes from impersonal figures on a TV screen. I'd love to teach a history course based on my life experience, but I'm told I'm too old and irrelevant."

"What a shame society doesn't treasure the wisdom of our older citizens more," Michael added.

"Kathryn, do you take any medications?"

"Only an occasional aspirin. I'm fortunate."

"Do you have your own?"

"No, I have to order it. All meds are administered by staff. Why do you ask?"

"I just wondered. I wouldn't if I were you."

"Wouldn't what?"

"Take drugs. I don't believe in them. I mean I suggest only taking what Michael personally brings." How could Nick say don't trust this place? Surely Kathryn wouldn't believe she could be in danger in these beautiful, soothing surroundings. Directive 99 seemed an unreal nightmare, even to him.

She eyed him sharply with a perceptive gaze, but to his relief said nothing.

Kathryn checked her watch. "Gentlemen, I have tea with my husband at 2, I mustn't keep him waiting." Kathryn selected a book to take with her and buzzed for an attendant. She explained to Nick, "I can walk fine, but I'm required to have an attendant escort me or I can't leave this wing." Her eyes twinkled. "They insist on keeping track of me every minute. I might be a dangerous subversive, you know."

Michael laughed and opened the door. The dour, musical concerto in the halls assailed their ears.

"Do you ever hear lively music?" Nick asked. "This would get on my nerves fast!"

Kathryn turned abruptly. "Mr. Trevor, I'd love something peppier. If you're suggesting changes, I understand your wife is the one to contact."

Nick lowered his head, and let Kathryn pass.

***

When she left, Nick and Michael headed for the sunroom. Happily, it was deserted and would allow them privacy.

Michael asked immediately, "Any luck getting info on the starting date of the directive?"

Nick shrugged and shook his head in the negative. He quietly jotted notes on his Priority Management notepad.

"If Directive 99 goes through, Aunt Kathryn would be among the first! I need to get her and my uncle out of here."

Nick's face grayed. "And my own wife would have a major part in it!" He dragged a hand across his forehead. "Has our government gone insane? God help us all."

Michael nodded. "What do you suggest, Nick?"

"To do anything in the legal arena, I need hard facts."

"That's your department. In the meantime, I'll try to talk families of these at-risk residents into moving them home or to a private center without letting on why, starting with my Aunt."

"Good. From what I picked up from Jennifer, there may not be a lot of time."

"Unfortunately, there aren't enough private centers left to move residents into anymore."

"Why is that?" Nick had never given a thought to elderly care.

"They couldn't compete with government centers due to the tax breaks and employment benefits the government can provide. Nobody can run a business that becomes less profitable every year. I wonder if this Directive 99 has been the plan all along. Otherwise, how could it be operational so fast?"

"Beats me. Until Jennifer mentioned it, I never heard a hint something like this was in the works."

"From my previous work with church members I know that's often the way with government programs. They take action before too many people get wind of it."

"Once Directive 99's classified procedure, stopping it will be like trying to hold back a herd of elephants. We've got to expose it now. I need factual data or else the government will deny it ever existed. With evidence I can use court action to delay implementation. Maybe I can cut the directive off at its base without Jennifer. I'll keep you posted."

"Please."

"Remember we're dealing with federal government, and it's hard to break this kind of policy. Give me several days to get the legal part in motion."

"I'll get our intercessory prayer people going, too."

"Can you trust them to keep quiet?"

"Implicitly, but, Nick," Michael's eyes cut into Nick, "you need to understand, I won't wait to discreetly move whomever I can."

"I understand."

"What about Jennifer?"

"She'll suspect I've told you when she sees Kathryn's name on the departure list, but that doesn't matter."

"Kathryn's happy here overall and she's too sharp to fool. It may be necessary to tell her the truth."

"Hold off as long as you can."

***

Nick's next stop was Jennifer's office since she was at her daylong conference. What he wanted could best be collected during her absence.

Jennifer's assistant was in her office word processing. Ellen's no-nonsense, matter-of-fact voice matched the spark of her powerful personality. Had she gotten a degree, Nick guessed she'd be in administration herself, but Jennifer said she'd dropped out her freshman year too impatient with the state tedium of useless, required courses.

Nick feigned surprise when she said, "I'm sorry, Mr. Trevor, Jennifer must have forgotten to tell you. A special meeting was called to discuss a new directive. Your wife and Jack are in Chicago for the day."

*Jack was in on Directive 99 plans, too.* Nick knew Jack was Jennifer's checkpoint, the only governmental employee out of her range of authority whom she had no personal control over. Nick guessed Jack would be quite willing to report any of Jennifer's slip-ups or delays on implementing Directive 99 which could put him into Number One position.

No wonder she was scared. Jennifer had said when Jack first arrived in a couple years he'd be a head director. She'd told Nick half-jokingly, "Just so it's not my Fullness of Life Centre." She fully understood the precariousness of her position even if on the exterior she seemed to shrug it off. Some nights she'd awake in a cold sweat and share her fears with Nick.

Even if Nick could convince Jennifer to stop or slow this directive, ambitious, aggressive Jack would make it work. Nick decided to go the route of public protest. But he needed more information.

"Would you like to leave a message, Mr. Trevor?" Jennifer's assistant asked.

Nick put on his biggest grin. "I'd like to leave a personal letter on my wife's desk, if I may, just for her eyes." His eyes gleamed.

"You're the most romantic man! I'm not supposed to let anyone...."

Assuming a yes answer, Nick took two strides toward Jennifer's office. "I'll be right out."

The phone on Ellen's desk rang. "I suppose it's okay for a minute," she called after him.

Nick closed the door behind him and listened as Ellen resumed her keyboard clicking.

He glanced around. Thank God for his wife's neatnik work habits. Pending files would probably be in the top file drawer or stacked on her desk. For important papers, she always liked hard data as well as computer files, despite efforts to do away with paper. The drawer glided open soundlessly. He pawed through files, checking labels and pulled several. A glance through the eighth folder assured him he'd found it.

Nick skimmed the papers in the Directive 99 file alluded to as positive, beneficial, essential. The file gave no time frames, precise methodology, no description of procedures. The federal government must be keeping the details verbal, a critical maneuver since the Clinton's White House scandals and Nixon's paper shredding sins. He read a lot of gobbledygook about "full life" and "mature choice."

The ambiguous language about euthanasia would have been comical if it wasn't taken seriously. "We will establish budgets based on the government's definition of 'full life.' If it's three quarters full or half full, what is your capacity for enjoyment? For productivity? How shall we measure?" Nick groaned as he quickly recorded notes on his pocket pad.

Next, he flipped through Jennifer's desk calendar and jotted down any future meeting dates referred to as D. 99.

Finished, he pulled a prewritten letter from his pocket and set it in the center of Jennifer's desk for Ellen's benefit in case she snooped later. It said, "Had a wonderful time with my princess in St. Augustine. Let's do it again soon. All my love, Prince Charming."

Nick slipped his pocket-sized pad back inside his suit. The whole process took less than eight minutes. Nick graced Ellen with a broad smile as he passed her desk.

"Have a great day."

***

Back in the quiet environment of his own office, Nick had just spread out his notes on his desk when his secretary, Dora, interrupted him to announce the arrival of a client.

Nick's eyebrows lifted. He glanced at his appointment book.

"Dora, it's nearly five. I don't have a client scheduled."

"I made the appointment while you were out. Mr. Jerson gave me the order. It's a Mr. Toracelli with Landworks, Inc."

The company name rang a bell, a big firm outside the area. Before Nick could recall further data a hefty, tall man appeared at the door.

Nick nodded a dismissal to Dora and sized up the man before him. Pirelli's corpulence, unsuccessfully camouflaged by an expensive tailored suit, busted out between buttons on his shirt that couldn't be a hair tighter. It was like a strait jacket. Thin eyebrows framed a ruddy face with alert brown eyes Nick observed roving quickly about his office taking in its oak paneled walls and dark grey-green carpeting.

90

Pirelli's gaze became direct. "Nice to meet you, Mr. Trevor." His voice was surprisingly rich and pleasant like a radio announcer's.

*Everyone has redeeming qualities,* Nick reminded himself, as he shook Mr. Toracelli's outstretched hand.

The client's long, thin mouth looked as though a knife sliced his lips into two. Nick guessed his age as probably late forties, maybe early fifties.

Pirelli, alias Toracelli, sat down uninvited.

"How can I be of service?"

"I appreciate your fitting me in. I'll get right to the point." He brushed a piece of lint off his pants leg. "Our company is working on a downtown development project on Broad Street. I want you to check over the zoning changes. There are a couple rough spots, plus we need to clarify escrow for sewer and road responsibility in the proposal."

Nick's eyebrows shot up. "If the project is routine, why bring it to me?"

"We need a second opinion from a local lawyer confirming all local ordinances have been addressed correctly. My boss likes to make sure every base is covered."

Nick remembered something else about the company now. They had a reputation as real-estate wheeler-dealers and were rumored to have Mafia connections.

The client pulled a manila folder from his briefcase. "My boss would like you to review this material tonight. The meeting of the City Common Council is next week. Tomorrow is the last day to get on the agenda. The letter inside will explain." The man studied Nick, as if he were sizing him up with a tape measure.

"I can't get to it that fast." Nick stated the obvious, businesslike.

"I explained the situation to your senior partner, and he said you'd review it tonight."

"Oh, he did." Nick's tone was clearly annoyed. He buzzed Dora. "Did Mr. Jerson leave instructions regarding Mr. Toracelli's proposal?"

"Yes, sir. He said give it top priority."

Nick mumbled thanks.

The company probably had also promised a big contribution to Jerson's campaign for his charity drive. Nick ran his hand through his hair, disheveling it as he flipped through the first three of five pages of data.

"Sorry about the rush; it's not complicated though. Shouldn't take more than an hour to read it through and comment. Could I pick it up tomorrow morning at your home around eight to save me a trip downtown?"

Nick raised his eyebrows. "You know where I live?"

"I check details on anybody we do business with, especially a lawyer trusted with important transactions." Pirelli grinned disarmingly, which made his face look even rounder, like a cartoon caricature.

Nick sighed. "Okay, but be sure it's between eight and eight-thirty. I have a nine o'clock appointment here."

"I won't be late." Moving incredibly fast for his girth, Pirelli shut the door behind himself.

"Darn it." Nick resisted an urge to swear as he shoved the papers into his briefcase. "Jerson's pulled this on me before. He's a sucker for rich companies who dangle wealth and power around for hungry lawyers to drool over."

***

Even though Sarah tried hard to put on a front for the boys, she wasn't able to find joy in anything, not even their activities. They seemed to understand.

"Give me a little time, guys," she'd told them. "I'll be there for you again, I promise, right now it's hard."

"Sure, Mom," her oldest had said. She was both relieved and proud of the way he took charge of his little brother.

Sarah began each day with fervent prayer often followed by more conversation with God during morning Mass at her church. She prayed something would be found on John's computer to explain the tragedy that had ripped apart their life. She ended each day by crossing the date off the calendar, a day closer until she'd get the laptop back, one of the few satisfactions she had. Soon she'd be able to investigate what he'd been working on that may have motivated his killer to murder him.

The days lumbered by.

On the fifth day Sarah began to fear she'd never see her husband's computer again. She called and was told the recovery specialists hadn't gotten to it yet.

She grit her teeth before asking why.

"Please be patient, Ms. Levinson. Yes, we know it's top priority. However, a huge bank had a computer crisis, and all our technicians are involved. We're doing the best we can."

***

"Thanks for coming, Jen. I absolutely had to talk to you."

Becky greeted Jennifer at the door of her estate. Jennifer had wanted to drive straight home after work, but couldn't ignore the plea of a friend.

"I'm still terribly distressed about Ella's death. I've cried myself inside out since she died on Sunday. How can you look wonderful? I'm such a mess." Becky tried to use a light tone, which only made her pain more evident.

One glance at Becky's gaunt and ravished face made Jennifer glad she'd taken the time to come. She'd never seen her friend with chalky streaks rimming her eyes.

"I know how hard this must be for you, Becky. You and Ella were always close."

"We used to be, but not recently." Becky started crying again softly, steadily and leaned into Jennifer's arms.

They gravitated toward the living room, where they settled on the richly woven tapestry of her oversized sofa.

"I'd been so busy building this new house." Becky waved her arm about. "I'm berating myself for neglecting her. I didn't know her depression was this serious, I swear. I thought I knew everything about her. I never meant to shut the poor dear out. I knew she drank too much, but never talked about it. Some friend I

93

was. I guess that doesn't matter now," Becky said, a fresh sob catching in her throat.

Jennifer wanted to say Oh yes, it does matter. If you knew she had problems with alcohol you should have suggested she get help, taken her even. Instead she said, "Don't be too hard on yourself, Becky."

"And now she's dead, Jennifer."

"It's terrible and so hard for poor Larry. He doted on her."

"On the night of my first party, of all times!" Becky looked up, instantly ashamed. "I'm sorry. I didn't mean to say that. What difference does it make what night she chose?"

Jennifer patted Becky's shoulder. "I'll get us a soft drink. I know where the kitchen is."

She made her way to the kitchen and pulled two canned iced teas from the huge stainless-steel refrigerator.

Becky took a deep breath before she snapped open her can. "Life isn't making sense, if something like this can happen to someone I know. You're probably used to this in your job, I'm not!"

Jennifer sensed the selfishness in Becky's grief as she took a swallow of her drink. *It would be nice if Becky would be considerate of other people's grief, too,* Jennifer thought. *Who helps professionals like me when they grieve? Forget it, she coached herself. Becky needs a listener; at least I can offer my presence.*

Jennifer tuned in to hear Becky saying, "What scares me most is that in a down moment I could easily have been as stupid as Ella. I'm supposed to be evolving, getting better. Sometimes I think actually I'm deteriorating. I can't hang on to even a physical skill. I practice to improve my golf and if I don't play for a week, I lose it. I want to be a good mother, am I? Mostly, no, it's depressing."

"Becky, this isn't helping you."

"Do I get older and better?" Her voice sounded like a shriek. "No! I'm declining to eventual death, nothingness, like Ella." Becky looked morose as she swigged her drink.

Jennifer felt like she was in a delayed play echo chamber. These had been her own words at times, the me-centered core of values. Poor Ella died, but for Becky the experience is all about me. And fear about her own inevitable aging and death. How selfish this sounds! Jennifer was grossly uncomfortable. Threads of guilt rippled through her. She had no response for Becky.

"You know what I'd like?" Becky's eyes had a pathetic glaze. "I'd like to know something is permanent and real. I feel as important as a rabbit."

Jennifer ventured a half smile.

"I'm serious. Love is supposed to last forever. Yet my love for Jed hasn't, nor his for me. His business is his first love. He'll never get enough of the sweet juice of accomplishment. The only thing we both care about is our daughter. And she's not ours to keep."

Jennifer bit her tongue. This wasn't a counseling session but a talk with a friend. Becky wanted sympathy, not intervention and change. Jennifer expressed sympathy and finished her tea. "I need to get home for the kids. Call me tomorrow and let me know how you're doing. If you sense a need for a formal counseling session, I can recommend a colleague who's quite good."

"Why not meet with you?"

"It's not ethical professionally for me to counsel friends."

Jennifer felt sad for her, but didn't expect her to follow up with counseling. She guessed Becky would quickly mask her pain, and be back on her merry-ground of thoughtless lifestyle again. Jennifer struggled to maintain respect for Becky, as awareness of her own self-focus nipped at her.

\*\*\*

Pirelli breathed more comfortably back in the subdued atmosphere of Lawrence Relton's plush leased office building. The executive assistant's chair was empty so he bypassed the reception area and knocked before entering Relton's inner office.

When Pirelli strode in, Relton shifted his attention from the computer monitor momentarily and swiveled over to his thick, black polystyrene desk. The burgundy and black drapes were closed. Fluorescent lighting gave an eerie cast to their faces.

Relton's thick dark brown hair and deep auburn eyes set in a smooth, ivory complexion might have made him appear effeminate except for his muscular body. Despite the coldness of his eyes, Relton exuded what Pirelli called charm and charisma.

"How'd it go?"

"Flawless. We're operational." Pirelli slid into a black leather side chair.

"Good."

Working for Lawrence Relton gave Pirelli a pleasant feeling of significance. He rarely paid attention to the physical characteristics of other men; a well-rounded woman was another story. But he realized Relton was the handsomest man he'd ever seen, and Pirelli found the quality of importance to him, a person with no comeliness. He valued his own street smarts, but believed Relton was brilliant.

The truth was Relton also scared Pirelli slightly, a rarity, which added to the aura of his boss' presence.

Relton's gaze pierced Pirelli. "Our business involvement will be so obvious that's it's inconceivable we could be responsible for what happens." He clamped his hands together with satisfaction. "It's perfect, because it's exactly the opposite of the way most people think."

"Shrewd, Mr. Relton."

"Still, I'd never risk it if I wasn't sure you and Shak and Bruter could be counted on."

"Don't worry, boss, they're professionals who never fail. Besides, how could they, when I'm handing Trevor over like a piece of lumber? We should get a break on their fee for making it so easy, but pricing's your business."

Relton threw back his head and chuckled in a coarse, diabolical tone. His voice was the only thing unpleasant about him. "When I want something done, price is never an object." They spent the next few minutes discussing the final details of the plan. "Is everything clear?"

Pirelli shifted uneasily in his chair. "Yeah, boss." He didn't want or need to know any more than necessary. I'm primarily a connection man, that's what he'd say. As Relton's right hand guy in this project, Pirelli already had more knowledge than he'd like.

I'm valuable and at the moment indispensable, Pirelli reassured himself. Still he'd avoid giving his boss any cause to worry about his loyalty.

Relton's executive assistant, Chad, returned and knocked discreetly.

"Come in."

Chad was six-foot-one, late twenties, with a pointy chin and rolled shoulders. He moved precisely, like he had stones inside his shoes.

"Dinner's arrived, Mr. Relton."

"Set it up in the conference room."

Chad nodded to his employer and hurried to the task.

"Pirelli, join me in a glass of sherry while I eat."

The room held a large center table surrounded by six chairs and a side table beneath the only window in the room. A granite countertop along the wall was covered with paper platters of egg rolls, rice, chow mein noodles, and two Chinese entrees. Relton filled a huge platter before taking a seat at the head and motioned for Pirelli and Chad to sit across.

At the table, Relton seemed in a gregarious mood. Pirelli observed he seemed to like preening before a doting audience. Maybe because he was high on the thought of Nick Trevor's removal, Relton indulged in more conversation than usual. He bragged, "Not that Nicholas Trevor has been a strong threat yet, but I'm intuitive enough to recognize the potential is present and escalating fast. My instinct has served me well."

Pirelli eyed the plate of egg rolls. Relton never offered one and he didn't dare ask.

He watched Relton shake crunchy chow mein noodles atop his beef chop suey as he sipped his sherry. "We're doing it! Trevor goes down tomorrow. Discrediting or disposing of the most threatening individuals in this country! My college buddy, the health czar in Washington, will be most pleased. His elderly care directive will have no opposition." Relton wiped soy sauce from his face and held up two fingers. "One success - one opponent out already in this state - from apparently 'natural' suicide and now tomorrow Trevor." He flashed a huge smile.

Relton had never spoken this freely to Pirelli before. He was both flattered and uncomfortable. No way did Pirelli want Relton regretting his loquaciousness.

Pirelli waited, sending frequent glances toward the food. Surely Relton would suggest he take at least one of the fortune cookies.

But Relton never offered him a bite! Pirelli finished his sherry, and left as quickly as he decently could.

On his way home, he stopped at Su Ming's and ordered his own Chinese feast.

## Chapter Twelve

"This is the coldest November we've had since the nineteen-fifties." Jack chattered in his charming way before the weekly staff meeting. The department heads of the Fullness of Life Centre sat in the walnut-paneled conference room on sofas and chairs ala the relaxed business environment. Jennifer opened the meeting and one by one staff members gave their reports.

As Jennifer listened her gaze settled on Jack who seemed to be in a particularly jolly mood. She wondered why.

As usual he was dressed like the nineteen-sixties Ken doll, Barbie's boyfriend, on his way to a party. Today he wore khaki pants, denim shirt with an open collar, and a tan corduroy blazer, the epitome of carefully studied casualness. She wondered if he ever got his hands covered with mud as a child.

Jack had maneuvered into his government position because his intellectual blandness gave no one reason not to approve his advancement. Jennifer knew the central office interrogation and training programs were thorough. She'd gone through the mind-numbing torture herself.

She had no reason not to rate Jack highly his first year. He'd passed training with flying colors, a true product of his Dewey-inspired environment with his pragmatic "If it works, do it" attitude.

Jack's every action, thus far, proved compatible with pro-establishment protocol. His allegiance was to headquarters first and last. He had an unquestioning attitude of blind acceptance to any procedures handed down by the power above him. Frighteningly like me Jennifer thought.

Once Jack was entrenched in his role, Jennifer liked him less and less. His behavior often became obnoxious and overbearing in her presence. She could only imagine how he interacted when alone with the residents. One other annoying problem came up from time to time, like now.

Jack, perched on the edge of a chair near her, leaned over and crooned in her ear, "I'd like to keep you warm, just call out my name and I'll be there."

Jennifer glared. "Stop it, Jack!"

When he'd first hit on Jennifer, she'd warned him, "I won't look for a harassment boogie man behind every remark you make, but watch yourself or you'll be out of here quicker than you can say, I didn't mean it."

Today she wouldn't let him annoy her. Her anger would only encourage further trouble even though his ridiculous songs and comments fit the parameters for sexual harassment. Jennifer had considered reporting him, but the risk was too great, especially since he wanted her job. Eight years younger than Jennifer, he'd resort to denial and she'd end up perceived as a foolish, over-reacting woman. No man was dragging her into any petty responses that would draw unfavorable attention to her work.

She'd taught women how to handle unprofessional flirting in her private counseling days. "If you don't like what a guy says, try confronting him tactfully. If confrontation doesn't work, you have two options, remove the guy or yourself." Simple? Anything but.

She also sympathized with men sexually harassed by women speaking in innuendoes. The nicest guys seemed to be the easiest quarry and often lost jobs and families by falling into female traps. If she saw harassment in her employees she stopped it fast. But she wouldn't over react.

Her philosophy was if you couldn't handle the male-female dynamic get out of the workplace. If the situation became unbearable, find another job. Only Jennifer held the position of boss and had no intention of leaving, and she couldn't get rid of Jack. She'd hit an impasse with him and he knew it.

"Jack, give your report now," Jennifer ordered authoritatively.

He reacted to her tone with a frown, but pulled out a paper and ceremoniously placed it atop his other folders. He announced with barely suppressed glee Carlie had been caught stealing drugs last Tuesday, the day Jennifer was in St. Augustine. "I called the police. She was charged and removed."

Jennifer heard the murmur among her department heads.

"This is unfortunate, but, as we all know, it's happened before. Even though drugs are now legal in this country, the shortage is great and prices exorbitant. There's as much if not more stealing than ever."

Jack interrupted, "One other thing. Carlie said she'd made a deal to pay the administrator $500 for access at certain times during the week."

"That's ridiculous." Jennifer was on her feet.

He shrugged. "The drug case was unlocked. We weren't able to determine how that might have happened."

Jennifer stared Jack in the eye. "Since when do you accept the statement of a thief and a drug addict? She probably picked the outside lock and figured out the code on the inside one. I hope you clarified that for the police."

"Of course."

Jennifer wondered if Carlie had even made that false accusation. Or had Jack unlocked the case tempting her? Jennifer made a note to look into this. How sad for Carlie and her daughter.

No administrator liked having charges of this nature floating through the air. How convincing had Jack been with the police anyway?

Having a key staff person like Jack whom she couldn't trust with her back infuriated Jennifer. Technically beneath her in seniority, he couldn't be fired by her and knew it. His primary responsibility as patient services co-coordinator was filing comprehensive reports which would be cross-analyzed side by side with hers at headquarters. Jack had degrees in psychology and counseling, but specialized in handling medical assistance procedures that changed with every new congressional administration. Eleven Fullness of Life Centre employees worked full time to process federal reimbursements.

Jennifer concentrated on the rest of Jack's dispassionate report recited in the tone of disinterest, which seemed too often to come with the profession these days. She hadn't discussed the advanced aspects of Directive 99 with Jack, but surely headquarters had.

Jack would have no problem following the new procedures. He'd once even said to her, "As far as I'm concerned residents are names on paper. I view their issues as textbook situations." Rarely had she run into such an unfeeling health care professional - not one who would admit it anyway.

Jennifer reminded herself Nick didn't think her compassion level was high lately either.

She doodled on a legal pad until Jack finished his last client summary. He used exquisite psycho-jargon. "Mr. D's using anger as a defense mechanism to avoid closeness. Interpersonal relationships are threatening to him. He's fixated on his mother and unmotivated to break his codependent behavior," and on and on.

Each primary staff person contributed updates on twenty residents each week, evaluated in alphabetical order for impartiality.

In the early days of her training, Jennifer, too, had used the jargon well. Now she was beyond the almost mystical belief that she really did have appropriate labels and all the answers to every human dilemma. She'd long ago decided a "tension of pain" existed in every person at times. Inner peace was unknown to her, and, therefore, she assumed it didn't exist.

It irritated Jennifer to listen to Jack using Freud's mechanical model of behavior. She pressed the point of her pencil so hard it slit her paper.

When Jack sat down, the group participants paused for a brief break to fill coffee cups and stretch. Jennifer commented aside to him, "You make diagnosis sound so simple."

"Tut, tut, Ms. Trevor, are you questioning Freud?" Jack asked mockingly.

Jennifer's face flushed. "We both know Freud's research was full of more holes than a sponge. Talk about using a biased sample for study! Wealthy females! Freud planted sexual diagnoses in their brains and watched his clients prove him right. He never healed them either."

The meeting resumed and droned on with several other reports from the nutrition team, medical staff, and chaplain who held weekly "services," an amalgamation of everything from Native American rituals to Wicca rites. The chaplain predated Jennifer's arrival. Nobody quite knew how the man got his position, but he was firmly anchored in it.

Finally, the reports ended. Detailed treatment recommendations were made and the tedious staffing was completed. Jennifer closed the meeting and the staff members filed out.

Her heels clicked on the tile floor as she rose abruptly from her chair.

Jack mumbled solicitously, "In a rush, beautiful? Are we a little out of sorts today?"

She scowled at him and returned to her office. How she disliked this man!

\*\*\*

The next morning Nick watched Jennifer leave for work through the window in his den as he finished up the Landworks report. He'd reviewed the documents at six-thirty A. M. when he was fresh, rather than last night. Everything seemed in order. A shrewd development project for them, not the best for their town. The City Council was giving a far larger tax break than Nick would have recommended, but the tax incentive had already been set.

He heard grinding gears of the school bus stopping outside to pick up the children. When he entered the kitchen to grab coffee to take, he was surprised to find Collin finishing breakfast.

"Collin, you're late." Nick nagged. "You missed the bus again!"

"Derek is driving me to school. Mom said it was okay."

As if on cue, a car honked.

"Okay, I didn't know. Have a good day, son."

Collin yelled, "See ya Dad!" as he bounded past Nick and ran to the driveway entrance, where his friend, Derek, waited in his Mazda.

Another car, a Black Cadillac, with two male passengers came by, slowed and drove past. Collin glanced briefly at the large, round-faced man behind the wheel before shutting the door of Derek's sports car.

***

Inside the auto Pirelli swore. "Rotten luck," he muttered, "the kid saw us. What's he doing here now?" After he passed the Trevor house he kept driving to the end of the subdivision of large homes on five-acre lots before turning around and coming back. Slowly he edged his car up Nick's driveway.

"I knew the family schedule and picked today because the maid comes Thursday and usually nobody's here now."

Pirelli spoke to the man with him dressed like a gardener. His first name was Phil, but his friends and enemies knew him as Bruter for so long almost no one remembered he had any other name.

Pirelli opened the car door and exited with caution after carefully checking no neighbors were out walking their dogs or gardening. Passing a row of fragrant evergreens, he inhaled deeply as he hurried to the front door.

Bruter crept out the passenger side and slipped over to a row of hedges next to the open garage door, where he hid.

Nick answered Pirelli's ring immediately and greeted him holding Torricelli's manila folder in his hands. He handed it over saying, "Good, you're on time. The notes I made are comprehensive and self-explanatory. If your boss has any further questions, I can be reached at my office after eleven."

104

Pirelli grunted, "Thanks."

Nick grabbed his trench coat, stuck his leather briefcase under his arm and walked out, pulling the door shut, and locking it behind him. Pirelli strode along at his side to the end of the sidewalk.

"See ya," Pirelli said.

Nick used the security keypad to open the garage door.

As he was about to step into his car, Pirelli called out, "One more thing, Mr. Trevor ..."

Nick halted and turned as Bruter rushed up beside him. His next sensation was a piece of hard, steel pressing into his back.

"Keep quiet or you're dead," Bruter spoke in a resonant, controlled voice. He'd had the advantage of surprise. It took precious seconds for Nick to make sense of what was happening.

"Get into your car," Bruter ordered.

In a split second, Nick considered his options. He'd always told his kids if you're being forced at gunpoint, take your chances fighting, especially where there might be people around who'll notice the noise. But Nick's neighbors were dual career families and most likely there'd be no witnesses to report what was happening. Still every impulse inside him said he had to try.

Nick turned and brought his knee up as hard as he could into Bruter's groin. His opponent doubled over but came up with a hard right hand into Nick's stomach driving Nick backwards. He fell onto Pirelli who he hoped had run up to help him.

No such luck Nick quickly realized. Pirelli attempted to pin his arms to his side, but missed and Nick's left leg shot out again. This time he tried to strike Bruter's hand and knock the gun away.

He missed.

With a surge of strength Nick yanked free from Pirelli and caught Bruter's free hand pressing his forefinger back.

They struggled, until Bruter spun loose.

How could someone as big as Bruter move like a gazelle? "Why are you doing this?" Nick screamed. "Don't you know kidnapping is a federal offense? It'll get you life!"

"Shut up or we'll gag you," Bruter growled. "You're due for a rubout, but it's not gonna happen in your yard."

Pirelli grabbed both Nick's hands behind his back. Bruter lifted his revolver to Nick's ear and growled. "This has a silencer on it. If I pull the trigger, nobody's gonna know."

Flinching and waiting for the bullet, Nick went limp. He exhaled when Bruter didn't fire immediately. For some reason they must want to take him alive.

Reddening from anger, Bruter brought the gun down. The hard butt slammed into Nick's skull, knocking him nearly unconscious. Everything turned to haze as time and place became unimportant.

Bruter pulled a rope from his pack and whipped it around Nick's wrists. He and Pirelli shoved Nick onto the back seat and tied his feet together.

When Nick started to stir, Bruter whipped the gun full force again on the back of Nick's head hoping he wasn't killing him, although at the moment didn't care.

With one hand lifting Nick's limp wrists, Bruter adjusted Nick's body across the back seat.

Pirelli pulled on tight, leather gloves and searched Nick's pocket for his keys. He used them to open the back door of the house.

After two wrong turns, Pirelli located the master bedroom. He withdrew a note from his pocket and placed it on the tall dresser. Pirelli withdrew and locked up. He gave Bruter Nick's keys, got behind the wheel of his own car and casually drove off.

Bruter backed out, shut the garage door with Nick's remote, and drove Nick's car with Nick semi-conscious on the back seat. He followed Pirelli's car to the entrance of the subdivision. When Pirelli turned right, Bruter went the opposite way.

***

That night, Jennifer forgot all about grieving over Ella, distracted by a devastating loss of her own. Where was her husband?

Nick's secretary, Dora, had called her at the Fullness of Life Centre when Nick failed to arrive at work. He never came home either, not that night, or the next. Jennifer called his business associates, his friends, everywhere except the police. She'd found the note left on her dresser at 10:30 P. M. when she got ready for bed. She read it with trembling hands. "Our marriage isn't working. I need time to think things through. Nick." In a moment all feeling left her body.

Closing herself in her room, on the pretense of dealing with a migraine as she'd told the children, she turned on the TV for background noise to cover her sobbing. What every wife fears had happened. Nick had become fed up with the constant tension and abandoned her.

She thought back over the last several weeks. He'd been gone a lot lately. Had another woman, perhaps one with his same beliefs, enticed him away? Memories of his talk about being followed and about wanting her to go to church more surfaced. Both could have been simply a cover-up for an affair. Jennifer wanted to think the best, but couldn't. A childhood of betrayal by those she loved and trusted affected her reaction.

One hour of wakefulness turned into two and soon three. Exhausted, she finally fell into a troubled sleep.

***

Bruter had driven five miles to a secluded cul-de-sac where a tan van waited for the transfer of Nick.

When Bruter pulled over and stopped, Nick began to regain consciousness and tried to sit up. His head throbbed so badly he dropped over on the seat.

A burly, black-haired man in frayed khakis and dirty sweatshirt hopped out of the dusty van. Several days' growth of beard added to his unkempt look.

"Hey, Shak, give me a hand," Bruter called out. He threw open the back door of the car, tossed a trench coat over Nick's shoulders to hide his tied hands. If anyone happened to pass, it would look like Bruter was helping a friend who had too much to drink.

Shak was the taller of the two. An inch-long scar above his lip twitched when he muttered his monosyllabic commands like, "Move."

Nick staggered forward. Shak dug his knee into Nick's right kidney to hurry him to the van. Nick flinched in pain.

"Take it easy, don't maul the guy." Among Bruter's faults, as he perceived it, was a tendency to kindness. Try as he might, he couldn't completely break it. "We don't want this messy. A nice, clean drop tomorrow in the Wisconsin River, remember we make it look like an intentional disappearance. Follow me to the airport to drop off the car first."

Bruter pulled out as soon as the van started.

*** 

At 4 a.m. Jennifer awoke to the sensation of tiny pistol triggers being pulled simultaneously throughout her brain. She pulled herself up on her elbows, unnerved by the disturbingly still air. It seemed as though, without her consent, a suspension of her life had occurred.

"If Nick's gone, I may as well die," she said aloud. "I've no joy without him." Jennifer dropped her head back onto the feather pillow. "It can't be true. He'd never leave me." What if something terrible had happened to him and he hadn't run off after all? It flitted into her awareness perhaps she should be afraid. Jennifer pounded her fist on her mattress. No, he left me! I can't bear it. With all these thoughts driving her crazy she yearned for the oblivion of sleep, but it was not to be. The nightmare had stimulated total wakefulness.

She wasn't ready to tell the children yet and deal with their reaction. She'd told them Nick was away on a short business trip. If only this were true.

One minute Jennifer persuaded herself she'd be fine, the next she couldn't contain her anxiety. "How could you treat me like this Nick?" she cried in the shower where she couldn't be heard.

She could understand his wanting out of the marriage. Christians got divorced, but like this? It can't be he hates me enough to abandon his work and his children.

Although why not? A cold ray of gloom and chagrin lay disgustingly in the bottom of her mind. "I'm ashamed," she said aloud, contemptuous of herself. But no matter how despicable I've been Nick was not capable of such a hurtful act, was he? If only she could make the puzzle of Nick's absence fit.

Jennifer balked at its irrationality. He was a good communicator. He'd have come to me at least and told me if he were terribly upset. Or was he trying to say this in St. Augustine? Why not show up for work either? He never missed scheduled appointments with clients. Irresponsibility was uncharacteristic of him. He must have been under extreme duress - maybe a nervous breakdown?

Or had he been abducted? Her brain reeled. If so, why hadn't there been a sign of struggle? The farewell note was typed. But Nick hated to type. And it wasn't addressed to her as "punkin" the way he usually started his notes. Maybe the word was too tender for him to use now. Her head began to throb. Making sense out of this was impossible. She drifted off on another wild, useless mental hunt for what went wrong.

She forced herself to get up and walk to the window, not that she saw anything. The moonless night only reflected the darkness of her spirit. She slammed her fist against the wall, bruising her knuckles, before falling in a heap on the bed. She sobbed until no tears remained in her body.

During the day she knew she could pretend, but at night emptiness etched itself into her brain revealing undeniable truth. She was a woman alone, worse, abandoned. Life without Nick was a distortion of the only adult reality she knew. Insecurity rippled through her waiting to erupt, undermining her already fragile self-image.

Jennifer looked at her clock again. "Nick, I need you." She pleaded into the air, as if it could surrender Nick's presence if she begged.

He'd be crazy to love me forever like he said. Deep down she knew she didn't deserve an unconditional kind of love and never totally believed in it. Did anybody? But she never expected betrayal to hurt like this. Finally, extreme exhaustion brought the temporary surcease of sleep.

## Chapter Thirteen

The haze in Nick's head cleared as throbbing pain took its place. After several tries he managed to wiggle to a semi-sitting position in the van and look around, quite a feat with his hands and feet tied. At least his abductors hadn't bothered to gag him. Nothing seemed familiar in the rural area flying past. The occasional farms had houses set way back from the road.

The van turned onto a narrow country road flanked on each side by large ditches. More farmhouses and tumbledown housing shacks dotted the countryside.

Nick hunted for identifying road signs, but didn't even find a speed limit. A few cars zoomed past going in the opposite direction.

"Bruter, look who's up."

"Where are you taking me?" Nick's effort to talk came out a mumble.

"Sit tight, buddy it won't be long now."

"You'll know soon enough," the driver added.

Nick grimaced and lowered his eyes. The aura of absolute unreality filling his mind changed to stark fear. His captors wore no disguise and made no effort to hide their names from him. This could mean one thing. They intended to kill him. His armpits dampened with sweat as he pleaded from his soul, *Please, God, let me see my family again.*

The two men in the front seats drove on in almost total silence.

After what Nick judged to be about two hours on the road the van sped through a small resort town closed up for the winter.

Streaks of gold sunshine illuminated the drying fall leaves. How could it be such a beautiful day? Nick wondered.

He looked up and silently mouthed words over and over. *Help me God, help me.*

The sky, bright seconds ago, began to fill with twisting dark clouds as if blackness would envelope the earth, without an instant of transition. *This must be what it feels like to be in the silent center of a tornado.* Nick shoved his feet against the seat in front of him to brace himself. But it wasn't tornado season. He was too drained to try to figure out this strange occurrence. As if he could.

Even with the van's brights on, the road in front of them was completely blocked from sight.

"I can't see a thing!" Bruter complained, his voice tinged with panic.

"You should care! I'm driving. What about me?" He slammed on the brakes and slowed to twenty miles an hour, ten, five, and now a crawl. Shak leaned out the driver's window straining to find the center road line. He didn't dare pull off. The ditches on either side were at least four-feet deep. Stopping wasn't an option for fear of being hit from behind.

The winding road forced the curly headed driver to inch forward cautiously.

Nick heard a loud thud. They'd hit something, a metal pipe, a rod of some sort. The van swerved as the wheels left the road. Every nerve in Nick's body strained. Flames of fire appeared out of nowhere, swirling in and around the van.

The back door sprang open. A force like a gigantic torpedo of power thrust Nick free of the van and into the ditch. Seconds later he heard an explosion. The next sound was silence.

Nick couldn't explain afterwards what had happened inside the van. How were the bindings on his hands loosened? Although his wrists were bloodied he could slip them through his cords. Fire blazed all around him, but didn't touch him.

Quickly untying his feet, he stood, stumbled and rose again. He began to walk with stiff legs at first. He broke into a run blindly heading in the opposite direction from which they'd come, able only to see a couple feet ahead of him at a time.

How had he escaped? Had Shak and Bruter gotten out before the inferno?

And now what?

***

The second evening after Nick's disappearance, Jennifer realized she had to tell the children. She called Tara and Collin and Jenna into the living room. Something in the tone of her voice must have alarmed them because they came immediately.

Jennifer had already played a script through her brain. How many stories like hers had she heard in counseling? She'd even coached women through it. Nothing helped her now. She took a deep breath and choked out the words, "Children, I want you to understand none of this is your fault, but, well, Daddy and I haven't been getting along well. He's gone away for a while to decide what he wants to do. Whatever happens will be for the best." What a lie, her heart screamed. I didn't choose this!

The children stared at her like zombies hearing a foreign language. Were her words sinking in?

"You mean you could be getting divorced?"

"If we do, it will be better for you. You won't have to listen to our arguing."

Tara spoke first. "You don't argue that much."

"Not in front of you, maybe."

"Daddy can't leave." Jenna flung herself to the floor and started crying.

"Honey, he already has." Tara tried to pull Jenna up into her arms, but she broke free. "It'll be okay."

Tara glared at Jennifer as her words tumbled out. "Dad didn't want to stay with you, Mom, because you always complain about everything he does."

"No, he was kidnapped," Jenna insisted, tearfully looking up. "I saw this happen to a man on TV. Maybe he's been killed." She crawled onto Jennifer's lap as her crying turned to wailing.

Jennifer shook her head. "No. Your Dad left because he needed some time alone."

"Where did he go?" Tara demanded.

"I don't know, sweetie."

"Didn't he even tell you?"

"Not yet."

"He'll be back. He'll get in touch with us tomorrow, you'll see," Collin said.

"I don't think we should expect contact anytime soon." Jennifer had to be honest. "I'm sure this is hard on him, too."

Tara tried to sound mature. "He wouldn't want us to feel bad."

"Will we ever see him again?" Jenna paused to wipe her nose on the sleeve of her sweater before resuming bawling.

"Sure. We'll set up custody arrangements." Jennifer tried to smile.

"Tara, please take Jenna to the bathroom to wash her face," Jennifer ordered. She couldn't stand hearing her youngest daughter cry another minute.

"Mom," Collin said when they were alone, "Dad said more than once that he'd always be here for us and for you, too. Being a Christian and all, are you sure he's okay?"

"Forever love doesn't exist, except in movies, Collin. I don't know much about Christian values, but being a Christian doesn't always stop a divorce."

Collin's head dropped.

"I'm sorry, Son."

***

Hours later, as Jennifer stepped out of the tub in her over-sized bathroom, a melodious voice chanted stereophonically. "The Lord's will is my will. God and I are unified beyond distinction. My desires are His to fulfill. I am holy."

Birds chirped as the sound of ocean waves lapped the shore. The bathroom ceiling speaker filled the air with sound. "I am God's form in physical reality. There is no risk in my decisions. They are God's choices for me."

The Freedom Tape, part of the SRS, Stress Reduction Series she used for residents was intended to create feelings of ultimate peace. Jennifer often found comfort concentrating on the soothing background sounds of nature, but tonight the words leapt out at her. She really heard them for the first time.

Was that true of her? Did she really only choose the best? As she dried herself she pondered her life and longed for the days when Collin, and Tara were babies. She'd bathed them in her vanity sink, carried them to the king-size bed, and rolled and powdered them as they giggled. She imagined herself tucking the children in bed at night when they were little.

"Mommy, mommy, do the cloud!" Collin would squeal and stay straight as a straw in happy anticipation. She'd shake his favorite blanket and swirl it lightly three feet above him. "A cloud is falling on you Collin Get ready, here it comes." Then she'd drop his lion-print blanket and he'd chuckle as it fell in soft folds around him. "Do it again, mommy." And Jennifer had, repeating the game over and over, while they laughed together.

Jennifer finished patting herself with her luxuriant, pristine, white bath towel. Towel-wrapped, she stepped into the peach floral wallpapered bedroom suite.

Her cleaning woman kept the place in sterile condition, even the corners. Anything out of place she shoved in a laundry basket in the utility room closet. Jennifer appreciated the help, yet at times resented it. It seemed everything was too perfect on the outside with mess inside, just like her life until now.

Tara's room had become the only unmanaged space. She tossed clothes wherever she removed them, and refused to move them even when threatened by Jennifer they wouldn't be washed. "I don't care, I'll wear them dirty," was her standard retort.

Tara's "I don't care attitude" toward any consequence Jennifer dreamt up disturbed her. But perhaps Tara only pretended to have a brazen front, Jennifer told herself, like I do at times. Maybe I'd be surprised at how much she does care about our family.

Jennifer lowered herself onto the bed, continuing her reverie. She couldn't remember the last time she'd laughed with the children. Had she lost the joy of them? When had she stopped going into their rooms to tuck them in at night? *And why, for heaven's sake?* Her inner voice accused and she knew why.

My schedule became more rigid. I eliminated any games that would be an excuse to delay bedtime. How foolish this little change seemed in retrospect. Did I think school-age children didn't need someone to talk to and reassure them as they crossed from wakefulness into sleep?

Nick had started one-on-one bedtime visits with the children again the year before. Many a night he was in the children's rooms reading or talking.

*Good for you darling,* she thought, *I wish you'd made me be there, too. Why didn't you?*

It was as if Nick had whispered in her ear. She knew the answer. Because you considered yourself an adequate mother, and didn't want suggestions, right? In her preoccupation with herself, her work, her friends, her "freedom" became a confinement. Face it, Jennifer, family intimacy disintegrated. Forgotten were the silly games with the children, private jokes, little things, but maybe, after all, these were the truly big things in life? She vaguely heard the background music still humming through the room.

Her trade-offs seemed stupid now. How muddled life had become. *Confused, dumb and disconnected, that's me. What's important in life?* She could answer with more clarity now than she would have three days ago. It seemed as if a closed curtain had been drawn open.

If Nick ever came back she'd be different...more nurturing. Could she win him back if she told him? Not if he never called. Her skin prickled with shame at his desertion.

Embarrassed Nick had left her, Jennifer had told no one at work about his absence. It was bad enough his office knew he'd taken off. She sighed. Soon the children would spread the news, and everyone will know. And it will seem final. Tears came unbidden again.

The tape was drawing to a conclusion with a dramatic rhapsody, "God is in you, you are god." The basis of the New

Worldview was the absence of a personal God willing and eager to be part of every individual's life. Jennifer reeled from the words, as if struck by weighted lead. Even with her limited Sunday school background, she recognized what used to be called blasphemy.

She sat down on the side of the bed, and reached for the Bible Nick had left behind. Opening to Genesis, she read about the sin in the Garden of Eden. Jennifer squirmed. The words were different, but the message was the same, wasn't it?

She'd pushed away these cumbersome, intruding traditional ideas about religion she'd heard and adamantly refused to have a receptive mind-set. Her life had to have answers, plain and irrefutable facts.

From among the thousand complex, preposterous ideas about the meaning of life, she knew nothing mattered more than understanding whether there was a power in control of this obviously crazy world, and if she and those she loved were safe. Jennifer heard a gentle voice in her head say, "There is only one God. Thou shall not put other gods before Him, not even yourself." Hadn't she? She addressed her soul accusingly.

Could it be? Was she a traitor to her own desire for truth? Totally exhausted though it was only eight, Jennifer leaned back against the lace and ribbon trimmed throw pillows and slipped into a light sleep.

In her dozing, it was summer time, days of joy when Collin was nine and Tara seven, enthusiasm bursting from their skin. Collin came into her dream and said, "Mom, I'm ready."

"Ready for what, my darling?"

"For the beach, I have to finish my castle for Lancelot. He's getting knighted in three days, and I haven't got it ready." Collin dragged his goldenrod yellow, indestructible Tonka bulldozer by the bucket.

Tara scurried past in seersucker bibbed shorts and slipped her plump toes out of faded navy sneakers. Jennifer heard the echo of her voice yelling out to them, "Scrumpkins, I hope you can repeat this rapid-fire readiness when I want to go somewhere."

"Oh we will, Mommy, right Tara?"

"Right. We love you Mommy."

How everything had changed, how Jennifer had changed! It started with an innocent inner drive seeking an elusive little state called "Fulfillment," the goal of every new woman. Jennifer was an innovator, her women's magazines said she belonged to the generation creating the futurist revision sweeping away female deterioration and boredom.

The New Worldview was all so plausible at her first contact. A new order of self-supremacy. No one suspected self would be a devouring, relentless god, more demanding than the Creator it replaced. Could she have made the wrong choice after all? She laughed aloud, the thought made her feel free for a moment and not sad as much as stupid.

Jennifer strove for personal completion and work insidiously sucked up her family time, her leisure, all of her, as though life itself had been liposuctioned away. How strange. She'd say her family was the underlying inspiration for all she did and she wanted nothing else more than living each day with them in joy.

Nick must have hated watching her sink in the shallow waters of self. His most powerful statement had been his love for her when she'd been so unloving toward him. Would she ever see him again? Oh my God, she sobbed. Who was she begging with all her heart?

*** 

Around eight-thirty Anne called to invite Jennifer, Nick and the children to her newly adopted daughter's dedication. "I'm sorry, did I wake you? You sound groggy?"

"No problem. I was reading."

During the light chitchat following, Jennifer considered whether to confide in Anne and decided to risk it.

Her friend listened patiently to her entire story.

Jennifer concluded with the admission, "I drove him away, Anne. I wish I could start over. I can't imagine life without Nick. I've never loved anyone else. I have no idea what to do."

Anne expressed tender sympathy and assurance. Nick would never leave her or his children. "I'm racking my brain to think what could have happened to him. Character qualities don't change overnight. I'm concerned for his safety. Are you sure the note's in his writing?"

"It was printed on his letterhead using a computer."

"Anyone could imitate that. Wouldn't he have hand-written?"

"Not always. Oh Anne. How do you redo years? How do you start over as a single mother?"

"You can't believe Nick's left you for good?"

"What else can I think?" Jennifer's fragile composure shattered and she struggled for control. "Anne, how could he! I'm so confused! If there's a God, Nick separated himself from Him, too, didn't he? Isn't a Christian supposed to be faithful? Now and forever."

"Ideally, yes."

"Not always, I know what I've witnessed in the news." Jennifer slumped on her bed. "It wasn't only our differences over religion. I believed I was an invincible career woman and an all-star mother. I thought I had a weirdo religious husband and problem kids, but never that I was the problem." She chuckled. "You're supposed to say, 'Don't be too hard on yourself, you did your best.'"

Anne couldn't see her wistful smile over the line.

"Whatever you did or didn't do, God forgives a truly repentant heart and I'm sure Nick would, too. Remember the Our Father prayer. You can count on God's love and mercy."

"I wish I could believe this, I'm like a child testing water depth." Jennifer added grimly. "If I trust this vague God figure and He's not real, I'll drown. I've nothing else."

"That's ultimately true for all of us. God understands."

Jennifer pushed back tendrils of hair that had slipped forward around her face.

"Have you reported Nick's disappearance?"

"I called missing persons, but nothing came of it. The police found his car parked at the airport. Without evidence of foul play they refuse to check further. They say he probably took a personal trip, supposedly it happens often that spouses take off."

"Michael has a friend who's a private investigator. Shall we have him look into Nick's disappearance?"

"I'd like him to, but let's keep it discreet. I don't want to add to my embarrassment." Jennifer shifted uncomfortably.

"There's no way Nick left you of his own accord unless he had a good reason. Don't think for a minute there's another woman."

"You read my mind." Pain stabbed at Jennifer's heart. "A neighbor saw his car driving off."

"What did his secretary say?"

"Nick's previous day had been normal. His last appointment was with a man named Torricelli, representing a Landworks Company, Inc. Nick took work home for him. It was the last project he handled."

"Did anyone call to check they got it?"

"Yes."

"Everything was in order, done professionally?"

Jennifer nodded. "None of this makes any sense to me. I feel like a basket case. I'm already under tension at work launching a new directive and making initial phase adjustment plans. Every spare minute is consumed and I can hardly think. I swear I'm falling apart."

"I'll be praying," Anne said. "I'll talk to Mike and get back to you. We're leaving tomorrow to pick up our adopted daughter. We'll call when we get back."

"Anne, I'm sorry to upset you during this special time of welcoming your new daughter."

"Never mind. You take care."

Jennifer hung up the phone slowly and sat for a time with her head bowed.

*** 

Collin put a chair outside his mother's bedroom door after she retired and stayed there from ten to midnight wondering

120

what to do. Jennifer tried, but couldn't persuade him to leave. He said, "Mom, Dad's gone and I want to be here for you if you need me."

She cried herself softly to sleep.

***

Saturday morning Jennifer had planned on spending the day catching up on the work she'd brought home with her, but changed her plans. She filled the kitchen with the smell of grilled French toast with strawberries, one of her Tara's favorites.

Tara's delighted squeal when she awoke and staggered in for breakfast gave Jennifer momentary pleasure.

She sat to eat with the children while picking at her food and then tossed hers in the garbage when no one was looking.

After breakfast was cleared, Jennifer said, "Please come in the family room a minute, Tara."

Tara gave her a look, but followed.

"Sit down, please."

Tara plopped on the other half of the loveseat.

Jennifer rested her arm lightly on her daughter's shoulder. "It's hard to put into words what I want to say." She stumbled through a couple false starts and finally said, "I didn't realize I'd forgotten the things that glue people together into a strong family until this happened with Daddy."

Tara sighed impatiently. "What are you saying?"

"It's important to take time to share thoughts and feelings and for plain old family fun. This might not sound like much to you, but whatever happens with Daddy, it's good for us to remember how important we are to each other."

Tara's next response took Jennifer by surprise. "Instead of being uncomfortable, Mom, I like hearing you speak about your feelings, although it seems foreign."

Jennifer half-smiled. She continued. "I just want you and I to have fun together. Soon you'll be a grown woman. I want to stay part of your life. I know it's a two-way street, but I'd like us to be closer now, too. How about we start by going out for lunch together while Collin is at soccer? Jenna can come with, too. Girl time only."

Tara looked at Jennifer quizzically. "Mom, this is far out. All I can say is if you want to have fun, I'm all for it."

"Great, Darling, that's all I wanted to hear." Jennifer smiled and removed her arm from Tara's shoulder.

The moment was over.

"Mom, one thing, cut our the darling, OK? I hate the word."

"Thanks for telling me, pumpkin," Jennifer said teasingly.

Tara rolled her eyes. "You're impossible!"

Jennifer caught a glimmer of a smile.

\*\*\*

Pirelli finished his favorite meal at Little Sicily, an Italian feast of mostaccioli, veal Parmesan, and crisp garlic bread. The truth was canned chili was almost as tasty to him for he was addicted to the process of eating, rather than any particular food.

He ate if he was happy, if he was busy, if he was bored, if he was feeling low, whatever his mood, he ate. He'd never considered getting counseling for his eating disorder, but if he had, his problems could have been resolved with sustained effort.

The disorder was a common one. Food was his only memory of comfort as a child.

As an adult food continued to be the one solace always available. It demanded nothing from him. The more he ate, the more he distanced himself from a normal male/female relationship because of his obesity.

Pirelli had learned to hide anger, joy and, reluctant as he was to admit it, even fear in the pleasant movement of his jaw, the succulent sensations of his taste buds.

Food never let him down. Every human being he met had. Food had never canceled an appointment, never talked back or rejected him. Why should he limit his food intake, even briefly?

Pirelli had never known a permanent home. His parents abandoned him when he was five. His Dad ran off with another woman, and his mother decided she didn't want anything to do with the "three brats" he'd left behind.

By the time his Dad pulled out of the drive, she was on the phone with social services putting them up for adoption. In more foster homes than he could count, Pirelli was a fat little kid tolerated only for the monthly check his presence provided.

Pirelli had created a picture of a pretend dad in his mind. He'd developed it from bits and pieces of Dads he's seen in old TV sitcoms and the Dad of his one close boyhood friend. Even this childhood friend, Jerry, had copped out on him dying of a drug overdose.

When Jerry's Dad had called to tell Pirelli, he found Jerry dead in bed, Pirelli raced to his home. He'd lifted Jerry's cold hard body into his arms and yelled, "Jerry, don't do this to me! Don't leave me!"

Sobbing, he'd flung himself into the arms of Jerry's Dad who was also crying. They sat like that for over an hour.

That night Pirelli vowed to bury his emotions so deep he could never be hurt again.

Shortly afterwards he subconsciously chose a forever friend - food. There'd never be any better gratification than the brief, but real, sensual pleasure of eating. He believed he could control his drive at will, but actually was powerless.

When Pirelli traveled he preferred to stay in a hotel suite with a small, stocked refrigerator and microwave - all he needed for his private heaven. He liked excellent accommodations such as Embassy Suites with its well-equipped kitchenettes like the one he was in now. The staff even performed shopping services for a slight additional fee.

A permanent residence was out of the question in his work - too risky. Pirelli was not the kind of person who could fade in and out of a locale and be easily forgotten. Witnesses might be apt to describe him in detail.

Pirelli had gotten connected with mob boss Relton by luck from another job he'd done for a guy they both knew. Relton liked to employ people with a weakness. If they ever proved to be a liability, in a bind he had something to use against them.

Pirelli was bright, self-trained and devious - perfect skills for Relton's organization. He was smarter than one would expect from his appearance. Relton had used him several times before behind the scenes and had confidence in him.

Pirelli had been ordered to make himself available each evening between 8 and 9 for communication from Relton.

From his drawer Pirelli pulled a bag of peanut butter kisses, and relaxed with the newspaper. He liked being a well-informed citizen, and never failed to read the daily paper.

***

At half past eight Pirelli's phone rang. He recognized Relton's voice without an introduction. Brusque as usual, Relton said, "Trevor escaped. The van was found overturned with Shak and Bruter inside, babbling and petrified. They claim a sudden fire broke out following an explosion. Maybe Trevor had matches to set it, but that's ridiculous. His hands were supposedly tied. They're scratched up and badly shaken, but I've sent them out to find Trevor. I need you to determine where the Trevor woman stands on Directive 99. It's imperative it gets implemented quickly. Get a bug on her."

Relton had confidence in Pirelli. Perhaps they had different reasons, but they were fighting the same war against traditional, law-abiding society, he realized. This made them comrades in his book. Save the pleasantries to deceive enemies. A brutal heart beat in the handsome, power-thirsty Relton.

"You recall what happened to Levinson, the correspondent who collected info on Directive 99 and its timetable?"

Pirelli twisted his hands nervously wondering where this conversation was going. "Yeah, boss, he had to be eliminated."

"Every now and then somebody cuts a deal. I'm still trying to find out who ratted information to that correspondent Levinson. Now I'm wondering who helped Trevor escape. I guarantee these traitors will never talk again."

Pirelli started to sweat. Why was Relton telling him this?

"The other problem is Bruter failed to take Levinson's laptop. He was stupid enough to think crashing the hard drive was sufficient. I need to get my hands on that computer and check it over."

"Idiot." Pirelli made the appropriate response.

"I'm giving Shak and Bruter one more chance to find Trevor and finish the job. I'll visit Levinson's widow myself to get the laptop. I'd send you, but I want you to get info on Trevor's wife at the Fullness of Life Centre."

"You're the boss."

"One more thing, Pirelli. Do I seem like a man who enjoys giving second chances?"

"No, sir."

"With these bugs I'll know the instant her husband contacts her. If Jennifer Trevor gets out of line, we'll deal with her immediately. Is that clear? You'll handle her while I take care of the Levinson woman." With that Relton hung up.

Pirelli felt squeamish. He had a bit of chivalrous thread in him. Destroying men's reputations, even being involved in murder was all in a day's work, but he had no experience eliminating women. He knew he was a softie where manipulation, extortion or endangerment of women was concerned. Fortunately, he'd never been in a situation like this before. He wished he wasn't now.

Pirelli reminded himself, "Anything can happen in a deal. I can handle it." He snapped open a Coke and started pacing.

It was his custom to avoid hard liquor, he allowed himself two glasses of wine with dinner. Clear thinking was the key to survival and survival was crucial in his trade.

What personage suited his needs now? He rejected the ruse of an eccentric Englishman. It had proved highly workable on occasion, but Pirelli decided on the dumb bumpkin role he played superbly. He was a good impersonator and knew it. In fact, he mused, it would be fun to try acting when and if he retired.

Pirelli walked over to the refrigerator, pulled out a half gallon of chocolate mint ice cream and consumed it while plotting his strategy. His approach to Ms. Trevor required careful thought. A few hours later his plan was ready.

***

Relton examined his image in his rearview mirror adjusting the blonde wig he'd selected from his disguise case. His fake mustache matched perfectly even to the few gray hairs added for authenticity. He was satisfied, along with the contacts he'd inserted to disguise his eye color, he was unrecognizable. *Nothing is exactly as it seems,* he mused. Duplicity was, after all, his business.

He noted again the address numbers on the mailbox before ringing Sarah Levinson's doorbell.

"Ms. Levinson? Agent Melton." He passed her a picture ID showing his affiliation with ANSA, the American National Security Agency.

Sarah opened the door wide. "I can't tell you how glad I was to receive your call. The media ignored all my statements after the first one. And the police act as if I'm crazy."

"I assure you the American National Security Office shares your concern about the cause of your husband's death. We decided to reexamine his supposed suicide."

Sarah began to weep. "I'm so grateful. John's office burglary two days ago was another horrid violation. Who'd do such a thing to a dead man?" She shook her head and wiped her eyes with the back of her hand. "Forgive me. This has been terribly difficult."

"Please, no need to excuse your tears, your reaction is totally natural under the circumstances." He lowered his gaze and pulled out a small notepad. Now, if I may ask a few questions."

"Certainly. Would you like to sit down?"

"That won't be necessary." They remained standing in the kitchen area of the great room. "I understand you have John's laptop in your possession?"

"Yes, I do, but oh…not at the moment. I've sent it to a data recovery company."

His blue eyes hardened as he glanced up. "What's their name and address for my file? I may need to contact them."

Sarah turned, pulled a card from the kitchen desk drawer and dutifully read aloud the name and address.

"When do you expect it back?"

"They couldn't give me a definite date."

"Please call me as soon as it arrives. Also did John have any stored disks? Perhaps in a safe, if you have one?"

"I haven't come across any and we don't have a safe."

"May I take a look in his home office?"

"Of course. Follow me."

They walked down the hall passing the two boy's bedrooms. Relton glanced in at the baseball and hockey posters as they passed. John's den, a mahogany paneled room, had two walls of bookshelves. Glancing at a few titles, Relton summarized the values of this man. Eliminating him had been wise.

"I've gone through everything. John rarely made paper copies or disks of his current work. He used an electronic back-up company, but only he knew the password. Even now they won't reveal it to me. I never thought to ask John for it, although I doubt he'd have told me. He often said his work was controversial, and he'd never wanted me to be in jeopardy. He was," she stifled a sob, "very caring and protective."

An hour later, Relton was satisfied nothing existed in Levinson's desk or office files. "Please call me as soon as you receive your husband's computer back." He passed a card into her outstretched hand. "Our equipment may be able to pull up data this recovery company misses."

You haven't lost your touch, he prided himself, as he drove back to his office complex. On the way, he stopped at a busy gas station to use the lavatory and in the stall removed his disguise. No one noticed he walked in one man and out another.

\*\*\*

Jennifer's loved that her office resembled a large private perch with an intercom system she could flip to different stations to overhear conversation and evaluate in-progress patient procedures. She finished her daily visual inspection and looked down as an unusually large man walked into the lobby. He paused at the information desk. Curious, Jennifer clicked her front desk speaker on.

To say the man was simply unattractive was inaccurate. This was one of the few cases where the word "ugly" applied, Jennifer decided. His dark hair fell in numerous directions around a childish round face, a strong contrast to his pallid skin. He had to be at least fifty pounds overweight, maybe more. Jennifer's repulsion mixed with sympathy toward him. He asked a question and must have been referred to her secretary as he was handed the house phone and looked up.

She heard her secretary, Ellen, respond over the intercom to the man's request to schedule an appointment with Mrs. Trevor to discuss his father's situation."

After a pause, Ellen said, "You're in luck. It's usually necessary to schedule a week in advance, but Ms. Trevor has half an hour free this afternoon at 3. She can see you then."

The large man checked his watch. "Three o'clock," he repeated with a thick voice. Pirelli eyed the front and back entrances, the habit served him well when a sudden exit was in order. "I'll be back."

***

Jennifer returned from a meeting with the staff dietitian a few minutes before three to find Ellen bent over the bottom file cabinet drawer, displaying thinning black hair in desperate need of a root touch-up.

She surmised her assistant was dieting again from the two Weight-Watcher cookies displayed on a saucer atop her computer waiting for break time. Across from her sat Mr. Pirone watching her intently.

Jennifer introduced herself.

"Mr. Pirone, follow me, please," she invited cordially.

Once inside her office he slumped onto the sofa, apparently eager to switch his poundage to a sedentary state. She sat across from him.

"Now, how may I be of help?" Jennifer was good at expediting conversation. Nick often joked she should have been a talk show host. The thought of him brought a haze over her eyes. She blinked a few times and composed herself.

As it turned out, Mr. Pirone was an eager talker. "My father, I take good care of him. It's no problem. His legs are bad, he's only about 110 pounds, carrying him's easy for me." He paused for breath and patted his belly, before adding, "Yeah ya gotta wonder how he got a son my size." Pirone shoved out his stomach as though it were a strong muscle he was proud of.

Jennifer shuddered. "It's a little chilly here, excuse me." She picked up the remote on her desk to raise the temperature.

"Yeah? I'm fine."

"So back to the reason for your visit. You'd like information on setting up an assisted living arrangement for him?"

"Yeah," he continued, "I can do what my Dad needs, but well, I gotta work. He gets lonely sitting by himself all day."

"I understand. Many of our residents were in similar circumstances. Here's a packet of information on our services. Would you like a cup of coffee or soft drink before we go through it together?"

Pirone waved his hand, "Sure! Black's fine."

Jennifer welcomed the chance to briefly turn her back.

She snapped on her intercom. "Ellen, bring Mr. Pirone a cup of coffee, please."

Jennifer extended her courtesy to compensate for her negative feelings. She was by instinct and professional training a caring person and prided herself on a high level of acceptance of others. It concerned her to feel repulsed by this man. Looking down she shuffled some papers on her desk composing herself.

She heard a low moan and turned toward Mr. Pirone. In one swift moment, Pirone's whole demeanor had changed. He pulled off his suit coat and began stabbing his arms into his pants

129

pockets. One hand emerged with wrapped candy, which he ripped open and stuck in his mouth before collapsing on the floor.

"Diabetic?" Jennifer uttered. She pressed the emergency beeper clipped to her waist and was on her feet in one smooth motion.

Leaning over him she asked, "Mr. Pirone, are you alright? Can you hear me?"

His words came out in short bursts. "I'm fine, just give me a minute."

A male nurse shot in with an aide trailing behind. Pirone gestured as if to push them away. "Leave me alone. I got dizzy, don't need nothing."

Jennifer interceded. "Please let the nurse check your vitals."

The nurse took heart rate and blood pressure. Jennifer requested a blood sugar test. The lab girl arrived within minutes.

"I'm kinda nervous. I gotta set my dad up here, that's all. It's hard, Ms. Trevor 's gonna get him good care. This sometimes happens when I get too excited, I'm okay now, really. Thanks all the same."

Jennifer made Mr. Pirone comfortable on the sofa and chatted until the test results were available.

"Do you mind closing the drapes?" Pirone asked.

Without a second's hesitation, Jennifer rushed to comply. *All I need is for someone to die in my office*, she thought. The regional director would love that.

Immediately, she felt a sting of guilt. Really Jennifer, he's a human being, what's come over you?

The suddenness of Pirone's recovery surprised Jennifer, but she'd seen many unusual physical responses in her work. Although if it was only a fainting spell, it was fairly typical.

The staff doctor strode in briskly. "Mr. Pirone, your blood sugar level appears normal. Temp and blood pressure too. I can only conclude your distress was caused by an acute anxiety reaction to whatever was happening at the time. We call this a vasovagal episode, but it simply means becoming faint. That's not uncommon. Falling over restored effective blood flow to your brain. Still, I suggest you visit your own doctor for a thorough check-up."

"Then why did he reach for sugar?" Jennifer asked.

"Perhaps simply from a habit formed by stress episodes in the past," the doctor explained.

"Thanks, doc, coincidentally, I got a appointment for later this week. Hey, I'm real sorry this happened."

"Never mind, Mr. Pirone, you're all right, that's the important thing." Jennifer assured him. "Just rest for a bit."

"Yeah, it feels good to lie down."

She touched his arm compassionately. "I need to leave for a family meeting. We can schedule another appointment when you're feeling better."

"You've keen kind. I think I have enough info to look over. " Mr. Pirone's voice became a whisper. "Maybe I will rest a bit before leaving." Jennifer melted at his innocent, distressed look.

"I'll have my office assistant sit with you until you're up to leaving."

"That's not necessary."

"I insist."

Jennifer left to get her, but Ellen wasn't at her desk. Jennifer checked her watch. It was almost her break time. She'd probably taken it a few minutes early.

She turned to go back into her office almost bumping into Anne.

"Hi, Jennifer. Glad I caught you. I finished visiting with Michael's aunt and wanted to say a quick hi." Anne observed the man in Jennifer's office behind her through the open door and instinctively lowered her voice. "I'm sorry, you're busy. I'll catch you another time."

"Wait, Anne, could you do me a huge favor? I'm late for a meeting. Can you stay with the gentlemen in my office for a few minutes? He's resting after what appears to have been an anxiety attack. I'd have Ellen do it, but she's on break."

Anne glanced at the clock on the wall. "I'd be delighted, I don't have to be home for another hour."

Jennifer brought Anne into her office and introduced her. "Anne, Mr. Pirone and I were discussing our center when he began to feel ill. He's resting now and will be leaving shortly. I'd prefer he not be left alone under the circumstances."

"Yeah," Pirone smacked his head. "I'll be up to going as soon as I get collected."

"Of course." Anne dropped her purse on Jennifer's desk.

Jennifer took one last tentative glance at the two of them, before excusing herself.

"Don't want to trouble you, but another glass of water would be real nice, Ms. Stasen."

"I'll get it."

"Thank you," Pirone said weakly.

As soon as Anne entered the private washroom at the opposite end of the room, Pirelli popped over to the desk where he'd observed Jennifer's open briefcase. He pulled a dime-sized, battery-operated microphone out of his pants pocket, quickly pulled off the self-stick backing, and taped it inside the base of the file-holder pocket inside the briefcase. He added another microphone beneath the desk phone, and staggered back toward the chair as Anne returned. She handed Pirone water in a paper cup and a paper towel.

"Thank you." He took several slow sips, dragging his hand across his forehead. "I just tried to stand, but got a little dizzy."

Anne rested her cool hand upon Mr. Pirone's forehead and said, "Just rest a bit. When someone is ill, I believe prayer helps. May I pray for you?"

He said, "Yeah, sure," thinking Anne meant at home later or at church. His eyes widened when she started right in.

"Jesus, this is one of your beloved children. For him you went to the cross and died. Lord, he needs your healing touch. I ask for your hand upon this man, let the fullness of life, his life and your life surge through his body. In Your precious name, I pray." To herself she added, *Lord if he doesn't already know you, lead him into relationship with you and forgive him his trespasses whatever they may be.*"

Pirelli leaned against the sofa back seeking more distance between him and Anne.

*This is downright weird,* he thought. *I don't get it.* This broad's doesn't seem the least uncomfortable being alone with me. She even left her purse in plain sight when she got my water. I believe she actually cares about me.

He remembered a long-forgotten moment as a little boy when he couldn't swim. He'd gone out too deep and started floundering. A female lifeguard pulled him out of the water. She checked to see if he needed CPR, saying a prayer over him until she was sure he was breathing okay.

Warmth surged through Pirelli and peace, like he'd known years ago. He didn't want to move for fear of disturbing this strange feeling he didn't understand. He vowed to think on it some time. "I feel better now - guess that prayer stuff works fast. I'll be leaving."

"Are you sure you're up to driving? I'd be glad to take you home. You could get your car tomorrow."

Anne's eyes brimmed with such tender concern, Pirelli turned away. He couldn't believe this broad was willing to let him in her car.

"I think I can make it. Sorry to make such a fuss." He heard himself apologizing sincerely. What was going on?"

"No problem, just be sure to see your doctor for a check-up."

\*\*\*

Sarah's heart stopped when she saw the name, Raybon Computer Specialists Company on her caller ID. She was afraid to answer. If the news were bad, could she handle another disappointment?

"Ms. Levinson, I'm happy to report a successful retrieval, that is, we've recovered some files. It may not be everything, but definitely some data will now be accessible to you.

From the jubilant tone of his voice, the man she dealt with named Stan took a personal pride in helping his customers.

"We'll send the computer back this afternoon. You should have it the day after tomorrow."

"Thank you so much!"

"We were able to keep the cost down to $1200. Would you like to put it on the Master Card we put on file for you?"

"Yes, please. Stan, one more question. No one reads these files during the retrieval process, do they?"

"No, Ma'm, we just check that there's data available the owner can access. Our policy is to respect your privacy as much as we can."

"Good, Stan." Sarah paused and added quickly, "I can't tell you how grateful I am."

*** 

Jennifer mouthed a silent thanks to Anne for showing up when she did. Jennifer couldn't alter her schedule. She needed to meet with the family members of new patients scheduled for orientation. Actually, her job was to convince family members it was best for them not to visit often. She'd tell them their presence interfered with patient stabilization. Family members were sometimes a nuisance and interfered with smooth programming and standardized patient maintenance.

Jennifer reached the conference room door where a young woman in a brown and green checked pants suit hurried up to her. "Dr. Trevor, do you remember me?"

Jennifer smiled recognizing her former client. She held out her hand politely while searching for a name to match the face. "Carol Stockman...my, you've matured. It's been what, five years?"

"Six, you counseled me senior year of high school. I never could have survived without you. I still remember the principles you taught me about self-esteem and dealing with anger. My family had all but given up on me ever getting my bulimia under control. I'm doing quite well now, but it will always be a challenge. No more hospitalizations though," she announced proudly.

"That's great. What are you doing here?"

A shadow crossed the green-eyed woman's face, erasing her smile.

"Daddy has Alzheimer's."

"I'm so sorry."

"I insisted Mother bring him across town to be here. Are you still counseling in your private practice?"

"No more one-on-one since my administrative responsibilities occupy most of my time."

"What a shame, you were so good! I know I sound like I'm gushing and I'm probably keeping you from something, I'm sorry."

"Don't be silly. It's nice to see former clients and hear good reports. What are you doing now?"

"I finished college and married my high school sweetheart, Don."

Jennifer and Carol entered the group conference room together and took chairs around the shiny walnut table that sat twenty. The circular table was designed to make everyone feel equal, minimizing staff/family separation. The room was already full. Four families were represented.

Jennifer introduced herself and welcomed everyone. She invited the genial, plump social worker to speak first. She knew the middle-aged woman's spiel by heart so her mind was free to muse.

Seeing Carol brought back reminders of the days when Jennifer had worked on the front lines with clients and could readily see the results of her efforts. She'd been idealistic and believed she could help everyone. How had she gotten buried in an office and paperwork and drifted so far from caring about people?

Jennifer tuned back in to the social worker's concluding words being spoken like an oft-played record. "Placing your loved one with us is the difficult and courageous solution to caring for your loved ones."

It still amazed Jennifer how adult children with histories of child abuse or parental neglect were often the most concerned their aged parents receive excellent care. You'd have thought it would be payback time. But psychologically the adult children still yearned for those missing expressions of love. Perhaps there was still some chance they could yet feel the affirmation they'd lacked all their lives.

Alas, for most it was not to be. Elderly parents ignored them or verbally abused them same as before. And when these adult children visited too infrequently, their parents reprimanded them, again like little children. It was painful to watch these interchanges. Grown children like hungry dogs wagging their tails and running in circles, yet never feeling the pat on the head they yearned for.

On the other hand, loving parents often told their children not to bother to visit. Enjoy these years of your own life is what one popular resident, Kathryn, reportedly said to her two adult children. But you couldn't keep people from visiting that gem. Every staff member wanted to be assigned to her.

Jennifer pursed her lips, thinking about what lie ahead for Kathryn, Michael and Anne Stasen's aunt. Jennifer had met eighty-five-year old Kathryn when she arrived to reside with her ill husband. She'd found the capable, intelligent woman charming. And now a disturbing piece didn't fit the Directive 99 death formula.

Did one person who perhaps should live longer make the whole directive wrong? She remembered what Nick said days before he disappeared, "We're not talking about policy decisions, but human lives."

***

Sarah and John had fallen in love with their property in Massachusetts the moment they saw it. Ten acres of land with a remodeled farm house and a huge oak tree with perfect limbs for a tree house for the boys.

As she walked through their fields now, she remembered those happy moments. They'd come here as newlyweds, with plenty of savings to invest acquired by marrying later, and immediately had their daughter and eventually two sons.

The tree house, built after Jacob turned seven, even had two windows John had bought at a farm supply store. He and their sons struggled to install them, but John was determined it would be a do-it-yourself project and refused to call a handyman.

When one went in a little crooked, John had jokingly reminded her no work of art was perfect. They'd laughed uproariously when he'd made the label, Levinson Construction, and attached it.

About thirty yards from the tree house stood a mature maple tree, which could be easily climbed. She and John called it their Lovetree and often sat in its branches or on the wooden bench beneath. They occasionally brought wine and chips and chatted while the children either played in the tree house or stayed behind to watch TV at the main house.

The maple was special in another way. It had become their message tree. Beneath the longest branch John had attached a metal box. After they'd argue, rare as that was, they left love notes of apology for each other. When Sarah came home from the hospital after delivering Eli by c-section, John had planned a ritual of celebration for when she was strong enough to climb the tree and retrieve the love notes he'd written to her during her absence.

An early snow had left the maple coated with snow and crusted the earth beneath in white. Sarah, wanting desperately to lift the melancholy she carried everywhere, impulsively climbed the tree for old times' sake.

She sat on a branch in the cold snow and gazed at the six by eight-inch metal box with its Master Key lock in the crook of the limbs. The key was taped on the bottom, the last place anyone would look for a key, John had said with a grin. Besides who would ever know the box was there?

What drew her to open it now was a sense of nostalgia, a longing for something that had been only theirs. She had no expectation of finding what she did.

## Chapter Fourteen

Tangled in a mess of bed sheets Jennifer dreamt she was running down a dark corridor searching frantically for Nick. In her bones she sensed a pervasive horror lurking nearby.

A door opened to a cavernous courtroom where Nick sat in a witness chair. Quickly assuming the role of lawyer for the opposition, Jennifer interrogated him ruthlessly destroying his testimony. While demanding a guilty verdict, she sought a way to shield him from the jury. Into his ear she pleaded, "Nick, I won't hurt you, but you're tearing me apart."

As the captain of the jury rose to give the verdict she awoke with a jolt.

Why dream such a cruel caricature of reality? Jennifer wondered. *And why do I feel so frightened?* I am still in control of my destiny with or without my husband.

The answer came unbidden. I fear being without him. I need his love and the comfort of his presence. We are one, and if he's destroyed so am I.

This is more than I can bear.

Jenna's wail interrupted Jennifer's disoriented agonizing. Her door opened and her daughter staggered into the room falling into her mother's arms.

"It's okay, sweetheart, just a bad dream, you can go back to sleep." Jennifer's soothing voice didn't dispel the fear in her daughter's quivering body. She continued to scream, "Mommy, Daddy."

Jennifer held her close and rocked her daughter against her breast. "Sleep with me?" she invited. Jenna resembled an eighttentacled octopus as a bedmate, but this was clearly the easiest alternative.

Jenna sobbed out a "Yes," snuggled up and soon was asleep again. Every few minutes, a pathetic sob escaped between her little breaths.

Fully awake now, Jennifer slipped out of bed and downed two extra-strength aspirin with a full glass of water before slipping back under the covers.

A remnant from third grade Sunday school leapt unbidden into her wakefulness. Repeating the verse was simple. She'd earned a giant yellow construction paper star with a lollipop scotch-taped across it for her memory work. "Be anxious about nothing, but in all things give thanks for that is the will of Christ Jesus for you."

Saying the words slowly now, she pondered their meaning for the first time, before rejecting such foolishness. Perhaps, if she could believe a great powerful God had a willful, wise plan, she could endure this confusion, this rejection. Or was Nick, as Anne insisted, being held against his will somewhere?

Pull yourself together, you're falling apart, her inner voice insisted as her silent monologue continued. There was no unclaimed body, no accidental death. Nick's car had been left in long term parking at the airport. Jennifer had to accept the fact he simply chose to leave.

After only four hours sleep, Jennifer's body was ravaged. Her nerves wreaked havoc on her mind, pushing further sleep out of reach.

She arose when her quartz alarm went off at four a.m. A shower revived her a bit. With a heavy heart she finalized packing for her trip to Washington, D.C. She and Jack would testify at the Senate hearing on the latest program in comprehensive elderly residential care. Her mom, a retired flight attendant, bless her heart, had spent the night in the guest room and would get the children off to school. When she wasn't traveling herself, Grandma Bee was the children's best and favorite babysitter.

After dressing, Jennifer sipped her morning coffee, and again opened Nick's Bible for her one comforting connection to him. A new thought popped into her mind. Why would Nick leave without this marked-up Bible he prized? Was he really kidnapped? The idea sent a frisson of fear mixed with hope down Jennifer's spine. "No," she said aloud and shook her head. Perhaps the book itself didn't mean that much, because he could easily buy another.

***

Washington, D.C.

The airport terminal at Dulles International vibrated with swarms of people, like locusts, seemingly unable to find a leaf to alight. Jennifer and her companion walked swiftly past the baggage area.

"I'm glad we didn't need luggage," Jack said, eyeing the circle of fliers around the baggage carousel waiting for bags to be coughed up.

They pulled their carry-ons packed with laptops and their presentation materials. Lengthy briefs for the committee members had already been shipped directly to the hearing chambers.

"Look at this mob! I don't believe it." Jack said when they walked outside. "There must be fifty people ahead of us waiting for a cab."

"Relax, Jack, the line's moving fast."

"By now you must know I don't do waits well."

"You could use a dose of patience." Jennifer experienced the uneasiness in her gut she often developed in Jack's presence. Too much push. She couldn't help think he'd as soon shove her under a cab as ride in one with her.

The sporadic starts and stops of aggressive cabbies made pedestrians jump back who stood too close. After twenty minutes in the taxi line, Jack and Jennifer ducked into a once-yellow, rust-coated vehicle.

"The Capitol," Jack directed sharply.

The cabbie smiled and started off. By a combination of gestures and straining to communicate they discovered the black driver was a Muslim who spoke little English. It took almost five minutes, while he drove madly through the airport exit lanes, for him to understand their destination. Finally, he raised his arm enthusiastically and smiled with huge white teeth, "Yes, Yes, Kappital, Senato."

Jennifer's elbow went into the hole where there'd once been a door handle as the cab careened to her side.

Jack's face was white when he handed the driver two twenties at their destination and refused to wait for change.

Jennifer hoped her anti-perspirant was still in effect as she climbed out at the Senate Office Building.

Trudging up the steps, Jack again expressed dismay. "Why couldn't the senators just read their data, and ask questions by fax, e-mail or conference call to save us this hassle?"

Jennifer silently agreed it was a nuisance to present in person, but wouldn't admit this to Jack. He'd likely use the statement as a direct quote against her in some future report. Instead she said, "This hearing of the Health Committee is required to appease the legal process even though individual members have previously been contacted and lobbied by headquarters."

Jennifer had no idea who made those presentations, but doubted the extra material she'd received recently on advanced phases of Directive 99 had been passed along to Congress. How convenient for a rush strategy. She hadn't had time to read everything through herself. Nor would she bring up these advanced phases today. They'd left her almost no time to organize the details for their implementation. This hearing was to be on the innocuous first phase, Sensitivity To End-of-life Issues Faced by the Elderly. Once endorsed the Directive would include all phases automatically.

They hurried up to the assigned room on the second floor of the Capitol. It seemed a plain, musty old courtroom of the nineteenth century, not at all the glamorous platform she'd expected, but the walls reeked of history. Days earlier the auspicious setting might have tickled her pride, no longer. She marveled at her different perspective as she checked to see her materials had been delivered and was relieved to see them on a side table.

Senators filed in groups of two and three, some individually. After a shuffling of chairs the meeting was called to order by the Chairperson. Jennifer's adrenaline went into high gear.

"Knock 'em dead. Excuse the pun," Jack whispered with a quick turn of his head. He stood when she was invited to the podium and began to distribute to each committee member abbreviated copies of the directive and other explanatory material to examine as Jennifer spoke.

She waited until everyone had a copy, and then began her presentation with an impressive detail. "The elderly group 65-85 years of age is the fastest growing part of the population. Swelling numbers of baby-boomers need care and create a great burden to our economy. Our government intends to take care of them, but is struggling to survive these costs due to burgeoning operational expenses."

Fifteen minutes after rattling off boring statistics, she'd lost all but the most analytical among her listeners. One elderly Senator began to snore lightly. Her professional composure remained inviolate before the committee. Jennifer concluded by waving a thick document in her hand as she said, "Our new Directive 99 program will efficiently reduce these expenditures by revisiting contractual commitments with major pharmaceuticals, new labor agreements with unions and various other cost-saving measures."

She never once referred to Fullness of Life Centre residents as people. It was advisable to stick to vague words like population or group to distance hearers from the reality that she was referring to needs of human beings.

Following her uninterrupted speech, the Senators took turns posing questions. Most had been written in advance by their aides. Some legislators seemed interested and open-minded; others dragged out words pompously like balloons overstuffed with air merely needing an outlet to express excess wind.

Jennifer and Jack noticed party lines weren't showing distinguishing responses. Everyone wanted to be on the side of concern for the elderly, a huge block of voters. Jennifer assumed this dictated their behavior. However, members differed in how this caring should be demonstrated.

After over an hour of interrogation a thin, no-nonsense female senator from New Hampshire spoke. "Please be seated Ms. Trevor. My fellow senators, I believe we can agree we're getting a sense of closure from Ms. Trevor's answers. Certainly, this highly qualified woman understands the ramifications of this program. And let's remember the health czar has given this his endorsement. I have every confidence in the implementation of Directive 99 at our national Fullness of Life Centres as a valuable adjunct to the current care provided at our sites."

Jack leaned toward Jennifer. "That was Congressese, did you recognize it?" She winced and nodded.

The vote was taken. There was no dissent and the meeting was adjourned.

"You won them over!" Jack was generous with his praise.

Jennifer sat frozen in her seat. The damage was done.

*** 

Jennifer and Jack caught the next plane back.

When she unpacked it occurred to Jennifer she hadn't checked their luggage to see what bag Nick had taken. Maybe its size would indicate how long he'd planned to stay away. All their suitcases were there. She went through them twice to be sure. When Nick traveled by car, he often took a change of suits and threw underwear and a folded shirt in his briefcase.

The police had found his car at the airport with nothing inside. He had to have brought clothes. She went through his suits sliding them one by one along the clothes pole. Suddenly her fingers froze on a hanger and she stopped. Jennifer had no idea how many suits or shirts her husband owned, so how could she tell what was missing? What kind of wife was she?

She grew rigid with anger, and screamed in her mind, *where are you, you louse?* Exhausted, she lay her head against the shoulder of a grey stripe flannel and cried. How much longer

143

could she stand these vacillating emotions? Has Nick actually left me? Or is he out there somewhere in danger? Her shoulders slumped as she tried to repress her feelings yet again.

***

A force like a strong wind pushed Nick forward through the darkness, even though the trees around him were still. He sensed something or someone was after him, but could hear nothing. He half wanted to succumb to whatever, whoever chased him and be done with it. "God help me!" he yelled into the emptiness.

Nick had no idea how long he'd been staggering through fields when he slipped on the wet leaf-strewn ground. His body slid forward. As he recovered his balance he saw before him the door of a farmer's old root cellar. He hastily descended the steps. Once upon the damp, cold ground, the cellar door above him slammed shut.

Physically spent, Nick failed to comprehend his strange deliverance. Alone on the chilling earth, he used all his strength and constant repetitions of the name of Jesus to resist the temptation toward uncontrollable fear. Two strong emotions tugged on him. One was God's calm, gracious Spirit assuring him of eventual rescue; the other inspired panic and reveled in cunning, revengeful plans for retaliation against his offenders.

Go back home. Wait with a loaded gun in your lap. When they come after you again, blow them apart. Who cares who they are! They're the enemy, destroy them! You have the right! They would have done it to you, but you were too smart and strong. You escaped. Get them, before it's too late!

Nick longed for surcease as he fought the trepidation creeping through his bones.

Initially, Nick discerned only a fine distinction between the urges, but as he prayed he knew which voice belonged to whom. God knew his agony and fortified his spirit with words of assurance. Nick remembered Scriptures he'd read. You're like Nathaniel, a man without guile. I will guide you with mine eye.

The same Holy Spirit, sent to King David when he wrote the Psalms comforted Nick.

He began to explore the area with his hands finding a thin pile of straw against the side. He rolled onto it and continued praying.

Eventually the solitude enveloped him and he fell into a restless sleep.

\*\*\*

Bruter pushed his thick curly hair under a hunter's cap and pulled a wool flannel shirt from the Walmart bag. He tossed a green and black plaid jacket to Shak, the big German with prematurely graying hair and rough cracked hands.

Shak spread out a map and drew a black circle around a hundred-mile radius. "I doubt he'd go beyond this, until he knows his family is safe. My guess is he's holing up close by."

"Why do we have to track him down? Sooner or later he'll go home and we'll get him there," Bruter grumbled.

"We can't wait." Relton was adamant.

"What if he escapes again?"

"That's not going to happen. You and me, we got a reputation to protect. You scare too easily."

Bruter stuck the cell phone into his waistband clip. He knew his tendency to be frightened and always see negatives didn't fit with his size. He'd fallen into crime because of his mean streak. It began with being beaten as a child and led to becoming a fearful and insecure adult. One school psychologist had pegged him in one session before he quit attending altogether.

He was phobic about getting physically hurt and still hadn't fully recovered from seeing the van explode in fire. Remembering the heat of the flames he realized it might have helped if he could figure out what caused it and how they could possibly have survived. "Something weird happened to our van. I'd rather not mess with this guy. Why not tell Relton the deal's off?"

"What! We'd never work again, if Relton let the word out. We gotta get Trevor. Let's get moving."

"I don't like this one bit." They climbed into a rented Praxis, the new energy efficient electric car, and headed North along the same road Nick had been on three hours earlier.

Bruter and Shak showed a picture of Nick at gas stations and restaurants and motels along the way explaining they were supposed to meet Shak's brother for a camping trip, but the brother never showed. They were getting worried.

***

Nick awoke to light shafts darting along the top edges of the cellar door. He dimly made out root vegetables hanging from the rafters - onions and carrots and Jerusalem artichokes. Grabbing some carrots, he stuffed one into his mouth and more into his pockets to assuage hunger.

He strained to stand straight and exerted cautious pressure on the overhead door. Nick shoved with all his might over and over, but nothing happened. It was either stuck or some kind of lock had kicked in when it shut last night.

Exhausted, he dropped back on the floor, lowered his head into his hands and prayed, *God, is this where I'm supposed to die? Jennifer needs me. I love her and want to be with her. And the kids, let me be there for them please, Jesus!*

Forcing himself up Nick wearily pushed again. Nothing happened. He gritted his teeth and shoved his shoulder as hard as he could at the door. A little creak sounded and he pushed again with all his strength. This time the door flipped open. Hastily he climbed out. A refreshing, cold splash of wind welcomed him back to the world of light.

He blinked rapidly several times and looked around. A boarded-up cedar-shingled country house about a twenty yards away was the only building within eyesight. He had no idea how he'd found this place, but the cellar had provided a secure, if damp, bed, and not the prison he'd feared.

Nick thanked God he was alive, but what shape was he is? He looked himself over for damage. Surprisingly, his suit was dusty, but not dirty. The leaves from the ditch and straw from the cellar brushed off easily. He checked his back pocket. He still had his wallet, good, but his cell phone clip must have come off in the van.

"God, thanks for giving me this temporary place of protection. Give me wisdom now," he prayed aloud, "I haven't a clue where I am or which way to go."

He took his direction from the sun and started striding North through desolate farm fields. For an hour and a half, he trudged along a gravel path. It finally came out on County Road W.

As Nick hiked, he tried to sort through the last twenty-four hours and make plans.

He knew he couldn't go home. *I'm a sitting duck there and I won't jeopardize Jennifer and the children,* he thought. Sweat formed in his armpits at the thought of his family. Jennifer must be frantic. He needed to contact Michael and make sure she and the children were okay.

If Torricelli did anything to them... His hands curled into fists. He couldn't think like this. They had to be safe. He muttered aloud to the wind longing for the comfort of a familiar, human voice. "It's me these people are after. I'm a danger, but why? For some reason, somebody thinks I'm a threat. I don't even know why!" All he could come up with was Jennifer's Directive 99.

Nick hated to involve Michael when his adopted child was arriving any day, but he needed help desperately. He knew Michael would want Nick to contact him.

If Nick could get hold of a phone he'd call him at his office at church to avoid jeopardizing Michael's family. How he wished he'd memorized Michael's cell number so he could call it. Without the directory of numbers in his cell phone, Nick was lost. *Whoever's after me may be checking my friends, too.*

Nick forced himself not to throw up. *How do you react when somebody wants you dead?* He reached a two-lane road with a bright yellow line and started hiking backwards hoping to hitchhike to the next town, wherever that was. Two cars zoomed by and the drivers gave him a curious look, but made no effort to stop.

A small truck approached with two women. Nick waved furiously. He may as well have been a pine tree; they never even glanced his way. How often does somebody try hitching a ride dressed in a fairly clean two-piece suit? They could have at least stopped to see if he needed gas. *Okay, I look suspicious,* he realized, *no car, okay.* He cooled his anger.

After another mile, he saw a sign, Oniah, forty miles. Nick figured he was close to Draxton, a mid-size city about three hours from home, close enough, but not too close.

An independent trucker in a dust-covered white semi whisked by and stopped about a hundred feet up the road and backed up toward him. "Hop in, buddy, car break down?" A congenial, broad shouldered Afro-American with a strong handshake welcomed him.

"Where're you heading?"

"To the next town." *Whatever that is,* Nick thought.

"Want me to CB for service on your vehicle?"

"Thanks, but I'll take care of my problem when I get into town." Why correct the trucker's assumption his car had broken down on a side road.

Nick leaned back and closed his eyes hoping to avoid further discussion. It didn't work. Joe, the trucker was the garrulous sort and jabbered non-stop first about his boss and then about walleyes and northerns, getting excited over his upcoming fishing trip. At least Nick's role was audience, nothing more. No questions worked fine by him. Nick was grateful the kidnappers hadn't taken his watch. He fingered his wedding band and prayed for Jennifer.

When the truck driver pulled into a Super America gas station, Nick hopped out. "While you gas up and get coffee, I need to grab something at Wal-Mart next door, buddy. Don't leave without me, I'll be quick, I've got to get to an appointment."

Nick walked inside and bought a cell phone with minutes. He covered his ear to block the sounds of the passing traffic while walking back and waiting for the connection. When Michael's answering machine came on, Nick pleaded into the phone. "Come on, pick up, pick up, and be there, please."

The recorder clicked off. He fought the urge to throw the phone in frustration.

"Everything okay?" The driver asked when Nick lifted himself back into the cab of the truck.

"Yeah, sure."

\*\*\*

Sarah's hands trembled as she stared at a bubble wrapper the size of a CD or DVD, she never could keep them straight.

Her gasp was almost inaudible. The name on the outside of the mailer was one she'd never seen before. Hudson Armor, P. O. Box 1225, Oniah, WI.

The sticky note stuck on the mailer said simply: "Sarah, in the event of my death mail this to the address indicated. My deepest love always. Your devoted husband, John."

She clutched her hand over her heart and started to cry, quietly at first. Soon tears tumbled forth, racking her body. She held tightly to the tree branch and the mailer for fear of falling or dropping the small package.

Perhaps this disk was what Agent Melton from ANSA was looking for. She wiped her face first with one sleeve, then the other, hurried down and ran all the way back to the house. She needed to call him immediately and play this disk. Dare she?

Why the intrigue? Did John know he was going to die? He had a file cabinet in his den with a Last Will and Testament. Why not leave the disk there? Had he hoped it would be found long after his death?

If she started immediately, she could burn copies and easily make the afternoon mail. She knew how to copy a disk.

No need to run, yet she did.

\*\*\*

Ever so tenderly, Jennifer opened the book on Nick's nightstand. The first thing she did, although it seemed foolish, was to smell the pages. She closed her eyes and a tiny smile flooded her face. The paper had the fragrance of Nick's after-shave. She held the open pages to her breast as a newborn child. This was the possession dearest to her husband.

149

Flipping slowly through the dog-eared pages she experienced curiosity for the first time about its contents.

What was it about this book Nick found so intriguing?

Like a duck foraging lake waters for food, she dipped into chapters here and there, sometimes circling back and immersing herself for an extended time in one chapter.

She discovered the book's two divisions and hunted in her memory for the words Old Testament and New Testament and recalled old and new covenants. Long ago in church school she'd learned the terms.

Finally, she slept. In her dream she repeated the word covenant over and over.

In the days to come reading Nick's Bible became a bedtime ritual, the only thing that could eventually lull her to sleep. She wouldn't admit to any spiritual interest, she simply wanted to touch anything valued by him.

The words became her primary source of a strange kind of comfort. In many ways her reading was like following a road map Nick had made, because he'd highlighted lots of sentences, even whole paragraphs, at times dating them, with more markings in the second half than the first. She read everything in yellow. Perhaps there was something in these pages to help her unravel the chaos her life had become.

*** 

An hour later, Nick thanked the truck driver as he jumped out in Oniah. The trucker refused Nick's offer of money and even looked insulted so Nick quickly pocketed his twenty bucks.

He waved as Joe roared back onto the highway.

Nick uttered quick prayers of relief to be back in civilization, thanking God for Joe. He found a quiet spot behind a local diner, and tried to call Michael again. Four rings with no answer. A machine clicked on. It was worth the call to hear Michael's rich, warm recorded voice again. He didn't dare leave a message.

Nick walked down the street and studied his surroundings. He saw a small Visitor Info Center a block from the center of town.

The office was closed, but a rack of brochures on the outside porch gave him what he needed. Nick picked out a small B & B inn and called their number. An advance reservation would cause less suspicion than just wandering in. "You have a corporate rate on weekdays, good. No need to guarantee, I'm close by."

Nick left his name as Mr. Nicholas and said he'd be arriving shortly. He rarely traveled outside large hotel chains, preferring Marriott, although he knew businessmen who often used small B & B's and inns, enjoying the more personal atmosphere.

By now it was late afternoon and he realized he was famished. In the distance he made out the name of a cafe, Happy Henrietta's.

He hurried over, glad no one seemed to take notice as he slid into a faded maroon vinyl booth except for his waitress with a bird's nest twist of coarse black hair locked in place atop her head. She ambled over, order pad ready. Her eyes never left the paper as he ordered the Plate Lunch Special, fried chicken, real mashed potatoes and corn with two flour dusted potato rolls, and a Decaf. When she plopped the cup of steaming brown liquid before him, he forced himself to control his shaking hands as he grabbed the cup.

Within five minutes, and none too soon, the food arrived. He raised his eyes to the ceiling for thanksgiving and blessing. It was his custom to look heavenward, not downward, when he prayed. God wasn't sitting in his lap or on his plate of food. Thanks for this feast, Lord, I'm starved. He ripped a roll apart and buttered it lavishly.

Nick devoured the main course, and washed down nutmeg-laced bread pudding, the finale to the special, with his third cup of coffee. With some nourishment in his body, it became a little easier to think. Nick reviewed his options. Should he call the police? He seriously considered it but was afraid to risk involving them. He needed more information first. There must be a library in this town. Hopefully, they'd have computers he could use on-line. He needed to research who might benefit from having him dead. What connection did he have with Landworks?

After he paid the bill, Nick counted the rest of his money carefully. No telling how long he'd have to stay at the inn. He might not be able to get funds transferred to him. Eventually he'd have to use his credit card, which could be traced. He'd probably have to use it to secure his room for seven days, but hopefully they wouldn't process it until he checked out. A week should buy him enough time to figure out and stop this madness.

Nick didn't want to call attention to himself at the Inn by arriving without toiletries so he asked his waitress for the location of a drug store. Fortunately, Walgreen's was three blocks away. He bought shaving supplies, toothpaste and brush, comb, shampoo and a toiletry bag.

Dusk dropped a shadowy mantle over the street as he emerged. His bones ached, and the six-block walk to the small inn tortured his knees. His old football injury didn't respond well to walking for miles, not to mention the mental strain of the last twenty-four hours.

Before going inside, Nick tried Michael's office two more times, but no one answered.


The inn was a quaint blue and yellow Tudor building decorated in Country French style. Outside lights around the front door and along the walkway twinkled as he approached. The brochure had promised television and a private bath in each room. Inside the lobby, decorative handmade wooden ducks, maybe a hobby of the host, were displayed on wall shelves. A small refrigerator and micro sat off to the side in the sitting room with a sign For Guest Use. A paper sign attached to the wicker basket next to it suggested fees for pop and snacks.

Nick scanned the place, praying it would be a safe house. He hoped to avoid extended conversation, although he'd have to pass the desk clerk every time to go in or out.

The innkeeper, a robust, handsome man Nick guessed to be in his early to mid-seventies with a grey beard and penetrating green eyes folded the newspaper he'd been reading behind the counter when Nick entered. He introduced himself as Hudson and the woman in jeans and a sweater busily watering ivy plants behind him as his wife, Marie.

Nick took a room with one double bed and a twin. He could have done with a single, but the inn had only ten rooms with the two singles already occupied.

"I'll help with your luggage," the innkeeper offered.

"That's not necessary. I'm traveling light." Hudson had to have noticed his lack of a suitcase.

"How long will you be staying?" he asked

"I'm not sure yet, perhaps a few days, maybe a week, depends how long my business takes." He answered quickly hoping to God he wouldn't be asked what his business was.

Hudson looked at him strangely, which made Nick's throat constrict. No luggage, yet an extended stay? Maybe the innkeeper would think he was a traveling salesman whose bags had been misdirected from a flight. Neither the innkeeper nor his smiley wife, Marie, commented further.

In a thick Scandinavian accent Marie said, "There's a basket in the hall with extra toiletry supplies for anything you may have forgotten."

"Thanks, I'm all set."

Why did they keep watching him intently? Suddenly, Nick wished he'd picked a big hotel chain. *There's not one within a hundred miles* he reminded himself.

"Tea and coffee are available in the sitting room every morning and afternoon. You're welcome to join us for our Continental breakfast of juice, coffee, muffins or toast at eight. You may eat with the other guests or take food to your room."

"Thanks. I may skip tomorrow. Now where's my room? I'm beat."

Hudson nodded and started for the stairs.

Nick protested. "I can find it if you'll give me the key."

"No trouble. We want to be sure you're satisfied." Hudson smiled.

At the top of the steps, he turned right, started down a long hall and halted at the second room. He flung open the door with a flourish.

Nick saw the plain walnut headboard and the chenille bedspread. *Sure beats last night's cellar,* he thought. Aloud he said, "This will be fine."

Hudson lingered. Nick started to perspire under his arms. It seemed as if this guy wanted to say something else, but maybe changed his mind. He wished Nick a good night's sleep and started back down the hall.

Nick locked the door behind Hudson and flopped down on the bed breathing deeply. The Inn seemed cozy; the colorful décor reminded him of Jennifer. He heard the noise of the toilet flushing from the room next to his. Soundproof the White Dove wasn't, but he found the noise strangely comforting.

Being totally alone seemed strange to him. Several months into Jennifer's pregnancy with their first child, he'd longed briefly for the freedom from responsibility being single had offered. Nick figured everybody wanted to be carefree, more or less, but he wanted Jennifer and his growing family even more. He treasured marriage, the permanence of it, the security of it, and the love of his fiery, emotional woman. Now he longed for her with every cell in his body. He sat up and dropped his head in his hands, overcome by anguish.

He had to pull himself together.

His body craved sleep, but he willed himself to stay awake so he could try once more to make contact with Michael. He wasn't eager to hit the streets again but didn't want to place a call from the Inn with its paper-thin walls.

Leafing through the literature on the table in his room, he came across the local Chamber of Commerce's brochure describing Oniah. It listed a couple of manufacturing plants and a small airport. Good, the town would be accustomed to strangers.

Next, he rummaged through drawers until he found a Bible in the end table next to the bed. Immediately, he flipped to Psalms142-145. He took comfort from the words about David whose run from enemies matched his own.

Nick found a pen and notepad next to the phone and started writing, which usually helped his thinking process. If only recording what had happened to him would help it make sense. "Who wants me dead?" he wrote across the top of the page.

After jotting down and re-thinking all his current work cases, he still couldn't come up with a motive to arouse fatal vengeance against him. It had to be Directive 99.

Around nine, Nick walked to town for ice cream and to use his phone.

Again no success reaching Michael. When he got back to his room he listened to the 10 p.m. news on the radio. The absence of an announcement about his disappearance made his spirits drop. It meant nobody was investigating what happened. Perhaps this was better. Publicity would make his hiding out more difficult.

Nick eyed the phone in his room longingly, knowing Jennifer could be on the other end of the line in a minute. He wanted to let her know he was okay, but didn't dare. Instead he'd work this out in a way no one could be connected to him. He wouldn't make one move that might harm his family or friends. He'd become like a leper who could infect those he loved.

Sleep didn't come as quickly as he'd hoped. The threat of death was still so real he could taste it. Like the smell of blood, it nauseated him.

At one, Nick was still awake. He scrunched the extra pillow in half and placed it at his side in the double bed wishing fervently it was Jennifer. She'd be frantic. He'd find a way to communicate somehow. *Please God, be with her*, he prayed.

\*\*\*

In the grey dawn of Saturday, Nick walked downtown and again called Michael's office. This time the answering machine message was "Sorry I missed your call. I'll be out of town until Sunday morning. My wife, Anne, and I are picking up our adopted daughter. Please leave your number and I'll get back to you as soon as possible. If this is an emergency, call the head church elder." Nick listened to Michael give the elder's home number holding the receiver next to his ear until the answering machine clicked off.

He'd been tempted to leave a message under another name, but his voice might be recognized by the person at church retrieving Michael's messages.

Now what? Nick cradled the phone against his chest. Other than Michael, I don't know anyone I can totally trust. He swiped at the moisture sliding unbidden from his eyes. Outside, on the short walk back to the inn, he examined the people heading in his direction. Until he knew who was after him, he suspected everyone.

# Chapter Fifteen

Jennifer watched as Collin clicked from picture to picture, her only show of anxiety wringing the Kleenex in her left hand.

"Mom, Dad disappeared days ago, I don't remember."

"Collin, try harder."

"Mom, I'm doing the best I can!" he exclaimed.

It had been a tough day at school, and for the past two hours Collin scanned mug shots at online sites recommended by the private investigator to see if any face matched the person in the car at their curb the morning Nick disappeared. The day their world shifted out of control.

"Mom, we don't even know for sure if this guy was involved with Dad's disappearance. You want to assume he was. I'm sorry I ever told you I saw a car drive by slowly." Collin slammed his fist on the table in frustration. "I'm sick of all this! If being a Christian is all it's cracked up to be, where is my father? Why did Dad leave us?"

Jennifer had no answer.

"Mom, I'm all mixed up. And now I'm late for my date time with Carolyn, the best part of my world. I planned to pick her up an hour ago."

"We're almost through. Carolyn won't mind waiting," Jennifer coaxed. "I know she'll understand. I'll call her."

"I already did. Do you think I'm a jerk, too?"

Jennifer bit her tongue. She approved of Collin's seeing Michael and Anne's seventeen-year-old niece. She lived with them in Lake Geneva after her parents died in an auto accident. Carolyn had a tender sensitivity endearing her to young and old.

Collin set his teeth and clicked to the next screen. "Mom, the more faces I see, the harder it gets and the more confused I become."

Half an hour later Collin dropped his head into his palms, rubbing his forehead and eyes as if that'd clear the haze in his brain.

"I'm going to take a ten-minute nap, pick up Carolyn, and take her to the late movies. My life's going on!" He stalked from the room.

Jennifer relented. "Be sure to grab your house keys. I'll be visiting Becky until around ten. Tara's coming with me and Jenna is spending the night at a friend's."

Collin rested on the sofa with the timer on his cell phone set, trying not to feel, but coming always against a wall of confusion. His Dad's disappearance didn't make sense, nothing made sense.

Sleepless, he rose to shower and shave before heading out.

***

Carolyn's smile radiated across her face when she opened the front door of the Stasen's ranch home. Suddenly the world seemed a bit less confusing to Collin.

"Anything new about your Dad?" she inquired as they walked toward Collin's car.

Responding more sharply than he intended, he said, "No, Carolyn, and for tonight I don't want to talk about him, okay?"

"Sure," she said softly.

He started feeling better by the minute. Carolyn always made him feel happy. Nothing else in his life came close.

He stared at her for a long moment, losing himself in her physical beauty as he admired her pink sweater set and the floral skirt, which flounced down to pink flats.

Noticing his gaze, she lifted one foot. "I spent some of my baby-sitting money on new shoes today. Do you like them?"

"Great!" He answered too quickly still staring at her face.

Carolyn blushed.

Suddenly the ideas he'd been toying with since awakening from his nap turned into fierce desires. *It's time*, he thought. *Just because the adults in my life want to destroy their lives, doesn't mean I have to mess up mine.*

"I need to stop at my house. Jenna said she might want to come," Collin announced unexpectedly, with every second of the drive increasing his desire. "You can come in, while I get her, in case she's not ready." He opened Carolyn's car door.

The house emitted an aura of silence. Even before she asked, "Where's everyone?" Carolyn sensed no one was at home.

Collin thought back to his Dad's admonitions.

Reading his mind, Carolyn said, "Collin, you know your Dad's rule about our not being here alone."

The sound of her voice enchanted Collin.

Wordlessly, Carolyn began to edge toward the door.

Collin abruptly pulled her into the living room. "Jenna will be home any second, don't worry."

His words reassured her, but his eyes spoke a different message.

He gazed at Carolyn's naturally pink lips and brushed his own against them lightly at first, then with the pressure of unfolding passion. "Carolyn, you're all that matters to me." He pulled her to his chest like a lifeline.

Carolyn sensed what was coming. "Collin, you know you're important to me, too, which is why we can't do this."

He was kissing her eyes, her cheeks, her neck.

She understood his fragile, hurt soul deep within even as she said, "No."

"I love the rise and fall of your voice, your laughter, I want to know every part of you, my love."

"Collin, are you writing a movie script?" She tried to joke. In the past it had always worked. "What you're wanting is flattering, but impossible. You know that!"

"Not if we let it happen."

"We discussed pre-marital sex and agreed it wasn't for us."

She pushed him away but he didn't budge. He was past the time to reason.

Carolyn was displeased, then turned red with anger. He wouldn't back off and she resented his using her as salve for the other problems in his life. More importantly, her love for Christ was too strong to settle for a casual violation of her virginity.

"It's okay, I want to marry you," Collin kept repeating, as he pushed her onto the sofa. He dropped on top of her and buried his head on her chest.

Carolyn didn't hesitate for an instant.

"Collin Trevor, No! No, I said!" She yelled inches from his ear.

"Why not? If you love me." He held her arms behind her back as he saw himself being pulled down a road he knew he should avoid, but didn't stop himself.

"Collin, I'll scream. This isn't love. I'll hate you forever if you do this! You know what's right. Don't do this to yourself, or me."

He ignored her objections.

She couldn't get her hand up to his face to slap him, but she screamed his name, "Collin!"

Realizing she wouldn't relent and unwilling to force her, he released her arms and started to back off. Carolyn jumped up.

For the second time that day Collin dropped his head into his hands. He moaned, "Carrie, I'm sorry. I love you and I want you so bad, but you're right. I want you to help stop the pain I'm feeling about my Dad. I've never had sex, because my Dad always told me it was wrong before marriage. Now he's run out on us, and I want to do the opposite of everything he ever said."

"Collin, premarital sex isn't the answer." Carolyn brushed the folds of her skirt into place. When she sat down it was at the far end of the sofa.

"Forgive me," Collin had swung from the depth of passion to the dredges of despair in moments feeling as though life itself was being drained from his body.

"Please don't let it happen again." Determination etched her face.

"I can't believe this. I almost hurt you badly," he said despondently. His reflection in the mirror showed him as an insecure, immature boy.

After a brief pause, Carolyn spoke. "I will, you know."

"Will what?"

"Hurt you, too, but not like this. You think our relationship will be wonderful when we're married, but we'll still have disagreements to work through like Michael and Anne, and your Mom and Dad."

"Only my dad just ran."

"Let's go, we can talk in the car. We missed the show, but we can go for ice cream. Jenna's not coming, is she?"

He shook his head.

***

They drove to the Dairy Queen in Walworth and ordered two hot fudge sundaes, strolled back to the car and sat on the hood.

A glint of tears sparkled on Carolyn's cheeks. She chose her words carefully. "I understand your Dad's strange disappearance is hard on you because I know the pain of abandonment firsthand having lost both my parents. But for me I at least knew what happened wasn't their fault. And I had Christ to turn to. You have no idea what a help He is. That's why this is hard for you."

"Really?"

"Sure."

Collin was silent several minutes.

Carolyn had once told him she'd only marry a man who shared her beliefs. He realized after what just happened, it was time to get off the fence and decide if he was going to make an all-out commitment to God and following His principles.

"Carolyn, are you an angel? You seem so wise. Sometimes I wonder."

"Just a girl who hopes to marry you." Her eyes shone clear as stars in a northern sky.

Collin covered her hand with his. "Someday, my angel with new shoes, I'll make you mine, and that'll be the end of no's."

She turned and kissed him lightly on the lips. Although she yearned for him with all her being, she wouldn't let herself act on feelings. "In God's perfect time," she smiled, "not ours."

***

The wind sent torrents of rainwater assertively slamming against trees, buildings, every object in its path. The unrelenting gale changed direction like a whimsical child, pushing its force first right, then left.

Only a need to connect with Michael could motivate Nick's venturing forth tonight. One block from the inn, he struggled to hold his body upright against the battering storm. Reaching the covered porch of a closed store, he pulled out his cell phone and tried to reach Michael. Hopefully, he and Anne had returned from picking up their adopted daughter.

Waiting for the connection Nick thought of Michael's daughter. Suddenly he imagined Tara and Jennifer's voice yelling, "Daddy." He'd never before had such longing for his children.

*How do dads handle separation and divorce?* he wondered. *Not seeing and talking with his children regularly would be hell,* he thought.

Michael's resonant, clear "Hello" made Nick clutch the phone to keep from dropping it. The familiar sound penetrated the madness he was living through with a semblance of sanity.

"Hi, buddy."

"Nick! Is it you? Where are you? Jennifer's been wild with worry. Omigosh. Hang on." Nick heard footsteps, perhaps Michael's walking to a more private room. A few seconds later he was back. "Are you okay?" Michael whispered anxiously.

"Shook up, otherwise fine," Nick yelled into the phone.

"It sounds like you're in a war zone."

"There's a bad storm here, but nothing compared to what's going on in my gut. I'm not going to talk long, in case your line's bugged."

"Lucky I heard the phone. I'm at church for a meeting. What's going on?"

Nick briefly recounted the story of his kidnapping as water soaked through his suit which had long ago lost its waterproofing. "How is Jennifer?"

"She's grieving. A note supposedly from you said you wanted out of your marriage."

"Surely she doesn't believe…"

"She's confused, but overall hanging strong, and doing a great job with the kids."

Nick experienced a surge of love mingled with respect for the wonderful woman God had joined him to.

"I'd like her to know I'm alright, but if you tell her you're in contact with me it could jeopardize her safety."

"We'll simply imply we're sure you're okay."

"Do what you can to keep her from worrying, but she mustn't know any details. I want you to hire a private investigator."

"We already did, to find you."

"I need to stay in hiding for now. Have him try to get data on a company named Landworks."

"The one you were doing work for when you disappeared?"

"I'm guessing it'll have a history of diabolical acts to sabotage this country and check out the messenger guy, Torricelli, although he's probably just a minion."

"I'll get right on it. Anything else?"

"Lots of prayer. I need to hear the Lord's voice on how to proceed. I've been pretty desperate and emotional."

Michael said, "I already called a prayer vigil at church. We're praying round the clock. I didn't say for you, but I said God's principles and life or death issues are ultimately at stake. My congregation, God bless them, trusts me and doesn't need details. Rest assured you've got an expanding prayer cover. Are you sure you can't tell me where you are?"

"Absolutely not. Knowing could put you in danger, too."

"Okay, have it your way. Give me twenty-four hours to collect information."

"That's too long, twelve. I'll call you tomorrow. What's your new cell phone number so I don't have to go through the church office?"

***

Sarah held the kitchen phone in her hand and punched in three numbers, but suddenly cancelled the call. Agent Melton had wanted to be informed of any new developments. Before she contacted him though, maybe she should try to find out something about the person John had wanted to receive this material.

She'd try to use the name and address to get a phone number, and devised a plan to call Hudson after two days to see if the disk had been received. Perhaps Hudson could tell her something about what her husband was doing to make him a threat. She hesitated. Her blood froze; hopefully, Hudson wasn't the person responsible for John's death.

She went through the directory on John's cell phone and the old Rolodex, but found no one by the name on the mailer.

Someone from his former office might know this Hudson or maybe Hudson even worked there. Sarah called Newspersons, which had been bought shortly after John died by a national news agency competitor. At the last second, she thought to disguise her voice by holding a Kleenex over the phone and using a drawl so no one would recognize her voice asking for Hudson.

"Sorry," the cheery receptionist said, "No one works here by that name."

Maybe Agent Melton could get this information for her. She'd have to tell him about their maple tree. He'd wonder why the disk hadn't turned up before. She didn't want to lie.

She anticipated what he'd ask. Was she sure John had been the one to put it there? Of course. Who else would know about their special hiding place?

Sarah sat down at her kitchen table and pulled the disk all the way out of the mailer. A small sheet of folded paper fluttered out - in her excitement she hadn't noticed it before. She opened it and read, "Precious Sarah, when you find this disk, DON'T read its contents, which could endanger you. TELL NO ONE about it and send it immediately to the address on the mailer."

Her heart started to pound. Was this information why John was killed? She picked up her phone again to notify American National Security. She was torn between following John's explicit instructions, and hoping Agent Melton could use this information somehow to solve the mystery of John's death.

Her spine stiffened as a horrid thought darted into her head. What if John was doing something he shouldn't? If he'd gotten this info illegally would Agent Melton think John had committed suicide from guilt and end his investigation?

Stop it, Sarah," she ordered herself aloud. She might be overwhelmed with grief, but she hadn't gone insane. John was an honorable man.

The beginning of a migraine throbbed across her forehead.

*** 

The next afternoon, with the smell of wood-burning fires in the air, Nick jogged to the park and eagerly punched in Michael's cell phone number.

To his delight, Michael answered immediately. "I've got news! You won't believe this."

"Try me."

"One of Landworks subsidiary businesses is called Lifeworks which handles financial affairs for retired people. A man named Howard Relton runs this. He encourages them to go into national life centers. The older people turn all their finances over to him, in return he cuts a deal with the government center and pays their incidental bills as long as they live."

"So, the sooner they die, the more money his company gets."

"Right. He's touted as being altruistic and concerned about providing loving respect for life in his promo material! Some suspect he has a handful of nursing staff from the centers on his payroll, too, who work on a percentage if the elderly resident is put out of their unhappy, unproductive life a little quicker than expected. Thus far, nothing's been proven."

"My connection to Jennifer makes me a threat?"

"So it appears. Plus, he hates all Christians, with their life values."

A ripple of disgust coursed through Nick's veins. "Sounds Satanic."

"Would the devil delight in this scheme? You bet."

"Anything else?"

"Relton makes all the operational decisions, as head of Landworks and Lifeworks, nice names, huh? He has a Washington address, but works out of different states in temporary rented office buildings. Catch this. He went to Harvard with the top health czar. They're good buddies."

Nick stated the obvious while his mind whirled through options, "Relton clearly doesn't want this directive stopped."

"And he's powerful as well as determined. He's already tried to kill you. I hate to say it, but if you and Jennifer are to be safe you may need to hide until the government has their final vote on this measure and Directive 99 goes forward."

"No. I intend to stop it."

"Jennifer will fight for it. Besides if they don't get it through this time, they'll simply try again."

"I'm not going to hide forever, just long enough to bring this down."

"I understand. Often Paul of Tarsus had to run for a while to survive."

"I'm safe at a B & B for now. How I wish Jennifer hadn't been involved. But for some reason, God allowed it, so who am I to question?"

"Job asked your questions already in the Old Testament," Michael reminded him. "Remember the good ending, a double portion of blessings, when God restored him."

Nick sighed. "Works for me, although that's not always the case."

Michael hesitated, before continuing. "Something's happening to Jennifer. There's a new softness about her. Your absence has hit her hard. She told Anne she's even been looking at your Bible."

"And the kids?"

"They're pretty confused, but it's to be expected."

Nick was silent a moment. "Michael, we've got to stop this guy, not just for us, for our kids and grandkids. I'm doing research on the Neanderthal library computers to see if Relton can be put away for any other illegalities. It's slow going. There's a newer one in the B & B lounge, but I'm not comfortable using it."

"If only we could prove he was directly involved with your abduction."

"What about Torricelli, the guy who came to my house?"

"Supposedly he's out of the country on business, but we're still trying to track him down and get him to talk," Michael continued.

"Who's we?"

"I've contacted the Christian underground; they're hoping to dig something up."

"Are you sure you're dealing with people who can be trusted?"

"I'd stake my life on it."

"I hate involving you, Michael. I don't want to jeopardize your family."

"I'm taking precautions, don't worry. Watch yourself, okay? Until we get Relton and his thugs behind bars, you're not safe."

A burly man approached the porch as Nick clicked off. He turned to leave, but froze momentarily when the man tapped his shoulder. "Just a minute, hey, I want to talk with you. Got any money for a pack of cigarettes?"

Nick didn't pause long enough to look twice. At first glance the big guy looked like one of his abductors. Maybe he just wanted money, but Nick wasn't waiting to find out.

He ran, not stopping till pain sheared across his chest because his lungs were starved for air. Finally, he found a protected alley and crouched behind a garbage bin until rested enough to venture forth.

Nick never saw the contingent of angels that surrounded him.

***

Anne gestured to the waitress at Uteri's Café for more coffee.

Jennifer sat across from her. "I'm so upset about Nick I can hardly function. Mom's helping a lot. I don't have many

167

emotional resources left for coping with the children at the end of the day."

"How I pray you and Nick will be together before long."

"Anne, do you think that's possible?"

"Trust the Lord."

The confidence in Anne's words made Jennifer scrutinize her. Did she know something? No, of course not, how could she?

"How I wish I could. Can you believe I'm actually reading the Bible? How many times Nick begged me to read it, and now I am, but I don't understand much." She flipped open to Romans 10, sliding her manicured fingernail down the page. Nick had written Roman Road in the margin. "Listen to this. 'If you confess with your mouth the Lord Jesus and believe in your heart God has raised Him from the dead, you will be saved.' From what? And why?" Jennifer's voice increased in volume. "These are trite phrases to me."

The waitress interrupted to refill their coffee cups. Jennifer reflexively covered hers, and waved the woman away with her free hand.

Anne wasn't sure Jennifer was ready to receive the next statement since it was contrary to her self-exaltation view, but knew she had to say it. "When we finally admit there's evil and imperfection in us, for example, greed, jealousy, resentment, we understand we're in need of a Savior. Because of His great love for us, Jesus is willing to forgive immediately and send us His Holy Spirit who empowers us to overcome our faults."

"Like Jesus' encounter with the repentant thief on the cross next to Him? I read with amazement when Jesus said, 'Assuredly, I say to you, today you will be with Me in Paradise.'"

"Extraordinary sounding, but true."

"I'm intrigued by the irony. To think Jesus would assure a thief of spending eternity in paradise is so bizarre. For some reason the idea gives me goose bumps."

Anne scarcely paused for breath. "That's how simple salvation is. Inviting Christ to work in us transforming us into His holiness."

"If I were a Christian, would I be expected to go to church every week, give lots of money, and work on committees?"

Anne smiled. "You may want to do some of that, but the only necessities are to love God with all your heart, soul and mind and love others as yourself. Everything else falls into place when the basics are straight."

"I'll think more about it someday. It's not the time for making life decisions with Nick gone."

Anne leaned back. "Remember, Michael and I are here to help any way we can."

"Michael's done plenty finding me a detective, and keeping tabs on the investigation." Guilt stabbed Jennifer. She felt like a hypocrite. *Run to Anne and Michael any time you have a problem, then when all is well, have no use for them.* Aloud she said, "I know I haven't been a dependable friend to you, Anne. I'm sorry. You've always been there for me."

"I think you're great," Anne said sweetly.

"Thanks for meeting me. Talking to someone who knows Nick and cares about him and me means more than I can say. I've got to run. I have a resident's family going through deathbed watch." Jennifer picked up the check from the table. "I'll get this on my way out."

Jennifer's first duty after lunch involved being present for a family whose seventy-eight-year-old husband and father was dying of congestive heart failure. If the death of a resident occurred during her shift she always put in an appearance, though she dreaded such moments.

She entered the room on tiptoes. His wife and three grown children, a son and two daughters were clustered about his bed. Three grandchildren sat on chairs along the left side of the room in perfect quiet, watching everything.

The resident's oxygen had been removed. No further medical intervention was possible, the family had been told by the hospice nurse.

Jennifer held her breath. All the world stills for death and birth.

She'd been through this with countless residents and with her Mom and Dad. She knew nothing else matters when you hold the hand of someone you love who has hours, perhaps minutes left on earth. So much to say, but words don't seem to matter any longer. Only the gentle closing of your hand on fingers too weak to hold on any more speaks of your presence and shows you respect the life about to flee this body.

The wife leaned over to kiss her dying husband on his forehead, both cheeks and finally on his lips. A stunning silver cross on a chain around her neck lightly brushed his chest.

Sealed with a kiss. Oh, the pain, oh the sweetness, as tears fell unnoticed. There was none of the hysterical crying here Jennifer often saw.

She didn't sense the other presence in the room waiting until the time came, the appointed moment.

Soon Jennifer would be witnessing deaths more frequently. She returned to her office, utterly drained.

# Chapter Sixteen

Five-year-old Maria, raven curls twisting every which way, stood in the church sacristy in an ivory lace dress looking like a dark-skinned cherub between her new parents, Anne and Michael.

Jennifer and two of her children, Jenna and Collin, entered Michael's church to attend his adopted daughter's dedication. Tara had spent the night with friends and wouldn't be home until evening.

Jennifer glanced at Anne's shining face riveted on her precious daughter. Anne and Michael's adopted niece, Carolyn, beamed like a mother herself at this addition to their family. She smiled as Jennifer passed and whispered, "Thank you for coming. You'll love Pastor Baxton. He's had eons of experience ministering and spent a zillion hours in God's Word."

Michael leaned over to Collin and whispered, "Don't leave until we speak." His voice was so low that no one else heard.

Jennifer selected seats halfway back and settled in between Collin and her daughter, Jenna, on the other side. This was Jennifer's third time in Pastor Michael's church, Nick's church too, she reminded herself. Nick had invited her each week since he became "religious" this past year, and often took the children despite her objection. Jennifer frowned. Was my husband fanatical about religion? Or am I fanatical against it?

She shrugged away the stab of pain. It didn't matter now, nothing did. Jennifer repressed a desire to speak Nick's name aloud. I'll think about him later, she promised herself using her characteristic escape mechanism.

For exactly fifteen minutes each night, Jennifer let herself dwell on worries or problems, a trick she'd learned from a time management seminar years ago to keep difficulties in perspective. The postponement strategy had worked well until Nick's disappearance. Now anxiety seemed to intrude into every moment.

Senior Pastor Braxton presiding over the dedication hobbled like a bent-over gnome, but spoke with the authority of a patriarch. His rich baritone rang through the church. "Michael, God has made you leader of this family and entrusted you to raise Maria and Carolyn and any other children He gives you in the way of the Lord."

He paused, letting the solemnity of his words hang in the air. "You have the honor of being a model and a provider for this child as she grows into womanhood and achieves the purposes God has for her life. It is the intention of the community gathered here to assist you any way we can."

Applause, followed by silence swept through the parishioners as they contemplated their own responsibilities to their children as well.

Only half-listening, Jennifer studied the nattily attired men and women. Even the children wore dress-up clothes. A dedication to God apparently rated as a special occasion. Silly sentimentality, perhaps, but there was extraordinary warmth here, Jennifer had to admit.

Pastor Baxton ceremoniously presented a white carnation to Anne, "This flower represents holiness. God has given you the privilege of nurturing Maria's life in the world just as His own mother, Mary, cared for Jesus. We know you will love and train your daughter in the way of truth and purity." Anne nodded and lifted her head higher.

The elderly pastor bent over and encircled little Maria in his arms. Tenderly he released her and gazed at the angelic face before him as tears filled his eyes.

Jennifer experienced a rare feeling of reverence. She disliked public display of emotion, but this was touching. The pleasure of interconnectedness, of sacrificing time and energy for the welfare

172

of a little one, and transforming the life of a child is an awesome privilege.

"Maria," Pastor Baxton focused on the well-behaved, five-year-old, wide-eyed before him. "You are precious in the eyes of your earthly father and mother, and even more precious to your Father in heaven." The pastor looked skyward. "Lord, we ask you to watch over Maria always. May she keep her spirit of wonder and her eagerness to love and trust You all the days of her life. Shower your richest blessings upon her!"

Finally the ceremony drew to a close. The church community clapped spontaneously delighted Maria had joined their spiritual family. It had only taken twenty minutes but seemed an hour to Jennifer.

The guests filed over to the reception hall.

On the way, Michael pulled Collin aside. Not having a son of his own, Michael had often attended Collin's basketball and baseball games and developed a friendship with him. "I need to talk to you privately; let's slip away."

Michael led the way over to the bell tower and they mounted the steps.

Alone on the top landing, he said, "What I'm about to tell you is totally confidential. You're to tell no one, not even your mom, promise?"

"Sure." Collin's throat constricted at the seriousness of Michael's tone.

"I've been in contact with your Dad. He believes you can be trusted with some important information."

Collin's eyes bulged and he shifted nervously from one foot to the other.

Michael laid a hand on his shoulder. "Your Dad was kidnapped, almost killed, but managed to escape. He can't return home safely until we find out who did this and why."

The color drained from Collin's face. He stood speechless.

"So far, we have no evidence, but we're working on leads. In the meantime, these people are presumably on your Dad's tail so he's still in danger. He said for you not to worry, God is protecting him."

Collin leaned against the support rail. "What about Mom? Will she be next?"

"We believe they won't touch her to avoid drawing publicity to Directive 99, a new policy she's working on. As long as your Dad doesn't return and try to stop her from implementing this directive, she should be safe."

Collin's brow beaded with perspiration. He sensed his mom's love acutely in this moment, and the thought of losing her was unbearable.

"But she thinks he's deserted her?" Collin's face lit up. "I thought somebody was hanging around the house. I couldn't be sure and didn't want to frighten Mom."

"You're right somebody's watching surreptitiously for your Dad's return. I expect the phone is bugged, too."

"How do you know this?"

"The detective we hired found out about the surveillance."

"Didn't you tell the police?"

"We're not sure who we can trust yet."

Collin wiped away the sweat beads forming on his forehead. "Mom doesn't know any of this?"

"The less information she has, the safer she is."

Collin hung on each word Michael said. "What can I do?"

"First of all, pray, especially for the men involved in the kidnapping."

Collin expelled his breath disgustedly, as if Michael had pulled a plug on his lungs. "You gotta be kidding!"

Michael continued kindly, "I know it's hard, Collin. This man has threatened the life of your Dad and my best friend. Yet God's Word commands us to pray for our enemies and not become bitter. Someday maybe you'll understand the wisdom of it."

Collin clenched his fists. "Do me a favor Michael? Skip the 'pie-in-the-sky' church stuff if you're really trying to help us."

"I am, Collin..."

"Well, I'll tell you something," Collin blurted out, "my dad didn't have these problems until he became a Christian. Since then he and my mom disagree constantly, now you say he's almost killed, and my mom's in danger. Praying for the jerks who did

174

this to my Dad isn't just stupid, it's impossible." Collin's voice increased in volume.

"Not so loud," Michael commanded.

Collin sputtered, "Dad's life is in jeopardy and he's separated from everyone in this world he loves and you want me to pray for his abductors!"

"Yes," Michael answered simply. "Believe me, I know it's not easy, Collin, because I'm doing it, and it's one of the hardest prayers I've prayed. Your Dad's like a brother to me." His voice broke. Michael struggled to compose himself. "If you aren't willing to forgive and pray for enemies, you can get trapped into the same net of hatred these men live in."

"I'll think about it." Collin unfurled his clenched fists and stared at his hands, without so much as a blink. "What else can I do?"

"So far their surveillance has been discreet. Let me know if it becomes more obvious."

Collin shivered although it wasn't cold in the tower.

"Your Dad wants you to keep an eye on your Mom, stick around the house at night." Michael looked around again to be sure no one had come up the stairs. "If anybody tries to get in, call this number. Don't let anyone else see it." He handed Collin a yellow slip of paper.

"Whose number is it?"

"An organization that handles Christian persecution." Collin stuck it in his pocket without looking at it.

He remembered the hunting gun in his Dad's closet his Dad had trained him to use. "I can handle this myself. Anybody comes in, I'll be ready." Collin tried to keep the trembling from his voice.

Michael's grip tightened on Collin's shoulder. "Don't take any chances. These men are dangerous." Less forcefully, he added, "Don't discuss any of this with your Mom. As soon as he can, your Dad will either come home or communicate to her somehow he's okay. In the meantime, we don't want her doing anything desperate or dumb endangering both of them further." Michael's eyes bored into Collin, "Understand?"

"Yes." Images of his Dad playing ball with him and lying in a casket swirled through his head. "Can I talk to him?"

"Not yet." Michael wrapped Collin in a bear hug. "Take care."

"Tell Dad I love him."

Michael nodded. "I'll call you on your cell when I have anything else you need to know. I'm going down now. Coming?"

"In a minute."

Michael understood the powerlessness Collin felt. In his emerging manhood, Collin expected to have control over the experiences of his life. He'd tasted an orderly, adult world. His dad, the man he respected most, had become a victim of madmen. It was hard to grasp God remained in control, no matter the circumstances, and would work all this for good. *Collin's a baby Christian, but he'll learn,* thought Michael as he descended the tower steps.

\*\*\*

Collin lingered in the tower. He'd do anything to help his Dad, but all the same he was seventeen and scared to death. He leaned over the half wall flanking the huge metal bell and gazed through the opening overlooking the city.

Fall's riot of color had been replaced by the drab grey landscape of winter.

Thousands of people swarmed below, and somewhere his Dad moved like a stalked animal in constant danger. How could God let this happen? The clear, little world he knew days ago had turned into a crazy place populated by insane men.

Michael had said prayer was first. Collin never needed anything desperately before and wasn't sure he even believed in God's help in daily situations. But he knew his Dad and Michael did.

Why not give it a try? Nobody could hear him up in the tower. He said aloud, "Please protect my Dad, and God, I want to forgive these guys who are after him, but I can do it a lot easier

176

when my Dad is home safe. Whatever has happened to screw up their heads to do this, get them straightened around, please, and fast!"

Okay, he'd prayed, but if and when the time for action came, he'd be ready, too.

The long flight of stairs gave Collin a few more minutes to collect his thoughts before returning to the celebration.

***

"Have you seen Collin?" Jennifer asked Carolyn.

Carolyn glanced around, "Uhh, there he is."

Jennifer followed her eyes to where Collin entered the church hall.

Carolyn said, "Michael's probably been giving him a pep talk about his Dad's disappearance and reminding him to take care of you."

Jennifer looked away to hide the tears quickly filling her eyes.

"I'm sorry, Jennifer, I shouldn't have mentioned your husband. How insensitive of me."

"No, it's not that, Carolyn. Don't stop talking about him." Jennifer took her hand and squeezed it tightly.

Carolyn wished she could give Jennifer spiritual strength through her physical contact, but was wise enough to know only God could.

***

Midmorning the next day, Jennifer's assistant, Ellen, popped into her office at the Fullness of Life Centre. "Excuse me, Dr. Trevor, one of the residents, Kathryn Dobbs, has requested a brief, private conference with you when you make your daily rounds. She says it's important."

Jennifer looked up from the report she was reading. "See if the social worker, Miss Davis, can help her instead. Hopefully, it's minor and she can handle it."

177

Thirty minutes later Miss Davis stuck her head in after knocking. "Kathryn's a dear, but won't be put off, says this requires your personal attention. I couldn't get any more out of her other than 'It's urgent, but not an emergency.' Sorry, Jennifer. What would you like me to tell her?"

"I'll go in a few minutes. I could use a break from this report."

Jennifer stepped into the open elevator, her thoughts focused on the paperwork on her desk. She needed to speed her progress to get home on time tonight. The kids deserved at least her presence at dinner, although she hated sitting across from Nick's empty chair. *One of us has to keep some consistency in our household,* she thought.

She pressed four, and rode up to Kathryn Dobb's independent living floor, the section with the largest rooms, actually 12 x 14. Patients furnished them with their favorite furniture from home. Most brought a dresser and a chair. Jennifer had never been in Kathryn's cramped, but cozy, room, but heard from other staff the decor was charming.

After knocking, Jennifer heard a welcoming, "Come in" spoken by a soft feminine voice. Jennifer pushed the door in slowly so as not to startle her resident. Upon entering, she did a visual double take.

Kathryn's room exuded the charm of a bygone romantic era exemplified in Battenberg laces and Victorian florals of muted olives and rose. A gorgeous re-creation, the setting reminded Jennifer of pictures of her great-grandmother's home of the early 1900's, a period when families and friendships flourished because relationships were carefully tended by frequent, reciprocal visiting.

Her glance took in the ornate Eastlake antique dresser with intricate carvings further beautified by a rich, white cotton embroidered dresser scarf. Heart-shaped wall hangings filled with dried flower arrangements emitted fragrance evoking Jennifer's memories of her great-grandmother. "How beautiful your room is, Kathryn!" she exclaimed.

The elderly woman's eyes beamed a thank-you. "Please sit down, Dr. Trevor," she invited.

Jennifer sank onto a thickly cushioned chair flounced with a ruffled chintz skirt and slid her arms along the utilitarian crocheted doilies, another of the myriad touches of Victorian creativity. Kathryn sat across from her in a Boston rocker.

"I appreciate your coming. I know you're busy and hated to bother you, but it was important to me to speak to you in person." Jennifer had just leaned back when Kathryn announced, "I've read on the Internet about some closed hearings in Washington and a new directive containing some changes for elderly care."

Jennifer bolted upright as Kathryn continued. "It's all so vague, no one seems to have any details to report. I've always believed in going to the top when I have a question. What can you tell me about it?"

*How much news is out there?* Jennifer hurriedly composed herself and mouthed reassurances to Kathryn. It surprised her how quickly she was able to recover.

"We've no plans to make any major changes in the program here." Guiltily she realized this lovely woman would be among those to die in Phase One. For the first time she allowed herself to wonder what would happen to the morale of the Fullness of Life Centre residents when Directive 99 went into effect.

Jennifer's cell phone rang and she excused herself to Kathryn, delighted to take her leave. Kathryn's gaze followed her out the door.

***

Anne had agreed to meet Jennifer for lunch at Gillie's specialty sandwich shop in the heart of downtown. When Jennifer entered the tiny deli throbbing with noon frenzy she was still stunned by Kathryn's question.

Anne arrived a few minutes later and slid in across from Jennifer, who had chosen a booth in the rear. This was one conversation she didn't want overheard.

"Any word from the private investigator, Anne?"

179

"Nothing new. I'm sorry." Anne patted her hand.

Jennifer lowered her head. "Life is almost unbearable without Nick. Every day I wake up with one thought, Where are you? Come back, I'll do anything!"

Their waitress, Mardel, as proclaimed on her tarnished, gold-colored nameplate, ran over for their order. Jennifer figured her Reeboks probably put on as many miles in a day as a tiger pacing in its cage all week. Except Mardel got tips. Jennifer handed her menu back. "BLT, Cole slaw, no fries, water without ice with lemon to drink."

"Sounds good to me, too, make mine the same with coffee though. Thanks," Anne added.

While waiting for their drinks, they chatted briefly about the children. It was hard for Jennifer to shift her mind even temporarily from Nick.

Unable to contain herself, she blurted out, "Anne, I'm so frightened. I have to sort this out. With all my heart I want to believe Nick cares and didn't abandon me! I've been going over our entire life together, starting with our courtship in college. I think we started out on solid ground, but how can I be sure? Tell me about you and Michael, how you met. I was so into my own life back at the time I don't remember."

"At a Campus Crusade meeting. He was a guest speaker, Michael Stasen, a hammer-em-hard independent business-type on his way to becoming an investment tycoon. He shared his newfound belief in God with us."

"Love at first sight?" Jennifer leaned back enjoying a few moments' reprieve of old-fashioned girl talk.

Anne nodded. "We ignited like two explosives lit by one match; a kaleidoscope formed from our blended personalities, enhanced through our budding knowledge of Christ."

"So, religion came first," Jennifer interrupted. "Followed by?"

Anne's eyes took on a dreamy glow. "Courtship - sunrise bike rides, evening runs along the Madison campus lakeshore trails, and lots of laughter. Michael's easy, steady personality complemented mine. Over late-night dinners we discussed theology, and struggled to maintain premarital virginity. How about you and Nick?"

Jennifer finished half her sandwich and pushed her plate away. "Nick and I hit it off from the second date. We thought alike on everything until..." Her voice trailed off. She pulled Nick's Bible from her sculptured leather briefcase. "Can you believe this? Me, pulling out a Bible?" She looked around nervously, as if anybody cared what she read. Pulling out a ticking bomb wouldn't have been noticed in Gillie's at 12:40 p.m.

Anne's eyes widened as she waited to follow Jennifer's stream of thought. The waitress poured steaming coffee unnoticed into her drained cup.

"I remember my great-grandmother saying she was forbidden to read the Bible growing up," Jennifer said. "Something about the church hierarchy fearing she'd become confused. Great-grandmother said that made her all the more curious. Well, I've never been curious, not even when I saw Nick study Scripture for hours."

Anne nodded, pushing up the sleeves of her ramie and cotton knit sweater, clearly intrigued.

Jennifer continued. "Why should I be? I learned from my graduate school philosophy classes that Biblical theology is outdated. What word did one of my professors use?" Jennifer twisted her face, paused and looked up at the ceiling. "Oh yes, irrelevant.'"

"He was wrong," Anne interjected.

"Anyway, I was surprised and annoyed when Nick started poring through the Bible every morning and night. I wanted none of it."

Anne smiled, understanding her reaction. "Happened to me at age twelve when I got confirmed. I've been excited about studying Scripture ever since. I want to know all I can about God."

"Anne, I'm almost forty years old and never wanted to read a word!"

"Yet, you're motivated now with Nick gone?"

Jennifer nodded. "I'm reading Scripture because it mattered so much to him." After a brief pause, she added, "I'm sorry, I know my unbelief separates you and me, Anne, as it did me from Nick. I wish I could believe. I know Nick wanted to share Christ with me but I shut him up like a pesky child, and especially hated when he said Christ was his best friend. I wanted this place."

Anne placed her hand over Jennifer's tenderly. "You don't have to be jealous of God. He loves you personally and wants you and Nick to be one unit as He says in His Word."

Jennifer patted the Bible. "These are only words to me, not the voice of God."

"The more you read the easier it becomes to recognize God's voice. But, Jennifer, you need to read for yourself not just with the idea of feeling connecting to Nick."

"I'm not there yet, maybe I never will be." Jennifer glanced at her watch. "Omigosh. I've got to run."

\*\*\*

The sun streamed into Sarah's kitchen sending rays across her corner kitchen counter specially designed as a desk for her silver laptop, only a year old. It served her well for looking up recipes and shopping from the Web. She often played iTunes or podcasts while she cooked and cleaned up. Sarah took pride in impressing her sons with her minimal computer use. They called her Techky Mom. She even played Scrabble online while waiting to take something from the oven.

Now, she realized she was about to do the most important thing she'd ever done with her computer. She wouldn't read the disk because John told her not to, but she had to make a copy to keep for Agent Melton before she sent it. She rationalized it might be lost and she'd have nothing. Why not do both, make a copy for the agent and send the original? She knew how to burn a copy.

Sarah clicked her computer on and waited for the beep alerting her all systems were ready.

Prayerfully, tenderly, she inserted the disk. It took several moments to battle the temptation one last time to read whatever was on the disk. She loved John and had always trusted him in life. Now she must in death.

She went to the burn disk utility and began to follow the procedure exactly. To her dismay when she tried to copy it, it wouldn't. Somehow, the disk had been protected from reproduction.

Her eyes filled with tears. She couldn't even do something as simple as this. Every which way she turned seemed to end in defeat.

Slowly she began to repack the CD-R in its bubble wrap. The crinkly, popping noise of the plastic wrap made her tense nerves even more raw.

\*\*\*

Bruter stood at the counter of the White Dove Inn waiting for Hudson to check in a female guest. What was taking the old guy so long? At how many inns and hotels had they already made this inquiry? *What a waste of energy,* he thought. Relton could have sent a woman to do this. Shak emerged from the bathroom and joined Bruter. Both had their backs to the front door.

Hudson finished and turned his two-hundred-and-fifty-pound frame to Bruter and Shak. He glanced sideways and noticed Nick enter the foyer. Instead of coming into the main reception area, Nick slipped through the open lounge door on the right and half closed it.

From behind the door Nick overheard Shak saying to Bruter, "Last lodging place in this town, Trevor's got to be somewhere. We know he didn't go home."

Nick tried to steady his nerves. How had they found him? He needed to think of an escape plan, but his brain seemed like concrete. At the moment, his fate was in Hudson's hands.

Through the partially open door, Nick watched Bruter pull a picture out of his jacket pocket and go through a spiel of being concerned about a missing brother.

Nick's blood froze. They hadn't seen him yet, but he was trapped. If he went back onto the street, Bruter would notice him leave. If Nick went to his room, Bruter and Shak could observe him walk past.

He heard Bruter saying, "Look at this picture carefully, please."

"Yeah, I know him. He stayed here one night. Nice guy, quiet. I can't help you with any information as to his whereabouts now. Why are you tracking him anyway?"

Nick let his breath out quietly. Clever and quick, Hudson had changed the subject. He didn't even lie, just said he didn't know anything, and couldn't give out any information about his present location.

Bruter and Shak were walking past the lounge. Nick stayed behind the door. He couldn't see out now, but sensed their shadows as they walked past.

*Did they believe Hudson?*

Nick prayed as he watched them walk down the street.

Hudson had protected him. Why?

# Chapter Seventeen

Jack was already seated in the Fullness of Life Centre conference room at the large center table waiting for their scheduled planning meeting when Jennifer entered. He looked trim and handsome in his pin stripe suit and checked dark brown tie. *He knows it, too,* thought Jennifer.

She glossed over his warm hello and remark about the weather.

"Let's skip the small talk, Jack, we have a busy afternoon drafting implementation strategies for the additional policy procedures we've received on Directive 99."

The subject Directive 99 made her cringe as she recalled her last conversation with Kathryn about it. She steeled her mind to ignore it.

"I've had Ellen print out the hundreds of new pages."

She spread papers over the walnut table. "We need to summarize the data in plain English. I want this entire document of legalese reduced to eighteen pages of simple stats and procedures. I've divided up the sections. I'll handle the rationale in the introduction, include my study of the initial operational phase, and draw up the formal conclusions at home tonight and tomorrow."

"Why the push? We don't start implementation for three to four weeks, and it's assured of federal approval."

"Nevertheless, we must follow standard guidelines. I want you to double check the starting date for each phase and re-evaluate the statistical figures for accuracy."

"I'll get right on it." Jack saluted. She'd just given him a ton of work and knew he didn't like it. To his credit he kept his tongue. He'd find somewhere else to dump a mouthful of criticism, she realized.

"Sorry, I'm being rather abrupt, but a lot's happening."

"How about a quiet dinner tomorrow night for a break. I understand your man's out of town and we both have to eat." He came around the desk and put his arm around her shoulders.

"Jack, stop it! You're out of line, and I've had it with your messing around."

"But at the moment you're lonely, which is exactly why you need me." He grinned enticingly.

"How would you like a sexual harassment lawsuit?" Jennifer asked, not joking.

"Okay. I get the message."

"Good, stop being incorrigible," Jennifer rose and opened her door. "Instead of working on this together, take your sections and work in your office. I want some of this material ready to go over at home tonight."

Jennifer's next scheduled orientation meeting with the family members of new residents was in the lounge. Her job was to convince them the Fullness of Life Centre was great for their dear ones, not an attempt to get rid of them. She explained the varied and smooth programming and standardized resident care.

A twinge of guilt pricked Jennifer. Her own mother had loved being in her home alone watching TV, knitting, reading and visiting by phone with friends. She hurriedly collected the necessary signatures on the intake forms and smiled her way out of the room.

*** 

Sarah endured one final struggle with her desire to open and read the disk material first, but John was so clear about what she must do. Strong-willed and independent, she'd knowingly married a strong, decisive man and been happily married, partly because when there had been an issue of wills she'd submit in the end to his.

This had been their agreement when they married, although she appreciated he always heard her out and considered her opinions respectfully. In fact, he sometimes revised his thinking afterwards.

Sarah missed the time for mail pick-up at her house while trying to burn a copy of the disk. She drove quickly to the post office before she could change her mind. If the information would truly endanger her or their family, she couldn't risk having them all killed as John was or have her children live as orphans without her.

How she wished John had chosen a different career. Why did he have to consider himself a truth-torch for the culture?

She shook her head, instantly ashamed.

The God she and John both believed in had a purpose for people's lives. As Christ had accepted His cross, she'd have to live the rest of her life without her man who had died doing what he believed was right. God's powerful grace would help her. Of this she was sure.

If only she knew what this all meant.

Sarah heard the clunk of the mailer hitting the bottom of the mailbox outside the post office, like burying another part of John.

\*\*\*

Nick's grey eyes surveyed the innkeeper. Hudson had stopped him on his way out. He'd never said a word about Shak and Bruter's earlier visit. Was he going to ask now?

Hudson's tall body dominated the 1900 mahogany desk in the comfortable parlor miniaturized by the massive antiques. He wore a weathered Izod golf shirt and khaki pants smeared in a variety of paint splotches matching the Victorian colors on the walls, apparently dressed to handle maintenance chores.

"I wanted to let you know, Mr. Nicholas, tomorrow I'll be processing your credit card for your stay thus far. It's our policy to handle charges for extended stays on the 15th and 30th of the month. We're happy to have you with us as long as you'd like to stay, of course."

Nick panicked. He'd chosen this small inn precisely because he hoped to avoid having his card processed until he checked out. A swift trace of his credit card could bring his hunters here. He decided on a bold step.

"Could we speak confidentially a moment?"

Hudson looked up at him surprised. "Sure, what's up?"

Nick looked around. Seeing no one, he continued. "I know this sounds strange, but I need to ask you to trust me. I promise you'll get your money, but I'd appreciate it if you'd hold off."

Nick mistook Hudson's speechlessness for refusal.

*Oh no,* he thought, *I've said too much already.* Aloud Nick said, "Never mind, run it through. I'll be checking out in the morning." He turned to leave.

Hudson grabbed Nick's arm almost catching him off balance. He pulled Nick into the adjoining lounge and closed the door behind them.

Nick acquiesced rather than cause a scene. Hudson was big and athletic, but much older. He knew he could take Hudson down, if he had to.

"You're the one!" Hudson exclaimed.

Nick broke into a sweat while eyeing the door ready to bolt.

Hudson tightened the firm grip on Nick's arm.

Nick tried to act cool. Maybe it would buy him a few minutes.

## Chapter Eighteen

*Another day survived,* Jennifer thought. If only she didn't have to deal with the emptiness that came with every sunset. She'd worked at home until 11:30 P. M. poring over the material she'd brought from her office on Directive 99. When she finally turned off the light, the gorgeous full moon sent shafts of brightness illuminating her solitary figure in the king-sized bed.

Nick had been gone almost a week.

Jennifer longed for him, his thoughts, the essence of who he was. She wanted him back more than she'd ever wanted anything in her life.

"How long can I keep functioning?" she wondered.

Restless and unable to sleep, Jennifer tossed from side to side. Her eyes were drawn to Nick's Bible on the bedside table. She pulled herself to a sitting position, and shoved pillows behind her head for support.

As she picked it up, Jennifer pictured their last night together after lengthy lovemaking,

Nick had tucked the bedcovers around her gently making a one-sided sheet tent, so the light wouldn't disturb her, and opened this Bible as he always did.

When she'd complained, he said, "Honey, I sleep better after I read."

"Okay," she'd mumbled.

He read twenty minutes or so before turning off the light. Maybe this would help her now. She turned the lights back on and read until sleep overcame her.

At one a.m. she was sound asleep in the darkened bedroom suite with only the nightlight in the master bath to take the edge off her uneasiness in case she awoke before morning.

She disliked being alone at night, a carryover from the depression of early evening, which settled over the household of her dysfunctional childhood.

A soft slap on her cheek brought her instantly to a state of wakefulness.

What was that? She awoke and opened her eyes but could see nothing. Yet she sensed swirls going round her in wide circles, becoming smaller and tighter by the second. It seemed as if the silence in the air would swallow her up.

"I'm still alive," she said to the emptiness. "Go away." But the swirls came closer as if she were looking into the heart of evil and Satan was trying to capture her in his nothingness. She resisted, but to no avail. Jennifer screamed. "God, help me."

As suddenly as the impenetrable silence began, it ended leaving her exhausted and soaked with perspiration.

"Oh God." She shivered. "What was that?" She asked herself, am I awake?

Jennifer saw a tiny square inch of light, so incredibly bright she couldn't take her eyes away. As ugly as the evil had been was the beauty of this light, almost as if Tiffany glass were in the square. What was white became a rainbow of color, and she sensed the beauty of God as He filtered into a life making it lovely.

Peace stole over Jennifer. Her last wakeful thought, *I want to live in the light with Nick forever.*

The next morning, she was sure her sensations of the previous night had all been a dream. She convinced herself she imagined everything.

*** 

Nick and Hudson stood face to face in the lounge next to the leaded glass Victorian window, sizing each other up.

Nick questioned whether his instincts about men could still be relied on. He hadn't been sharp enough to pick up on Torricelli. The large man before him, totally grey and partially bald except for a fringe of wavy locks, moved agilely. Something about Hudson's inquisitive eyes reassured Nick he needn't be wary.

Hudson pulled a book from a shelf. "Have you ever seen one of these?"

"You dragged me here to see a book?"

"Do you know what this is?" He held out a small paperback Bible. The respectful way he handled it in his huge palms further relaxed Nick.

"Sure do." Nick's eyes riveted on Hudson's.

Hudson's next words tumbled out. "During my morning prayer, several days before you arrived, God revealed He was sending a special guest for me to protect, someone in desperate straits. I wondered if it was you when you checked in, but I figured you were too self-assured to have any major problems, even if your habits did seem a bit strange."

"I put on a good front," Nick said, still a bit nervous. "When I saw those two guys at your desk I thought I was done for."

"That's when I suspected you were the one. Tell me about yourself and how you came to be here."

For the next half hour Nick explained about Directive 99 and his previous Christian legal defense actions. "I spend every hour now planning how to expose this directive. It disgusts me." He mimicked, "Now once again, for your safety and protection the government is wasting billions of your dollars developing and implementing a new system of mass murder. Aren't American citizens lucky!" Nick ended on a flourish of sarcasm.

"But why stay way out here?"

"A safe hiding place. If I return home, I'm an open target and my family is in jeopardy. I couldn't let you process my card yet because obviously I could be traced by it."

"Well, you're welcome to remain as long as you like as our guest. I'd had word something like this directive was in the works, when we were tackling privacy issues, but didn't realize it would be this soon."

"You know about subjects like this?"

Hudson nodded. "Yes, and don't get me started on privacy. I used to be a reporter at CNA years ago. I wrote the first news items on the development of a magnetic code for the ultimate in sophisticated tracing of human beings. Everyone with only one number, never before such accuracy! How could there be a missing person again? Even children would have their codes. Between cell phones and magnetic strips on credit cards anonymity disappeared."

Nick nodded. "Right. Loss of privacy, the ultimate intrusion into personal life! Every subtle measure of control initially sounding logical with most citizens oblivious to its real threat."

Hudson added, "Because the public is persuaded with false arguments about safety along with other verbal deceptions calculated to prey upon public fear. No need to worry, people were told."

"What happened to your job at CNA?"

"Lost it because I refused to relay the biased information fed to us, lies in the place of truth, propaganda masquerading as news. I switched to the National Ezine, a popular conservative on-line and print magazine until the publication went under. John Levinson got similar media going again with Newspersons. By the way, something suspicious happened to him recently, remind me to tell you about it another time. Anyway, there aren't many honest and bold voices left now in media.

"I remember how the entrepreneurial spirit evaporated when unemployed numbers rose and more than 65% of the country got some kind of government hand-out. Many able-bodied people haven't worked in years. With taxes exceeding many American workers' take home pay, people can't afford full care at private centers even if there were enough left." Nick shook his head sadly. "Always government intervention is for your, catch the phrase, 'ultimate benefit'."

"Let's sit." Hudson led the way to two armchairs in front of the stone fireplace.

"I checked into the inn under just my first name Nicholas, hoping you wouldn't process my card until I left. I never expected to be in a Christian accommodation with someone knowledgeable about current society. I'm overwhelmed."

"You know who to thank."

"You better believe I do."

"I have connections with one part of the Christian underground called Leviathan. It takes its name from the large fish providing shelter for Jonah. We could use you in our organization when this is over. For now, we're willing to help with your investigation. I know a computer hack who may be able to get into the files of this guy's company who's after you and help us get evidence against him."

"I didn't know Leviathan existed. That'd be great."

Hudson smiled. "There are various sub-groups in the underground. We'll be as interested as you in exposing this Directive 99."

"I'd appreciate your help. Once it's law, It won't be easy to shoot down in court."

Hudson hurried over to lock the door, then sat down at the computer set up on the table for guest use. "We may already have a file on you." He punched a couple of keys and typed in a password for a computer insta-check. "Now I know your real name, and can tell you what our records say about you."

Nick joined him in front of the screen.

He read, "'Nicholas Trevor. Identified as a powerfully dangerous Christian because of his work on anti-pornography cases.' Each case is described and its outcome summarized. Impressive legal victories. There's a list of the letters to the editors you've written on various issues over the last five years." Hudson complimented Nick while reading his file.

"How did you compile this?"

"Some is gathered from public domain information, except for the last summary," Hudson said. "You might have been safe ad infinitum because of your public status. Unfortunately, some fanatics have arisen who seem to be the cohorts of Satan himself, speeding though the world in these last days."

"Tell me about it." Nick rubbed the bruises on his wrists.

"This is what you've run up against, my friend. The opposition has more knowledge than we do about what's happening at your wife's work. You've obviously become a threat there, too."

"Makes sense, but doesn't make fighting any easier."

Hudson nodded. "This attack is spiritual as well as physical."

"Right."

"God will protect you."

"He has. You should have seen what God did to get me here! After I was abducted, suddenly the van filled with fire, rolled and I was free."

"What happened to your kidnappers?"

"I didn't stick around to find out, but apparently Shak and Bruter, the guys you met, survived."

A bell chimed. "Nick, we'll talk again. I need to check in some guests arriving. Do you want me to send someone to watch over your wife?"

"Thanks, my friend Michael is handling her protection. She isn't a Christian. This is very hard for her, as you can imagine."

"Absolutely. We'll add her to our prayer list."

\*\*\*

Pirelli sat with his shoes off and his stocking feet up on the coffee table listening to Jennifer's conversation with Anne through his earpiece. He had the five-hour shift from two to seven. So far, except for Jack's discussion of assisted suicide procedures, he'd been incessantly bored by this eavesdropping task.

He was half dozing as he heard Jennifer punching in a phone number. "Anne, can you come help me? I've made a decision to try to stop Directive 99."

In his darkened suite Pirelli instantly shifted upright from his slouched position on the chair.

"What? How wonderful. I'll come as soon as Michael gets home."

"Don't tell him yet. I'm not sure my idea will work. Just ask him to pray."

Pirelli stood and began to pace. He had to notify Relton immediately, but something inside him didn't want to act.

Anne's image floated up from memory. If she helped Jennifer, he'd have to eliminate her. Pirelli knew Relton would make him stop them both.

Like an animal attaches to a human who befriends it, he remembered how Anne had treated him and prayed for him. For a reason he couldn't fully explain he didn't want her endangered.

When Relton called later for his report, Pirelli resolved to say nothing about Jennifer's plan, only mention she questioned Jack about the assisted suicide procedures.

*** 

Instead of calling at the usual time, Relton chose to visit Pirelli in person.

"Mr. Relton, hey, this is a surprise."

Relton's eyes swept the suite at a glance. The place was neat, except for two metal trashcans, one bulging with aluminum cans, the other with candy wrappers and empty food containers. "I decided to see where you're holing up. Apparently, there's been a lot of eating going on. I trust that's not all."

Relton dusted a chair with his handkerchief, before sitting on it. "What info have you collected so far from the Trevor woman's briefcase and phone bugs?"

"Nothing of value."

"Well?" Relton's eyebrows lifted. "Is she hanging tight on Directive 99?"

Pirelli shifted his weight from one foot to the other. "Boss, this miniature microphone system isn't working well, I can barely hear conversations."

"Strange. It's always worked before."

"Don't know. Maybe too much interference from the electronics at the care center, I have to listen through an earful of static."

Relton crossed his arms. "I'm tired of incompetence."

195

"Relax. The good news is as far as I can tell everything is moving along on schedule with the directive."

"Has she heard from Trevor?"

"No contact came through our channels. And if she's heard from him, she's a good actress, because she sure plays the part of the jilted wife well."

"Maybe you should go in and reset the bugs."

Pirelli shook his head. "I can't get inside again without arousing suspicion."

"Do I have anyone capable working for me?" Relton obsessed. "It's been days since the abduction and those goons, Shak and Bruter, still don't have a clue where to find Trevor."

"Unless he uses a credit card, the chances of tracing him are slim."

"I hoped this microphone bug would produce some dirt on his wife and the guy working with her."

"It still may." Pirelli carefully avoided any mention of Anne. "Relax, boss."

"I'll calm down when Trevor's taken out for good." Relton rose and crossed the room. He pulled a gun with a silencer from his attaché case and put it on the coffee table between him and Pirelli. "I keep a couple of these on hand precisely for situations like this. I want you to use this on Jennifer Trevor if she even squeaks about interfering. This woman's key because of her connections in Washington. We're this close to changing the future." Relton held up his thumb and forefinger a sixteenth inch apart.

Pirelli tasted stomach bile in his throat. "Be careful. Make it look like suicide, as if she's grieving over her husband's betrayal. Don't get sloppy on me!" Relton warned.

"Just so you know, this isn't my usual line, boss. I'm not a hit man, I just deliver. And I never took out a woman before."

"No difference." Relton interrupted, "You'll follow my orders."

"Sure, boss, I was thinking of packing one, one of these days." Pirelli wanted time to think, but Relton wasn't giving him any. He took the only safe course he saw in the moment. "Guess

I'll start sooner than I planned. Hey, I thought it was hard to find guns nowadays?" he added to lighten the mood.

"Anybody can get them if they have the cash." Relton's perfect white teeth gleamed as he smiled. "The only challenge is, finding the best price. And getting silencers, I always prefer quiet deaths."

"Isn't money always on everybody's mind?" *After all, wasn't this why he did what he did?* Pirelli's comment was uncharacteristic and his tone melancholic.

Relton ignored it to his peril. "Unless we find Trevor in twenty-four hours I'm going to contact the DEC office in Washington and sic their team on him, his wife and anybody close to them."

Pirelli inhaled. He understood the acronym only too well. "A zealous organization, Discredit Every Christian. Except discredit meant destroy in every possible way a person's reputation for integrity, distorting income tax records, health issues, a little HIV report, cell phone records for telephone sex, on and on. Good idea. DEC can be more painful than physical death." But the thought of this happening to the nice women he'd met at the Fullness of Life Centre, Jennifer Trevor and Anne Stasen sickened him.

"This will smoke Nicholas Trevor out."

Pirelli picked up the gun. "Don't you worry for a minute, Boss, I'll handle Jennifer Trevor for you."

Relton took his leave as quickly as he'd come.

Pirelli's heart pounded as he gaped at the gun. The surprise visit had distressed him. To try to keep his brain from freezing up he sat quietly reviewing what he knew about DEC. As with many things evil, truth and accuracy were grossly violated by DEC. They intended to destroy every person who proclaimed belief in Jesus Christ by defamation. Violence would be too obvious.

Most believers were too innocuous to be a threat, anyway, living like the pendulum on a clock swinging one way or the other depending on the convenience of the moment. DEC was dedicated only to discrediting every Christian who posed a threat, those not cold or lukewarm, but sold out even to the point of death for this Jesus person. Like Nick Trevor and Anne and Michael Stasen.

*** 

In the basement of the inn, all the doors were sealed. No illumination was allowed, except for two thick, tall candles. Yet to Nick, the concrete enclosure seemed brighter than the day outside, so shining were the countenances of those who attended the meeting.

Nick prayed silently, *My Lord and my God. Thank you for this place of refuge.*

Hudson's arm brushed against Nick's shoulder as they sat down side by side.

Nick sensed the overwhelming presence of the Spirit of God. "If only all our churches could all be like this place," he whispered to Hudson.

"Yes. These people take Christ seriously and the call to pray is a sacred joy, not an obligation."

The leader, a grey bearded man who appeared to be in his seventies opened with prayer. "Lord, we ask for Your wisdom and peace." Nick left his chair and knelt on the concrete basement floor. It may as well have been a pillow. He prayed, unaware of his surroundings. *Lord, I love you. Wrap your arms around my loved ones upon the earth this night. You can reach them, I cannot.* Tears streamed down his face from emotion born of agony and of hope for them all.

About forty people attended the meeting over the two-hour period coming and going. Most of this time was spent in fervent prayer. Hudson chose not to reveal details about Nick's situation to the others but at the end, Hudson asked Nick if he'd like special prayer. Nick nodded.

Hudson and a couple other men formed a circle enclosing Nick with the symbolic protection of their bodies. God's peace permeated Nick as they placed their hands on his shoulders and prayed for his special intentions.

Nick prayed along in the silence of his heart, *Lead Jennifer into your light, heavenly Father. Jesus, let Your righteousness prevail. Holy Spirit, give me wisdom and discernment to guard the elderly.*

Outside the meeting, Hudson pulled Nick aside in the hall. "One of the guys here is a brilliant computer nerd. He can help you get information you never dreamed you'd see. Want to talk to him?"

"Sure."

Nick was introduced to Ted Dyad, blonde, late twenties, with wire-rim spectacles.

"What do you need?" Ted asked without preamble.

"Info on a businessman, Howard Relton, who may have mob connections and another guy named Torricelli."

"Give me a few hours. Where can I reach you?"

"Right here." Nick gave Ted his room number.

Nick climbed the stairs to his room shaking his head in amazement. How lucky he was to be at this B & B. He laughed aloud. Luck had nothing to do with it.

***

Ted knocked on his door around midnight. carrying a laptop with wireless access. Nick ushered him in.

Ted grinned. "I assume you're ready for the results of my data search?"

"You bet!" Nick pulled a notepad and pen out of the desk drawer as Ted opened his computer.

"Relton has six companies: carpet business, restaurants, construction, land development, three hotels in the Cayman Islands and private home health care facilities in twenty-three states. These are the people he probably feeds into the federal elderly care system and gets a kickback from their financial resources.

Two businesses are currently in Chapter 11. Last year he had three other companies, but it appears what he did was change names. He made major campaign contributions, $500,000 each to two politicians. One of them is a militant gay and the other a racism agitator."

Nick scribbled notes as fast as he could write.

"I wouldn't suggest going near Relton, he's reputed to have mob affiliation. I've got pictures I want you to see." He pulled two prints from his folder. "Here's Relton and one of his cronies. Is this Torricelli, alias Pirelli?"

Nick jabbed his forefinger at the print. "That's the guy who picked up the work the morning I was kidnapped."

"I thought so. He's got a clean record - three arrests, no convictions. It looks like he's done jobs for Relton off and on for several years."

"He set me up, for sure."

"I got into Relton's system and downloaded files, although we can't use them as evidence, it's illegal. I'm trying to find out if there's an association between Relton and John Levinson, the Catholic journalist who supposedly committed suicide shortly before you were kidnapped. Under highly questionable circumstances according to his wife."

"You suspect a connection?"

"Don't know, something stinks there. It's going to take some time before we can be sure."

## Chapter Nineteen

Jennifer looked tiny behind her huge desk sitting alone in her glassed-in office perch above the dinner rush hour hustle below. She was too unsettled to eat.

This afternoon a piece of startling information had arrived in the latest packet on Directive 99. In tiny print buried in legalistic text, she discovered the innocuous phrase, "Once optimal level of average age has been uniformly achieved throughout each state, the age parameter will be gradually reduced downward, up to but not limited by, five years increments. Eventually termination may be mandated as young as sixty-five. This is an unspecified future time period."

She reflected sadly. *Many members of this generation didn't want their babies, now they're killing off their parents.*

Jennifer continued to read. "Injection, as simple as an immunization flu shot, is the preferred method for those who acquiesce and don't want to be a burden on their loved ones. Those less compliant will be subjected to a flu epidemic of our creation against which staff and younger patients will be inoculated. Never will any resident experience an iota of pain. Politicians and federal and state employees will be exempt from a shortened life termination."

How thoughtful, she raged.

For a long time Jennifer sat pondering. Her eyes were attracted to a frame on her desk. Nick had given her a picture of the two of them posing on a ski hill for their fifteenth anniversary. She'd loved it, but ignored the verse below. She read it now. Psalm 17:15 (NKJ), "As for me, I will see Your face in righteousness; I shall be satisfied when I awake in Your likeness."

Righteousness, how do I define it? Your likeness? What is the likeness of God? I don't know, but I know what righteousness is not, she mused. She spent the next hour in deep contemplation writing her thoughts.

Jennifer's initial shock at the age sixty-five parameter intensified. She lifted her eyes to stare out the window and watch the evening shadows settling imperceptibly at first, quickly transforming the day into total darkness. How similar dusk was to the directive lying on her desk, innocent, imperceptible at first and totally evil in consequences.

*** 

On the tenth day since Sarah had sent John's computer off, a UPS truck pulled into her driveway.

The deliveryman in traditional brown smiled as he handed the box to her. Sarah thanked him profusely.

She slammed the door behind her, put the package on the credenza in the foyer and tried to tear it open. Unable to break the tape, she ran to the kitchen for a knife and carefully slit the tape. She gulped once and prayed before opening the bubble wrap and lifting the computer out.

It took only a few moments to set it up and plug it in.

Her eyes skimmed the files, starting with the two weeks prior to John's death.

As the files marched onto the screen, anger surged inside her. Why hadn't the police attempted this recovery? They were quick to assume her husband had committed suicide and had no desire to check further. Her theory was perfectly plausible. Someone working at the hotel had been bribed to leave the patio door unlocked and relock it at a prescribed time after John's killer had left. The employee would never even know John's dead body was in the bathroom. Afterwards, he'd be afraid to come forward and be considered an accomplice.

What did the police care? A simple suicide meant one less case to deal with. But she had three huge reasons to search for the truth. Her daughter and two sons needed to know their father was a man they could honor and respect.

She worked backwards to see what John had been working on the week of his death. A little gasp escaped her throat when she saw the file marked 99-URGENT and opened it.

\*\*\*

A little after seven, Jennifer rose from her desk to follow through with the plan she'd decided upon. She'd called Anne and explained her idea.

At half past eight she went to the front door of the residential center to greet Anne. "Thanks for coming. I really need you. I hope it wasn't too inconvenient to get away."

"No problem. Michael's working on a sermon, and Carolyn's happy to have a special time with Maria all to herself." Anne hugged her hard. "When you told me, I knew I'd be honored to have a part."

Jennifer became teary, but swiped her eyes with a Kleenex. "This isn't going to be easy."

"Just like the old days at college – you and I out to save the world, only this time it's really true." Anne's caring gaze examined Jennifer. "How are you holding up?"

"Pretty good. I'm excited. Look what I've put together."

Before Anne had even removed her trench coat, Jennifer handed her a manila folder. "This holds the power to impact life or death for countless people."

\*\*\*

The file marked Urgent 99 included a time line and a book manuscript with a deadline two weeks after John's death.

*How ironic*, Sarah thought. Her husband had never missed a deadline before this, his last work.

The book manuscript was titled The Death Code: Ninety-Nine. The words both fascinated and frightened her.

She took her laptop into John's office and connected the USB cord to the HP printer. After checking the nearly empty paper tray, she retrieved more from the supply cabinet and filled the printer to capacity.

With shaking fingers she hit control P on her laptop keyboard. Her heart pounded as she waited for the sheets to click out.

When she had all the pages assembled Sarah sat down in John's recliner and began reading.

Shock, sadness, and cold fear pulsed through her as she read. When she finished much later, she wasn't sure what to do. She had to take action, but what?

\*\*\*

Anne drew in her breath with amazement, as she rifled through summaries of Directive 99's long-term goals.

Jennifer waited.

A few minutes later Anne said, "I want to read this in detail later but, just from a glance, I can see it's dynamite. I can't believe our government would do such a thing."

"I feel disgusted with myself I've let things get this far. Today it's like I raised a window shade on what I'm capable of and it's scary."

Anne listened nonjudgmentally while Jennifer exploded. "I look around and finally see. These haven't been human beings, only names to me, marks on paper. The closest I got to anyone personally is when I met families prior to check-in or consoled them upon their elderly loved one's death. The rest of the time I viewed residents from my glassed-in perch. How could I sink so low and allow Directive 99 to get this far?"

"You probably were deceived by the initial cover-up."

"I'd like to think so, but I was right in the middle and blind. I created parts of it! But I know for Kathryn to die is wrong! Jennifer waved her arm about. "This was supposed to be the fulfillment of my great potential! Sitting here playing God - getting bodies lined up to be laid on the altar of expediency. The greedy adults who drained the resources of their hard-working parents can play with their technological toys and enjoy their leisure without taking responsibility for lovingly providing for the aging in society."

"It's a tragedy," Anne agreed.

"I can't blame them. They were trained to be selfish! We all were. I hated your integrity and your Christian ideals. I'm still not sure about this Jesus stuff, but I know what I've been doing isn't right either. Somewhere I took a wrong turn, and lost my values. Nick and you and Michael helped me see what I've been hiding from."

"Not us, Jennifer, the Holy Spirit inspired your heart, not Nick or me, or Michael or any human being."

Jennifer smiled and chuckled. "Well, I wish He'd done it sooner. I finally get what's most important in life, and the reason why I'm here. I've got some important calls to make tonight."

"No doubt His power was at work, but people need to co-operate."

Jennifer sighed. "I'm not sure I can ever take the spiritual road all the way to this God stuff, but I've certainly been a foolish woman. I only hope my action tonight will stop Directive 99. It may be too late."

"With God nothing's ever too late." Anne said.

"I don't know. It may be for Nick and me. He's disgusted with the person I've become. I only hope he's safe somewhere. "

"Always remember he loves you," Anne said firmly, putting her arms around Jennifer.

They were both crying again. Anne pulled two Kleenex from her purse. Jennifer wiped away her tears and straightened up.

"Time for this later, Anne. We need to get everything taken care of quickly, because I think Jack may realize I'm not pleased with the advanced phase procedures. If he suspects something, he'll try to stop me or to destroy my credibility before I can act."

"How can I help?"

The copier was already humming in the next room churning off copies of the letter Jennifer had written. The printer was spitting out mailing labels.

"After I sign these cover letters, stuff one, along with this manila folder, in each large brown envelope. Affix a mailing label on the front from this sheet. With a little luck," Jennifer paused correcting herself, "with a lot of prayer, Jack's going to be helpless to do anything."

"Why the mailings, Jennifer? Aren't your calls enough?" Anne asked.

"We need both. The paperwork is back-up data, but I also must make personal contact. These packets may be intercepted. Send only to newspapers starred on the list. Can you help me think up good headlines? The media will probably distort what I send with their own slanted headlines, but with the minimal help they have now, one of the original headlines I write may get through. They'll have to include the actual content, but the title they give an article can cause the reader to question its authenticity even before reading it. I'll have to risk this distortion or miss too many powerful readers if I ignore the newspaper batch going out."

"Okay, let's cover this mailing in prayer." Anne placed her hands over the box, bowed her head and prayed before inserting the letters.

Jennifer pulled up her contact directory of names and numbers. A minute later she firmly punched a number into her I-phone. She drummed her fingers on the desk waiting for the connection. "This isn't much, Anne, but it's something and just might work."

"Senator Odling, Jennifer Trevor here, how are you? Good. Yes, I know I've called your private line. There's something you need to know as head of the committee initiating the Directive 99 bill."

"And it's important enough to interrupt me during my dinner party?" he asked icily.

"Yes. I have additional information of importance to clear up misconceptions regarding implementation of Directive 99. I only recently received the final program with the advanced procedures. You cannot appreciate the full extent of Directive 99 without this data."

He was listening now. She heard him breathing slowly.

"Senator," Jennifer spoke authoritatively, "Directive 99 is not the panacea I originally believed, quite the contrary."

"What do you mean?" he asked in a crisp tone.

"To summarize, Directive 99 makes human life a commodity subject to random manipulation. It states the termination of life is immaterial even at age sixty-five, but, Senator Odling, that's totally false. Let me explain." Jennifer gripped the phone more tightly.

"The Directive first approves the killing of the elderly through withholding extraordinary measures of medical care, nothing unusual there. But shortly moves to withholding food and water. What comes next in Phase Three is death achieved by administering 'death-productive drugs" based upon age criteria without consideration of other factors like physical health and mental acuity." Jennifer paused for breath before adding, "Sometimes it occurs with residents' knowledge after persuasive verbal manipulation."

Anne's ears focused on Jennifer while her hands worked.

"News releases to this effect will be out shortly, Senator. Since you were so courteous to me personally during the hearings, I wanted you to have an opportunity to avoid the bad publicity this could cause you by publicly withdrawing your support before the news hits the wire."

"I need to think this over. As you must know, Directive 99 has become a popular measure among budget conscious lawmakers," Senator Odling said.

Jennifer stifled the temptation to reply Congress merely wanted to preserve funds for their own pet programs and perks.

Instead she said, "I understand, but once the public gets wind of the full implications the Directive will lose its popularity overnight and its supporters in the legislature will more than likely be removed from office in the next election."

He thought he heard a threatening tone in her voice. He was smart enough not to comment.

"I understand this is a top-secret measure, Ms. Trevor. How will the public receive this information?"

"I assure you Senator, it's happening at this moment. I urge you to protect yourself. You've been given the first opportunity, Sir."

"Ms. Trevor, I appreciate your consideration. Your opinions are certainly important, but I must have factual data. If you have any evidence to back up these assertions I want to see it. It was my understanding the stipulation stated simply no extraordinary measures would be taken to keep older people alive."

"Senator, food and water are now considered extraordinary measures." She continued, "The complete data sheet describing these new procedures will be on your aide's desk tomorrow morning, along with every other Senator's desk and at the offices of the major news services. Good evening, sir."

Something about her firm, cold tone convinced him. He'd believe her because she had no reason to lie, nothing to gain, and everything to lose. As a lawmaker, it was increasingly difficult to gauge truth, but he sensed he'd just heard it.

Jennifer was satisfied she'd left him no alternative.

Her oral statement would arouse sufficient interest to keep the overnight express letters Anne was now sealing from being conspiratorially suppressed in the mail heap or garbage can by a biased press.

Senator Odling didn't return to his dinner guests immediately. After he hung up, he sat motionless in his leather swivel chair and tapped his cupped fingers together thoughtfully.

Ten minutes later he called his top aide, "Get this statement on the 10:00 news. Senator Odling has serious reservations about the new measure pending for the National Fullness of Life Centres. He's withdrawn his support from Directive 99."

"What reason shall I give, Sir?" the aide asked.

"Tell them my complete statement will be out tomorrow afternoon. And get Senators Bradford and Comiskey on the line." He hung up and expelled a long low whistle.

His Dad, a Senator before him had often said, "Political issues are like the stock market, you have to know when to get in and when to get out." Jennifer Trevor had given him inside information, and when one of the people in the know was willing to put her career on the line, the stink had to be real.

He wished he could tell himself he was doing this on ideological grounds, but he knew he'd lost his ideals years ago to the god of expediency. This Trevor woman he both pitied and admired.

Jennifer went to the next name on her list. "Senator Davis, I need to talk with you." She explained over and over to each Senator information withheld or distorted in the bill, often pacing the floor as she spoke. Her tension was an express train surging through her. She reached for her water bottle.

Anne said excitedly, "Jennifer you're doing great. I like this material I'm mailing. You state the issues in unequivocal terms in this written summary." Anne read aloud from one of the papers she'd been stuffing. "Senate Bill 99 calls ultimately for the death of millions of the elderly who currently reside in National Fullness of Life Centres....," she paused, "I had no idea how huge these numbers are." Anne shook her head. "This would make up for billions of dollars wasted in government corruption and mismanagement."

Jennifer responded emphatically, "As if shortening a human life is worth any amount of money."

"How could the government expect to get away with this?"

"Easy," Jennifer studied her list of Senators names. "Almost no one would know the details until it's too late."

Suddenly Anne whispered in a frightened voice, "Someone's in our office area. A light came on in the hall."

"Are you sure? I may have left the outer office light on."

"They both heard a sound like the clap of thunder or a door slamming. The two women froze.

*** 

Prior to finding the disk and recovering data from John's computer, the only ray of hope Sarah had experienced since John's death had come from Agent Melton of the American National Security Agency. Surely, he could be trusted with this information. He was probably already using the resources of his agency to stop the horrid Directive 99 John had written about. Sarah needed to tell him immediately about her computer retrieval success and what she'd found.

Yet, Sarah debated. She stared at Agent Melton's business card taped on her kitchen cabinet door, picked up the phone and put it down several times. What was holding her back from making contact? Agent Melton was polished, professional, yet ...what? Something bothered her.

Had she ever heard of his agency before?

Don't be silly, she chided herself. Ever since 9/11/2001 new government agencies were created and reorganized. With the introduction of the czars in 2009 with their special domains the names of departments changed so many times who could keep track? Sometimes she wondered if the government even knew. Still there should be some record.

She turned on her computer, opened her browser to Google and typed in American National Security Agency. She studied the options on her screen - National Security Council and the words American national security, but no office or agency by the ANSA name.

Sarah was troubled. If ANSA existed, it had to have a site somewhere unless it was top secret, but Melton hadn't indicated it was. Was she being silly?

Finally, she decided to call Agent Melton and ask him where his office was.

He hesitated not a moment. "How wise of you to check us out. After all you've been through, you can't be too careful."

Melton's voice was so sympathetic, Sarah was taken off guard.

"Our office is in Washington, under the umbrella of general security. We keep a low profile. You won't find ANSA listed in public data files."

Although she'd been emotionally exhausted by recent events, Sarah was a smart woman. His explanation was smooth, but perhaps too polished, and vague to suit her.

"Forgive my need to check. Thanks for being understanding."

"You'll let me know when John's laptop arrives?"

"Of course you'll know."

Agent Melton hung up the phone and sat thoughtfully studying a spider on the wall.

***

Jennifer checked the outer offices. "No one's there, but the light is on."

"Funny, I thought the noise came from the reception area."

They waited, but the sound wasn't repeated.

Anne glanced around one more time, before she resumed stuffing envelopes. She paled as she read additional glimpses of Directive 99's content. "How sad this is. Ultimately the directive endangers the life and well-being of all of us, young or old, because it desecrates the dignity of life."

Suddenly, they heard a loud thud.

Jennifer's assistant, Jack, jerked open the door and barged in. "I've heard enough. I can't let you do this, Jennifer. I intend to stop you."

Anne shrank from the door.

"Jack! I thought you'd left."

"I did, but forgot something and returned for it. Good thing. Jennifer, I'm officially replacing you as administrator."

"Says who?"

"I've already notified the transition team by cell phone. They'll be here tomorrow demanding your resignation. I order you to stop spreading this propaganda about Directive 99 until we have a complete investigation of your behavior tonight."

"You're in no position to be making ultimatums. Leave, Jack."

Jack stammered, "No way." He stomped over to the door, locked it and stood in front. He put the key in his pocket. "Nothing and nobody leaves here."

"Don't be a fool. I have a key, too. Besides, you're too late."

211

He turned an ugly crimson. "You're the fool. I heard your last phone conversation. You've lost your dedication as a professional. I'm staying here until..."

"Until what? Until people like you from headquarters arrive who haven't had a thought of their own in five years!"

"Watch it." Jack focused on Anne for the first time. "What's this woman doing in these offices after visitor hours? Another rule violation!"

"Leave Anne out of this. She had no idea what was happening here until tonight."

Jack glared at Jennifer. "As new Administrator of this Fullness of Life Centre, I insist you write your letter of resignation. You're interfering with authorized protocol."

"I already wrote it. I'm disgusted with myself - I almost let this reprehensible directive pass." Jennifer flung the words at him.

"Isn't it a bit late to be developing a conscience?" Jack sneered.

Anne interjected, "Jack, help us. The power of people can stop this. The press won't be able to ignore Jennifer's report!"

Jack laughed. "Watch them." He sat down in the leather swivel chair behind Jennifer's desk. "I may as well start getting used to this."

Jennifer angrily thrust a packet of papers at Jack. "Why don't you read the directive 99 you want to enforce? Here's eight pages of statistics and descriptions of procedures about withholding food and water with doctor's approval. Poisons are to be phased in discriminately once the foundation has been laid. This constitutes Phase A. Methods of Administration and the schedules follow."

A surge of boldness hit Jennifer. She was angry, and no longer frightened of anything. "How do you like this evaluation I wrote? Emotional prose, Jack, but true..." Jennifer read, "When man has discovered the treasury of the snow and hail, when man can send forth lightning, and can make the eagle mount up on command, perhaps then man can decree death." Taken from the book of Job in the Bible. When I read those phrases, they stuck in my mind. Good Lord," she stopped, "If my husband could hear me now." A sensation of sadness dropped on her and she prayed silently he was alive.

Anne picked up where Jennifer left off and read more of the original Directive 99 rationale aloud: "The primary selling point of this new elderly care policy among government officials is it's economically feasible. It was assumed welfare mothers would have the majority of abortions, thereby reducing the welfare rolls which didn't happen. Middle class women whose children would be working and paying for future welfare costs were often choosing abortions. Our dependent class now exceeds our working class."

"Jennifer's response follows: 'Abortion is murder, opposed to natural, spontaneous miscarriages, just as euthanasia is murder of the less young with less life as opposed to dying a natural death.'"

Jack held up his hand to quiet her. "I've heard enough."

"Listen to my last section," Jennifer said, "and tell me if you think it's clear enough. Directive 99 will murder the elderly, irrespective of their physical or mental condition. The only criteria to qualify for extermination is being above a certain age. Yet many of these people in our Fullness of Life Centres are still productive members of our society like Kathryn Stasen. Tell Anne what happens to the finances of residents here after their death according to Directive 99, Jack. You know."

"Those who are in life centers give their inheritances to the state for the privilege of having been housed as long as they lived," Jack spouted.

"Only we make sure it's not long. Greed is responsible for the hellish Directive 99 proposal spewed forth from this government. The less time a resident is housed the greater the profit to the state."

"You'll never stop Directive 99. Frankly, I don't care if you do or not. I'm protecting my future here. I've been looking forward to being chief administrator since the day I walked through this door. You've given me what I want. You're toast, Jennifer Trevor. I don't need to know any more. In fact, I'll even unlock the door and let you commit professional suicide."

"You're despicable."

"I take this as a compliment." His face turned an ugly purple. "I'm not even going to try to stop your mailings. I'll enjoy knowing you've destroyed yourself." Jack gloated as he stomped out.

Anne finished stuffing the large envelopes.

"Take them and go, Anne. If you hurry, you'll make tonight's mail."

Anne grabbed her coat. "Get some sleep, okay?" she said with concern, as she wrapped her trench coat around her.

"After a few more calls I'm going home." Their eyes met and Anne noticed again the brightness deep within Jennifer's.

"Talk to you tomorrow."

Anne hugged her before racing off to deposit the packets in the Fed Ex Overnight Mail center. "In by midnight, out by eight," was the guarantee. The timing was perfect.

*The ball's in your court now, Lord, and I know you're in this game.* Anne prayed silently.

Jennifer watched the Fed Ex packets go onto the truck from her office window. She turned back to her desk and deleted the letter she'd written on the computer, but couldn't wipe out the file. No matter.

For the next two hours Jennifer made more calls and reached at least two-thirds of the members present at the Washington hearing.

All the steps were in motion. Jennifer closed her briefcase and went home.

***

The eleven p.m. news carried Senator Odling's statement as well as statements from three other members of Congress denouncing Directive 99. The public outcry the next day would become a national uproar.

Nick had gone to bed at ten, but couldn't sleep. At eleven he got up and turned on the news. The anchorman was announcing a late-breaking story. He listened in shock to the announcement about Directive 99 being postponed indefinitely.

His first reaction was to thank God. Nick's second was concern for Jennifer. He loved her too much not to care how this affected her.

What could have happened? The directive had been sewn up tight. Anyone who protested would be called an enemy of life, taking away freedom of choice for thirty, forty and fifty-year-old Americans who would be burdened by caring for their adult parents. They'd be called unpatriotic, too, because they wouldn't sacrifice their loved ones for the good of the country.

"God, this is your victory!" If anyone told Nick it was Jennifer's too, he 'd have laughed with joy.

# Chapter Twenty

Jennifer braced herself against the harsh winds impeding the path from the Fullness of Life Centre to her car. The blackness at midnight mirrored the darkness in her soul. She was exhilarated and depressed at the same time. Tomorrow she'd be returning to her office to pack her things.

Jennifer re-entered the castle-like door of what had once been her family's safe, exclusive world. She tiptoed into the rooms of her sleeping children one by one, and stood silently several seconds over each bed.

Tara stirred at her presence. "Oh, it's you, Mom." Sleepily she dropped her head back on the pillow.

Jennifer stroked her cheek. "I'm home, Hon, thanks for babysitting Jenna after Grandma had to leave. Just checking you're okay. Go back to sleep."

Tara grunted and rolled over.

Satisfied all the children were safe, she walked down the hall to her room, and snapped on the lamp next to her bed.

"I hoped I'd feel better tonight," she said aloud. She knew exposing the horrors of Directive 99 was right. *I only wish it didn't mean my job.* Ironically most residents will never know I stopped their holocaust.

Why do I feel so empty? she wondered. The answer came swiftly with overwhelming sadness. Life without Nick seems like death. I've put my precious husband in such jeopardy even if he wanted to return, he's not safe in his own home. Without him all meaning had been stolen from the little events comprising her life. Visions of swimming through deep seas of nothingness taunted her.

To her amazement she addressed God. *"Lord, the Book of Genesis describes how You filled the void of the world with Your creation. Can you fill the void in my life? Not only with peace, but wonders and miracles, too?"* At two, Jennifer finally turned off the light, and for the first night since Nick's absence, she slept soundly.

***

Sarah Levinson finished the preface to the book as best she could working late into the night, including detailed information about what she believed to be her husband's supposed suicide set-up. "This is what happens to people who dare to defy the death march of our government." She added the last sentence as an afterthought and titled the Preface "A Book Without an Ending."

John had described in his Introduction the backlash his book would provoke: "Of course, the so called newspapers which have become prop-papers, instruments for government propaganda, will be filled with public denials, and attacks against so-called radicals like myself, who are trying to upset the sacred system entrenched in place."

"Who are these radicals who object? We the people of America. This country was founded by intelligent, compassionate men and women who valued their independence and resourcefulness and respected others' rights to life and freedom. Surely a nation as great as ours can find a respectful way to care for our elderly up to and including natural death. And a nation as great as America can treasure its unborn and newborn citizens treating them with the dignity our future posterity deserves."

Sarah would have liked to verify the information contained in the directive, but whom could she trust to give her accurate information? Fearing becoming paranoid, maybe she already was, she made the decision to simply go with what John had already uncovered. Her husband was a man of journalistic integrity; if he wrote something it was based on truth. His writing would be the beacon she'd trust.

217

She made a call to her husband's previous, conservative publisher. He was willing to consider posthumously publishing John's exposé book on Directive 99. He couldn't promise her, but if "it's what she said, and written by John, it would almost certainly see print," were his exact words.

She attached the word document file to an e-mail and sent it with a prayer.

***

Killing two women was too much. Pirelli had told Relton he wasn't a hit man. He wanted out. He never should have allowed his mind to linger on the incredible kindness of Anne. But he did and thought of her again now as he packed his bags. Why not keep the little ladies safe on his way out?

He needed to destroy Relton's files anyway because the name Pirelli could be in there somewhere.

What's it to me if, for a time, these Jesus-lovers will be safe?

When he had everything ready for departure, he settled in the overstuffed recliner chair and opened the Gideon Bible he'd seen in a drawer when he was stashing his snacks. Pirelli spread it open on his ample lap.

As a boy, he remembered hearing about the sacrifice of Isaac and about the love of a Father God for all his children. Now, for the first time, he read the account for himself. The thought of checking the fridge flitted into his consciousness, but the desire to eat suddenly escaped him. He fell asleep and slept like a baby pleased with himself, a foreign feeling for Pirelli.

He awoke at midnight. After splashing his face with water and changing from his white shirt to a charcoal turtleneck, he went to the closet and reached for the shoeshine kit. He lifted the top panel and removed his lock picking kit.

***

An hour later Pirelli let himself into Relton's office. No need to hurry. Keep the flashlight low, Pirelli told himself. Stay cool.

He went straight to the computer desk and searched through the files marked "Active" or "Dangerous" first. There were several hundred names of conservatives, Jews, Muslims and Christians under surveillance. Over and over he punched "Delete." He took care to empty the computer trash file. He didn't know much about building files, but destroying them was his specialty. Relton had hired him often to do this to their opposition, be it political or business.

Pirelli looked into the computer data disk storage cabinet and removed all Relton's disks. He pulled a folded nylon duffel bag from his leather coat, shook it to full size and deposited the files in it. He slipped the bag's strap over his shoulder in full view. No one would suspect he was walking away with valuable data disks.

As shrewd as Pirelli was, he failed to notice the camera eye hidden in the ivy plant atop the bookshelf.

***

Back in his suite, Pirelli rekindled the dying embers in his fireplace, added a few sheets of newspaper and watched the CD's contort and shrivel before his eyes. He especially enjoyed tossing the data disk entitled, "Pogrom" into the fire. He expected Nick's name was on there and Anne's, too. He wasn't computer literate enough to know there might be back up copies elsewhere.

After all, his primary job was working behind the scenes, and he did it well, one person at a time.

Pirelli questioned himself as the smell of fire subsided and he settled into the lounge chair. What had happened to dispel the aura he'd experienced about Relton enabling him to take this bold action? Being treated as a man, nothing more or less, being accepted and cared for in a situation of personal need even though it was a contrived situation at the elderly care center had affected him deeply. Anne had looked at him without ridicule, and with respect. When, for even a second, had he ever experienced selfless concern for him by anyone!

Relton was starting to suffocate him, just like his dad did. Pirelli sighed, knowing he might have to deal with the wrath of

Relton. But he could endure it, just like he did his Dad's anger. After Relton ranted a bit, maybe beat on him, which Pirelli steeled himself to take, it would be all over.

Nothing to do but wait and get through the night. Outside the hotel a wind started to howl. Thunder cracked and an occasional flash of lightning illuminated Pirelli's face. If Relton comes it will be alone, he decided. He wouldn't risk sending anyone else after the foul-up with Trevor. *Better here than anywhere else*, he thought. *Maybe I'll get lucky and catch my plane tomorrow before Relton discovers his loss.*

Pirelli had been dozing about an hour when a noise brought him to sudden wakefulness. He opened his eyes warily.

In between crashes of thunder, his finely tuned hearing had picked up the click of a lock. Since Relton paid the hotel bill, he had a key. Subconsciously, Pirelli had been waiting for this sound. Every muscle in his body tensed.

Seconds later, Relton hovered over Pirelli with a Glock revolver pointed at his chest.

"Fool! My hidden camera picked up your picture and set the alarm off at my home. Relton snarled and swore, his tone threatening. "Where are my files?"

"Boss, whadda ya mean? Put your gun away. Give me a chance to explain. I'm glad you came, 'cause I want to talk to you. I'm getting too old for this work. I didn't know how to tell you, but I need to get out. I don't have the stomach for this business anymore."

"I hate traitors. There's only one way you're going out." Relton stared menacingly.

"Put the gun away," Pirelli repeated. "I only destroyed CD's with reference to me. I had to. I promise you'll never hear from me again! I'm never going to leave the Cayman Islands. I've got enough money to keep me for life."

Relton growled. "Nobody double-crosses me!"

"Killing me could blow your whole operation. My picture in the paper will be tied to the Fullness of Life Centre. They know me there."

"I'll take the chance."

Pirelli started to sweat. *He's really going to shoot me.* Pirelli's right leg shot up striking Relton in the stomach. Relton staggered off balance but got a shot off. The bullet struck the ceiling tile.

Quick as a cat, Pirelli, lunged for the gun in Relton's hand. He tumbled atop Relton knocking the air out of him. "You've treated me like dirt for the last time." An end table flipped and a lamp shattered as it hit the floor, just missing Pirelli's head.

The two men rolled across the carpeted floor in broken glass until they hit the wall. Relton's fingers were still frozen on the gun. Pirelli lifted Relton's arm and slammed it against the wall as Relton squeezed off another shot wide of its target.

From a half-sitting position, his back against the wall, Relton pushed hard with both legs to get to a standing position. Pirelli pinned him to the wall, but Relton broke loose.

Pirelli got his hand on the gun and held on.

Back and forth they went like two arm wrestlers with the gun first pointing to Pirelli, next toward Relton.

Pirelli's viselike grip crushed Relton's trigger finger against the housing of the gun. He couldn't get off a shot.

Pirelli directed the revolver away from himself and toward Relton's left side. Relton tried to break loose as the gun exploded.

Relton staggered away from Pirelli and grabbed for the wall, breathing deeply. He coughed and collapsed to the floor.

He made a vain attempt to stop the bleeding with his hand where a bullet had ripped through his chest into his lungs. He moaned loudly, then became still.

Pirelli scrambled to his feet, heart racing. He swiped the perspiration from his forehead with his sleeve. Taking deep, gasping breaths, he turned Relton over and checked a non-existent pulse. He saw a trickle of crimson flow from the corner of Relton's mouth.

Quickly, with a calm that surprised him, Pirelli went to the sink and washed his hands. He pulled on black vinyl gloves before wrapping a blanket around Relton. Pirelli heaved him over his shoulder to carry him to his car.

Letting himself out the door of his suite, Pirelli kicked it shut behind him. He took the back exit to avoid being seen. Fortunately, no one was roaming the halls at this hour.

After settling Relton's body in his car, Pirelli drove to a semi-deserted spot two miles across town near a landfill. There he propped the body behind the steering wheel, wiped his prints off every surface and started his walk back, leaving the car on a gravel side road. He welcomed the physical activity to get his adrenaline level closer to normal.

When Pirelli re-entered his suite, it was nearly dawn. He cleaned up the broken glass, washed everything down, and cleaned the fireplace ashes before he picked up his luggage and left.

***

"Is this Mrs. Sarah Levinson?"

"Yes." Sarah said tremulously to the unfamiliar voice.

"My name is Hudson, I was a friend of your husband's. We worked together unofficially for years. I'm the man to whom he sent the disk."

Sarah had been in her living room straightening the sofa pillows. She kept her cell phone clipped to her waist at all times. "Mr. Hudson!" She flopped onto the chair nearest her. "I've been wanting to speak with you. Was the information I sent helpful?"

"Immeasurably. Do you know what it contained?"

"No."

"I believe it's safe for you to be told now. The disk held the names of people at high levels of government involved with a powerful mob boss named Relton. These officials had decided ending the life of elderly citizens was in the best economic interest of America. Relton would benefit to the tune of millions. Thanks to your husband's work and the help of other key individuals, Directive 99 is stopped, at least for now."

"Thank God!"

"On the disk John also sent me a copy of the book manuscript he'd just finished. His death, I presume, was intended to prevent it from coming out. I assume you've already submitted the material to his publisher?"

"Yes."

"Good. Perhaps his work will encourage other men and women in their pursuit of honest, investigative journalism. Would you like me to write an endorsement for the back cover?"

"I'm sure John would be honored." Sarah's tears began to flow uncontrollably. She made arrangements to meet with Hudson later in the week.

***

At another home this same morning at 7:30 A. M. Anne Stasen answered her phone.

"Ms. Stasen, this is Mr. Pirone. I'm calling from the airport because I need to leave on an extended trip, and I'd like you to deliver a message to Ms. Trevor for me."

"I'd be happy to or I can give you her number and you can reach her direct."

"Thanks, but I'd appreciate it if you'd pass this on. Tell her I'm taking my Dad with me." His next words made Ann's blood dance. "And let her know her husband can return home. The man who was after him is no longer a threat. I doubt we'll meet again, Ms. Stasen, but I'll remember you and your kind prayer for me always. Thank you."

Anne stammered, "You're so welcome, but Mr. Pirone. I don't understand how you knew about Nick, but if what you say is true it's wonderful news."

"It's true alright, you can depend upon it."

"Are you sure you're okay physically and up to traveling after your health incident?"

"I'm fine, never been better."

"How do you know Nicolas Trevor?"

"Gotta go, sorry." Pirelli hung up.

Anne set the phone down with trembling fingers.

"Michael!" she yelled upstairs.

Half-dressed, Michael sensed her urgency and ran down.

Anne repeated the details of the phone conversation almost sword for word.

"When did you meet this man?"

She told Michael about her encounter with him at the Fullness of Life Centre.

Michael sat her down. "Anne, this is extremely important, please describe him in detail."

When she finished, Michael gasped. "There couldn't be two people with such unique girth and height. Mr. Pirone sounds identical to the Mr. Torricelli Nick described!"

"He must have used an assumed name. If you knew where he was, why didn't you have him arrested immediately?"

"We were told by Landworks Company he left the country for business and would return in six weeks. We've been trying unsuccessfully to track him down. We think he may have been one of the men responsible for Nick's disappearance."

"I doubt it, but if so, Mr. Pirelli may have been following orders he now regrets."

"To think he was at the Fullness of Life Centre!" Michael muttered. "Right under our noses. Why his change of heart, Anne? What makes you think we can trust him now? This might be a trap to get Nick out of hiding."

"He seemed sincere. I just know."

"We need to pray this through, darling."

Michael's doubt was dispelled when he picked up the evening paper and read confirmation of Pirelli's message. A one by two column in the stated, "Mr. Relton, a prominent local real-estate investor, lost his life last night. Foul play is suspected. His body was found in his car parked at a landfill by the police acting on an anonymous tip. Mr. Relton had no immediate family."

\*\*\*

"Don't you think you should have called and talked to Jennifer first before going home?" Hudson asked Nick.

Nick shook his head side to side. "Michael told her I'm coming and gave an approximate time. I want our first contact to be face to face."

It was the day after Leviathan spread the news about Relton's death and Michael had delivered Pirelli's message to Nick. Hudson arranged for his wife to handle the inn so he could drive Nick home.

"I'm forever indebted to you, Hudson. At seventy-three-years old, you're my inspiration for staying strong on the front lines for Christ. This reunion between me and my wife, might have been the delivery of my dead body in a casket if you hadn't protected me from Shak and Bruter."

"Could you be a little more graphic?" Hudson joked.

"I'm serious. You saved my life in more ways than one. And the mattresses at the White Dove Inn were decent, too, not to mention the great muffins Marie made."

"I'll tell her."

"I already did, many times."

"There are a few projects we can use your help with after you settle in. I may give you a chance for payback."

"Fine. Keep in touch."

***

Jennifer was watching at the window when Hudson's car pulled up the drive.

The instant Nick opened the door, she ran down the walkway into in his open arms. The two hugged and kissed like a soldier and his wife reunited after war.

Nick drew back and looked deep into her eyes misting over. He tenderly kissed each eyelid. Hudson had exited from the driver's side and grinned as he dropped the bag with Nick's few belongings on the sidewalk. Nick remembered his manners and introduced him to Jennifer.

Gratitude welled up inside her. "How can I thank you for all you did for my husband?" She held out her hand, which was quickly surrounded by earthy hands twice the size of hers.

225

"Don't mention it. I'm glad God gave me the privilege of helping out. Now I'll leave the two of you to your reunion." He gave Nick's hand a final shake and patted his shoulder. "Call me."

Hudson backed out with a smile and a wave.

Nick and Jennifer walked arm in arm down the garden path to the side of the house and into the glass enclosed porch. Nick kicked the door shut and pulled her onto the chaise as he wrapped Jennifer in his arms. His lips sought hers again.

"I've missed you so much," Nick whispered in her ear.

"Me, too. I don't ever want to let you go." She took his hand with its wedding band, a little loose, and held it to her chin wanting the feeling of his pulse against her, reassuring her he was truly alive and home again.

He nuzzled his face against her neck. "You smell delicious – my favorite perfume?"

"Of course, White Shoulders."

His voice became hoarse. He seemed to fight back the urge to cry.

She knew he never cried. Instead he asked, "Where are the kids? I can't wait to see them."

"At Anne and Michael's. They're excited to see you too. I didn't want you overwhelmed by all of us at once." She laughed. "Actually I wanted you all to myself first."

"I'm glad." His lips resettled on hers.

When they paused for breath she added, "We're invited for dinner later."

"Great. You've no idea what an ordinary night with family and friends means to me." Jennifer thought a snippet of Scripture escaped his lips as he looked toward the display of dried hydrangea: "The fullness of joy."

The snow was melting. Drops of water trickled from the eaves and the patches of dormant grass drank them greedily. They both recognized the essence of new life. The cycle of life and death in its natural unfolding would continue. She'd done her part.

"Nick, I'm so sorry I put you through this." He drew her closer against his chest.

"What matters is you recognized the horror of Directive 99 and stopped it. I'm proud of you for standing up for what's right."

"Nick, it came this close." She snapped her fingers. "But we killed it, for now anyway," she said with no small measure of pleasure.

Jennifer drew back and opened her mouth to speak again, but hesitated. She had to express the thought troubled her every hour since Nick's disappearance. "I was afraid you left because you didn't want to be married to someone like me."

Nick looked at her wide-eyed. "How could you think for a minute I'd ever leave you?" He touched his finger to Jennifer's lips. "Enough of this."

With a tremulous smile she reached up to caress the cheek of this man she loved so much. "You had every reason, Nick."

He rocked her softly against his body. "No way. Not ever."

His soft and gentle tone reassured her. "I love you," her lips trembled, "more than I even realized. I don't care that professional colleagues will probably shun me; my employability has shriveled to zip. It doesn't seem important. By the way, you'll get to be our sole breadwinner for a while."

"We'll get through with God's help." The confidence in his voice was soothing.

She nodded. "You're here, and people like Kathryn won't die before their natural time, that's all that matters." Jennifer smiled and shook her head. "You know, I'm still spinning. Rather amazing things have happened in this week. I think there may be something to this prayer thing. I'm actually open to learning more about this God of yours."

"Awesome." The fervor in Nick's kiss made Jennifer's heart overflow.

He picked her up and carried her to the bedroom, desire in his eyes lighting the way. "Don't drop me," she teased, as their mixed laughter filled the air. It was awhile before they made it to Anne and Michael's.

*\*\**

Sarah Levinson held the memorial service she'd long delayed for her husband.

She wanted her children to hear the truth about how their dad's final days on earth were spent using his wisdom and communication skills to expose an evil being perpetrated on our nation.

John's murder couldn't be proved. With Relton dead further investigation had been impossible. But Sarah and the children knew John didn't commit suicide and so did their close friends. Having the people who mattered most know the facts was enough.

The initial success of John's exposé book and the subsequent arrests in Washington were her private, but real, comfort for having John prematurely snatched from this world. Her deepest joy came from knowing he was now in the presence of the God they both loved.

The day was unseasonably warm and sunny. Although Sarah arrived a half hour early, the church was already nearly full.

She fanned herself with one of the programs she'd had printed for each guest. It pleased her to see her new friends Michael and Anne Stasen and Jennifer and Nick Trevor across the aisle.

Kathryn Stasen, Michael's aunt, listened enrapt. Michael and Anne had picked her up at the Fullness of Life Centre and driven her to the service. She was honored with a poem about elderly who would benefit from the demise of Directive 99.

Sarah's pastor began his message saying, "We have martyrs in the history of our church and they're among us still. John Levinson died as a martyr rather than live as a coward. He was killed for promoting his belief in the beauty and sanctity of all life. I can't think of a more noble cause. May his example embolden us all!" Brief eulogies given by several friends followed.

Sarah experienced a sweet peace knowing her sons, Jacob and Eli, and her married daughter and her family would remember forever the valor of this man whose life-giving genes they carried.

The next day, several newspapers carried small articles about the career of journalist, John Levinson, believed to have committed suicide who was memorialized by his family at St. Sebastian's Catholic Church. Nothing was mentioned about the significance of his work.

Only two made reference to the speeches made by John Levinson's wife, Sarah, and by Jennifer Trevor standing together on the church steps after the service.

However, both women's comments were carried by You Tube and viewed by millions.

In the video, Jennifer described the demise of the life-threatening Directive 99, speaking in a slow, sincere manner and instantly winning over the audience.

Sarah accepted the microphone from Jennifer. "These months have been hard on our family and the future may be even more difficult. My husband knew the challenge of delivering truth in our culture. He paid for it with his life." She paused to regain composure.

Jennifer slid her arm around Sarah.

"Although I'm unaccustomed to the public role," Sarah continued, "I'm carrying on his purpose. It's true, I'm a nobody. But, as John would say, 'We're all somebodies in the eyes of our Creator with contributions to make to the world."

Jennifer concluded the interview. "We've assumed our new responsibility as spokespersons for human life with humility and deep joy in partnership together. Honoring the value of every life at every age must prevail." She grinned as Nick cheered and whistled.

*Visit Judith Rolfs' amazon author page for her other books.*
*YouTube Channel: Judith Rolfs*